SKYLANDERS™

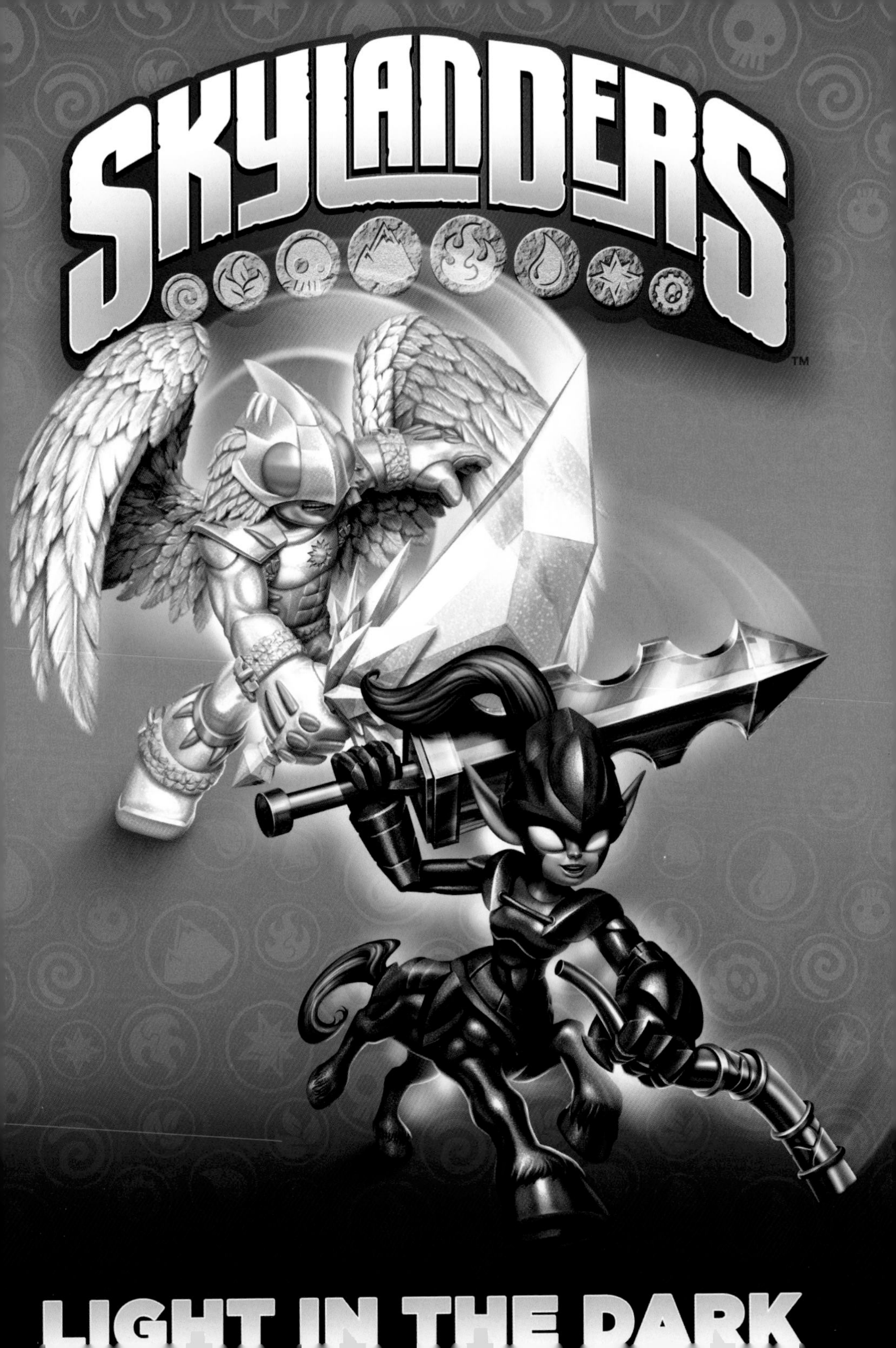

LIGHT IN THE DARK

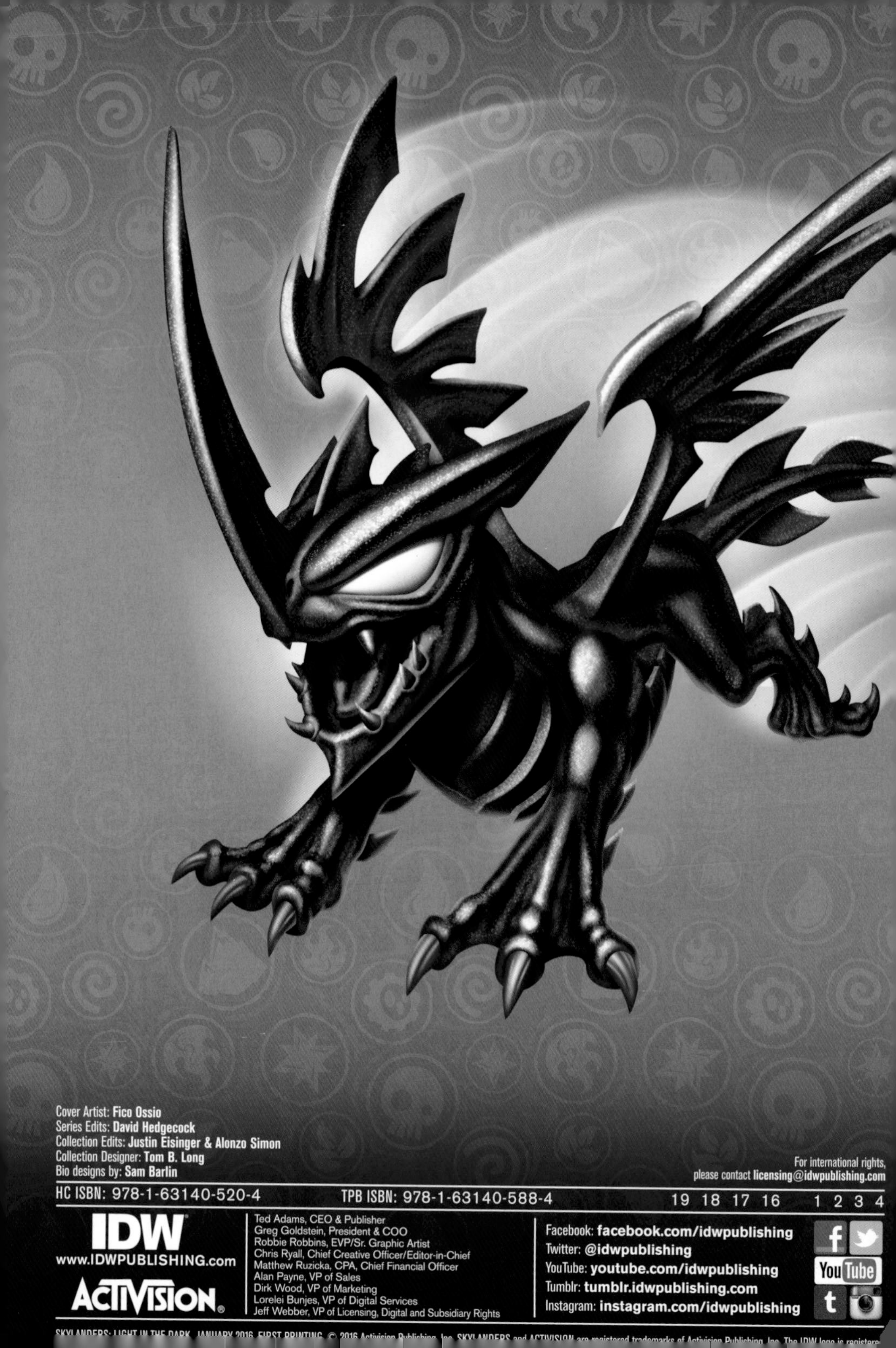

Cover Artist: **Fico Ossio**
Series Edits: **David Hedgecock**
Collection Edits: **Justin Eisinger & Alonzo Simon**
Collection Designer: **Tom B. Long**
Bio designs by: **Sam Barlin**

HC ISBN: 978-1-63140-520-4 TPB ISBN: 978-1-63140-588-4

19 18 17 16 1 2 3 4

IDW
www.IDWPUBLISHING.com
ACTIVISION.

Ted Adams, CEO & Publisher
Greg Goldstein, President & COO
Robbie Robbins, EVP/Sr. Graphic Artist
Chris Ryall, Chief Creative Officer/Editor-in-Chief
Matthew Ruzicka, CPA, Chief Financial Officer
Alan Payne, VP of Sales
Dirk Wood, VP of Marketing
Lorelei Bunjes, VP of Digital Services
Jeff Webber, VP of Licensing, Digital and Subsidiary Rights

Facebook: **facebook.com/idwpublishing**
Twitter: **@idwpublishing**
YouTube: **youtube.com/idwpublishing**
Tumblr: **tumblr.idwpublishing.com**
Instagram: **instagram.com/idwpublishing**

SKYLANDERS: LIGHT IN THE DARK. JANUARY 2016. FIRST PRINTING.

SKYLANDERS™

LIGHT IN THE DARK

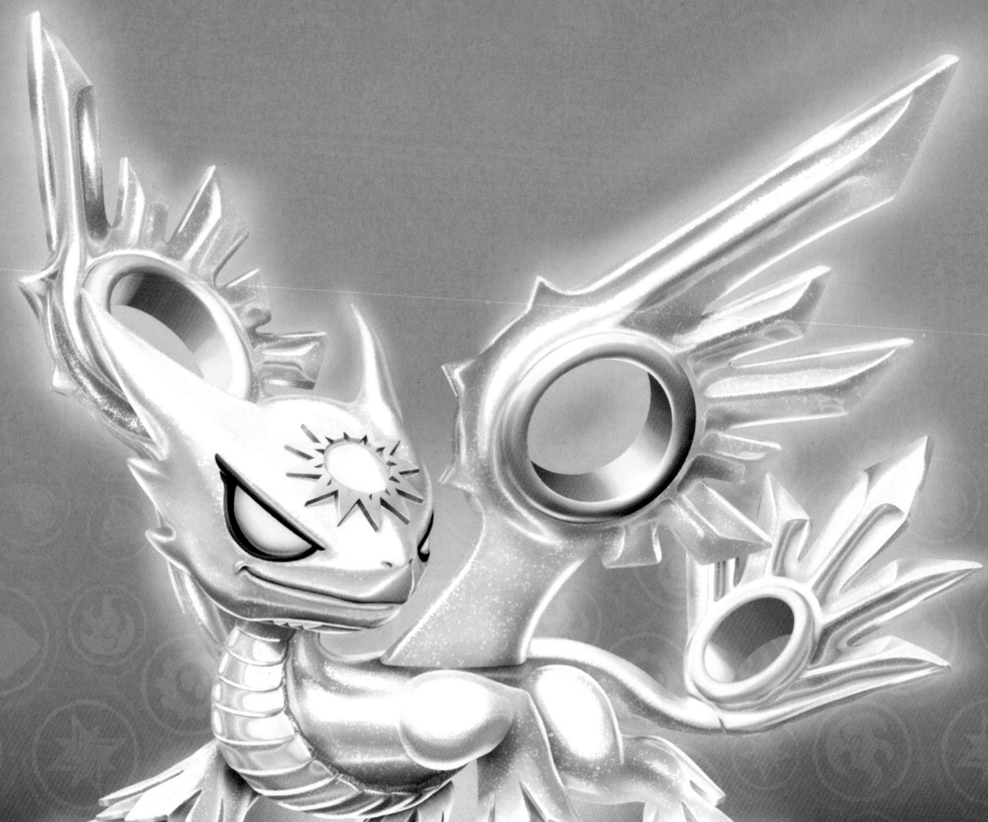

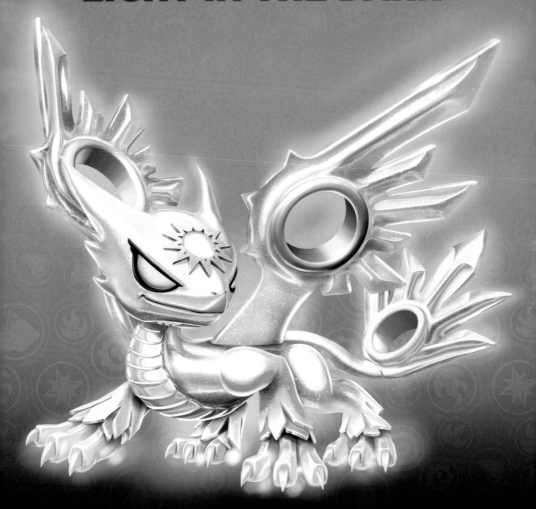

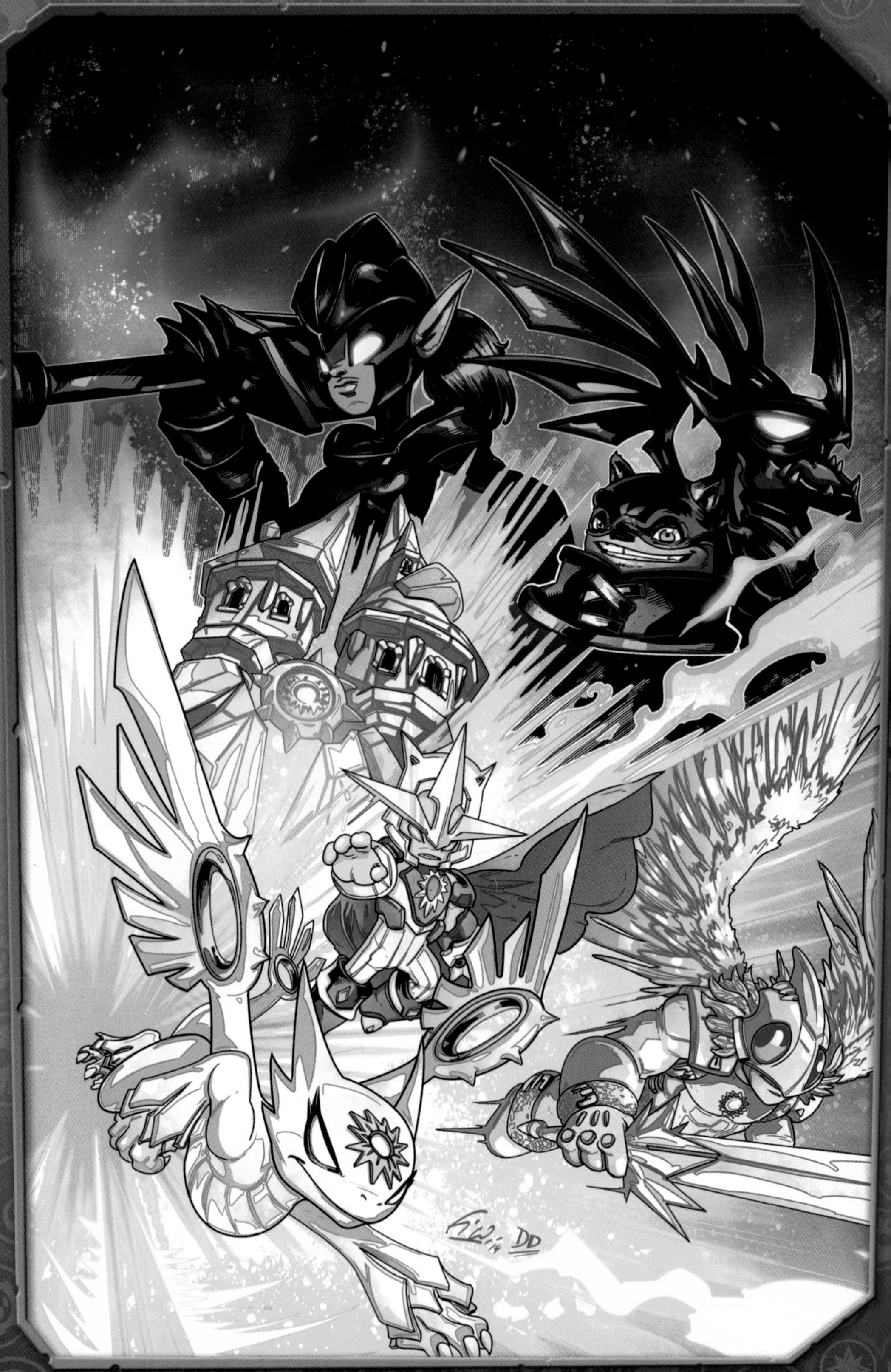

LIGHT SHOW!

Written by: **RON MARZ & DAVID A. RODRIGUEZ**
Art by: **FICO OSSIO**
Colors by: **DAVID GARCIA CRUZ**
Letters by: **DERON BENNETT**
Edits by: **DAVID HEDGECOCK**

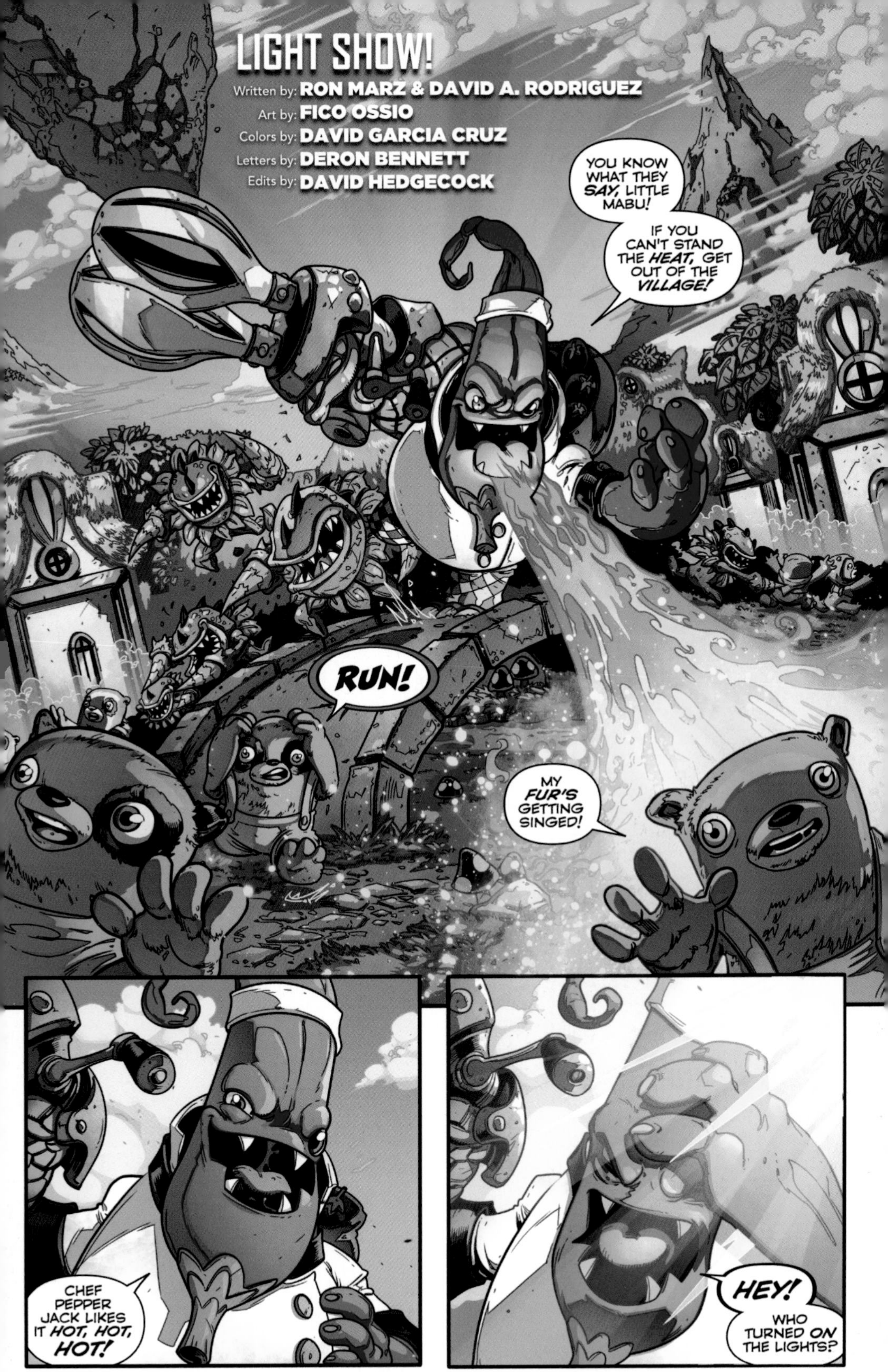
YOU KNOW WHAT THEY *SAY,* LITTLE MABU!
IF YOU CAN'T STAND THE *HEAT,* GET OUT OF THE *VILLAGE!*
RUN!
MY *FUR'S* GETTING SINGED!
CHEF PEPPER JACK LIKES IT *HOT, HOT, HOT!*
HEY!
WHO TURNED *ON* THE LIGHTS?

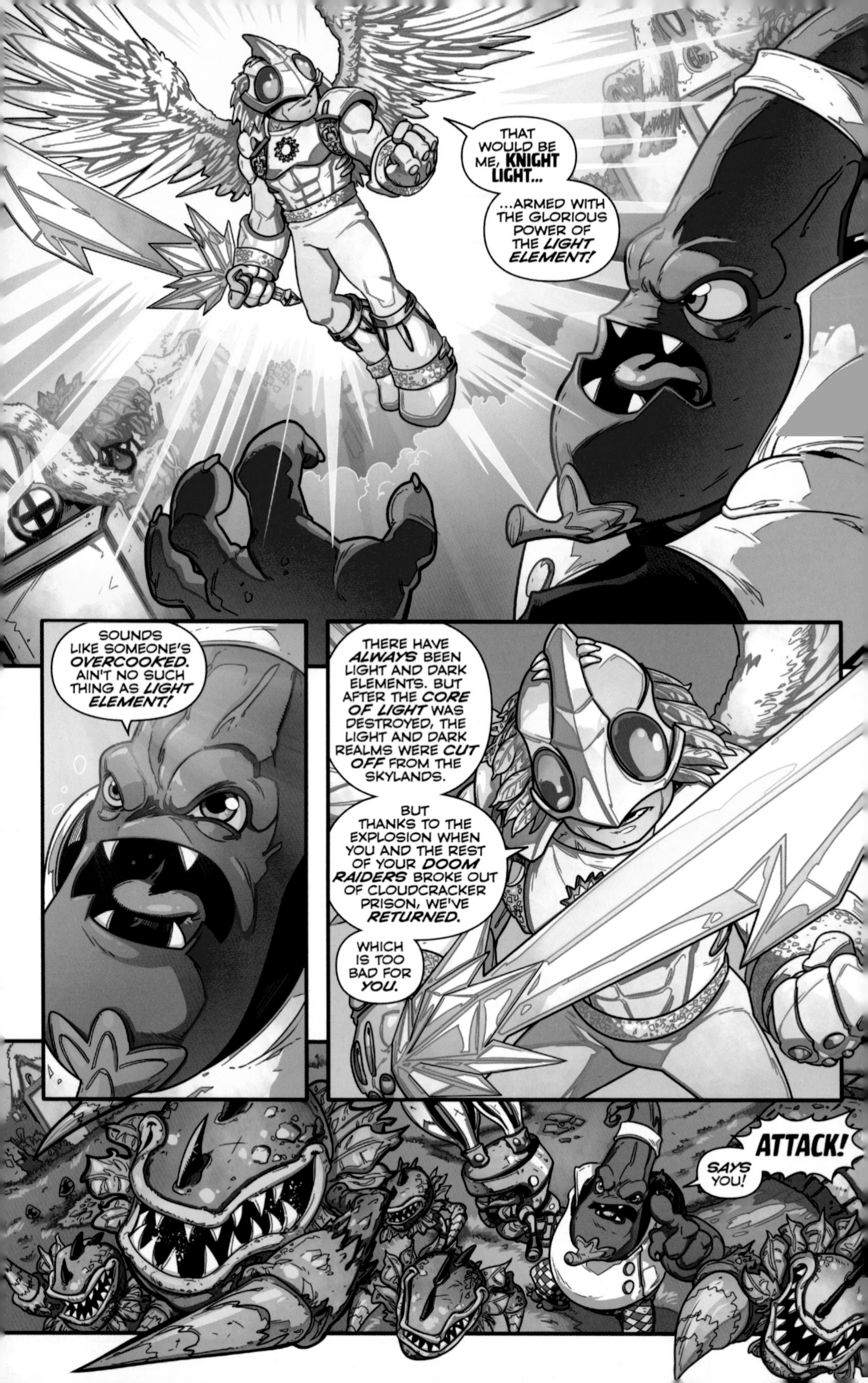

THAT WOULD BE ME, KNIGHT LIGHT...
...ARMED WITH THE GLORIOUS POWER OF THE LIGHT ELEMENT!
SOUNDS LIKE SOMEONE'S OVERCOOKED. AIN'T NO SUCH THING AS LIGHT ELEMENT!
THERE HAVE ALWAYS BEEN LIGHT AND DARK ELEMENTS. BUT AFTER THE CORE OF LIGHT WAS DESTROYED, THE LIGHT AND DARK REALMS WERE CUT OFF FROM THE SKYLANDS.
BUT THANKS TO THE EXPLOSION WHEN YOU AND THE REST OF YOUR DOOM RAIDERS BROKE OUT OF CLOUDCRACKER PRISON, WE'VE RETURNED.
WHICH IS TOO BAD FOR YOU.
SAYS YOU!
ATTACK!

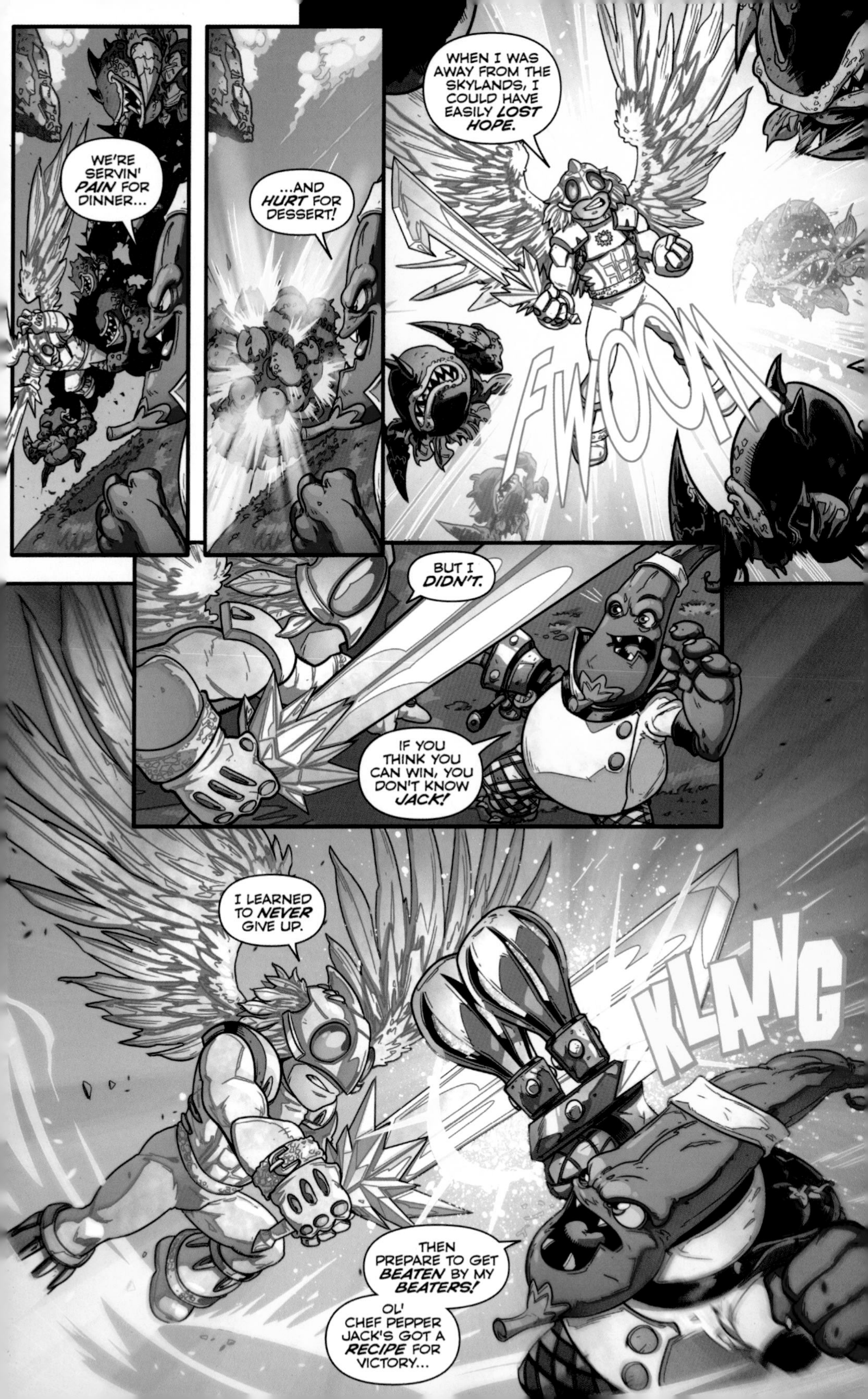

WE'RE SERVIN' PAIN FOR DINNER...
...AND HURT FOR DESSERT!
WHEN I WAS AWAY FROM THE SKYLANDS, I COULD HAVE EASILY LOST HOPE.
FWOOM
BUT I DIDN'T.
IF YOU THINK YOU CAN WIN, YOU DON'T KNOW JACK!
I LEARNED TO NEVER GIVE UP.
KLANG
THEN PREPARE TO GET BEATEN BY MY BEATERS!
OL' CHEF PEPPER JACK'S GOT A RECIPE FOR VICTORY...

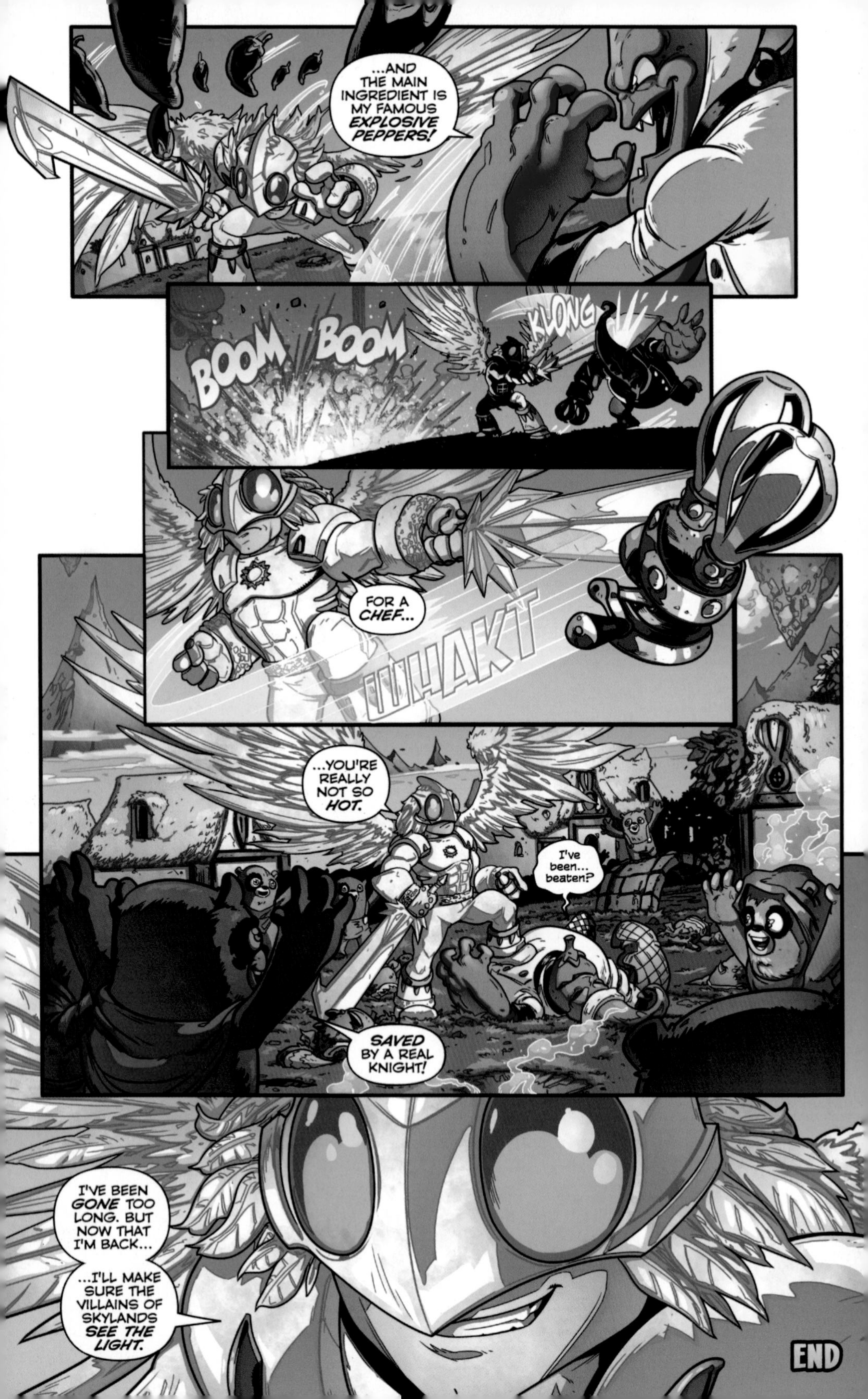
...AND THE MAIN INGREDIENT IS MY FAMOUS *EXPLOSIVE PEPPERS!*
BOOM
BOOM
KLONG
FOR A *CHEF*...
WHAKT
...YOU'RE REALLY NOT SO *HOT*.
I've been... beaten?
SAVED BY A REAL KNIGHT!
I'VE BEEN *GONE* TOO LONG. BUT NOW THAT I'M BACK...
...I'LL MAKE SURE THE VILLAINS OF SKYLANDS *SEE THE LIGHT*.
END

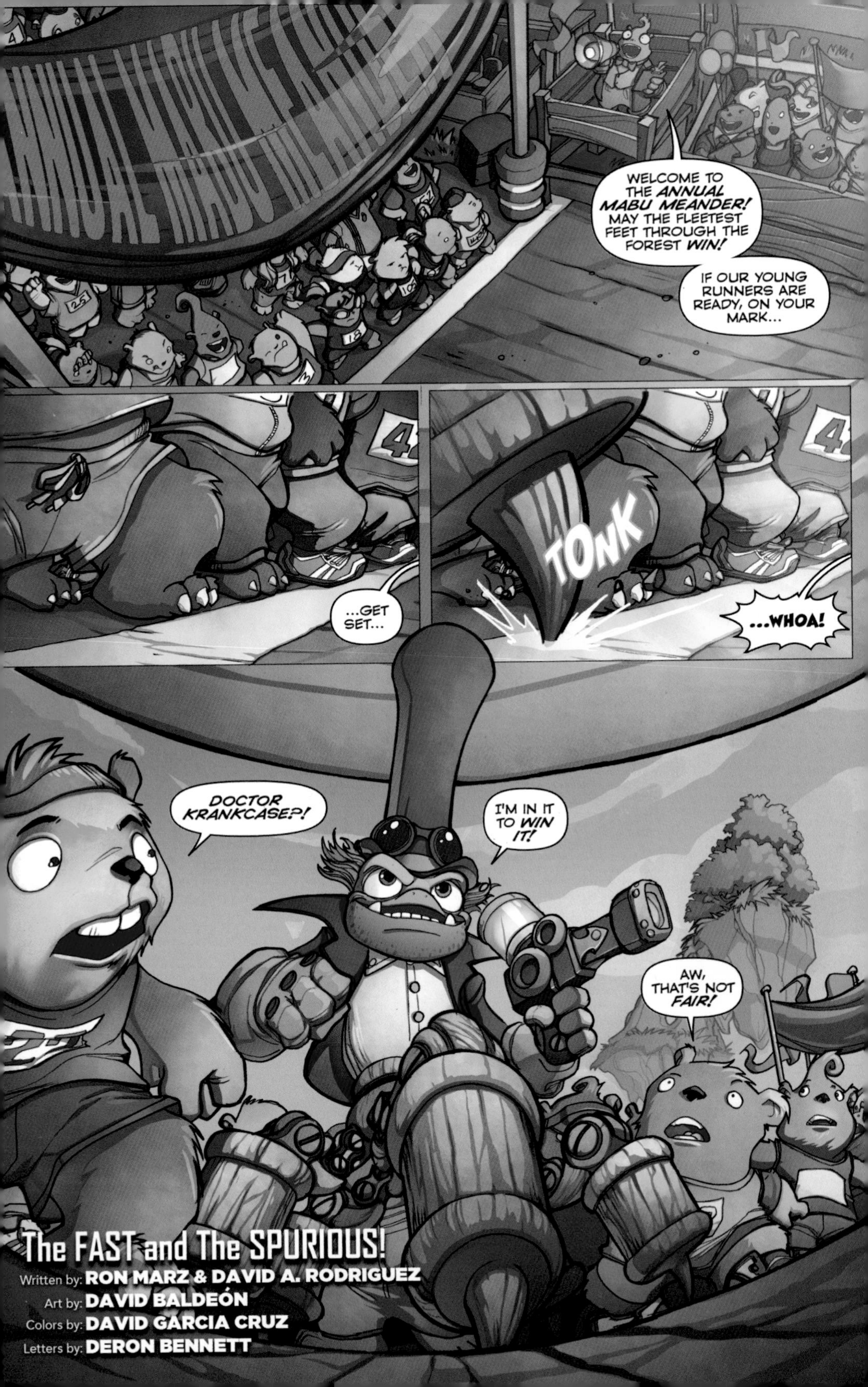
WELCOME TO THE ANNUAL MABU MEANDER! MAY THE FLEETEST FEET THROUGH THE FOREST WIN!
IF OUR YOUNG RUNNERS ARE READY, ON YOUR MARK...
...GET SET...
TONK
...WHOA!
DOCTOR KRANKCASE?!
I'M IN IT TO WIN IT!
AW, THAT'S NOT FAIR!

The FAST and The SPURIOUS!

Written by: **RON MARZ & DAVID A. RODRIGUEZ**
Art by: **DAVID BALDEÓN**
Colors by: **DAVID GARCIA CRUZ**
Letters by: **DERON BENNETT**

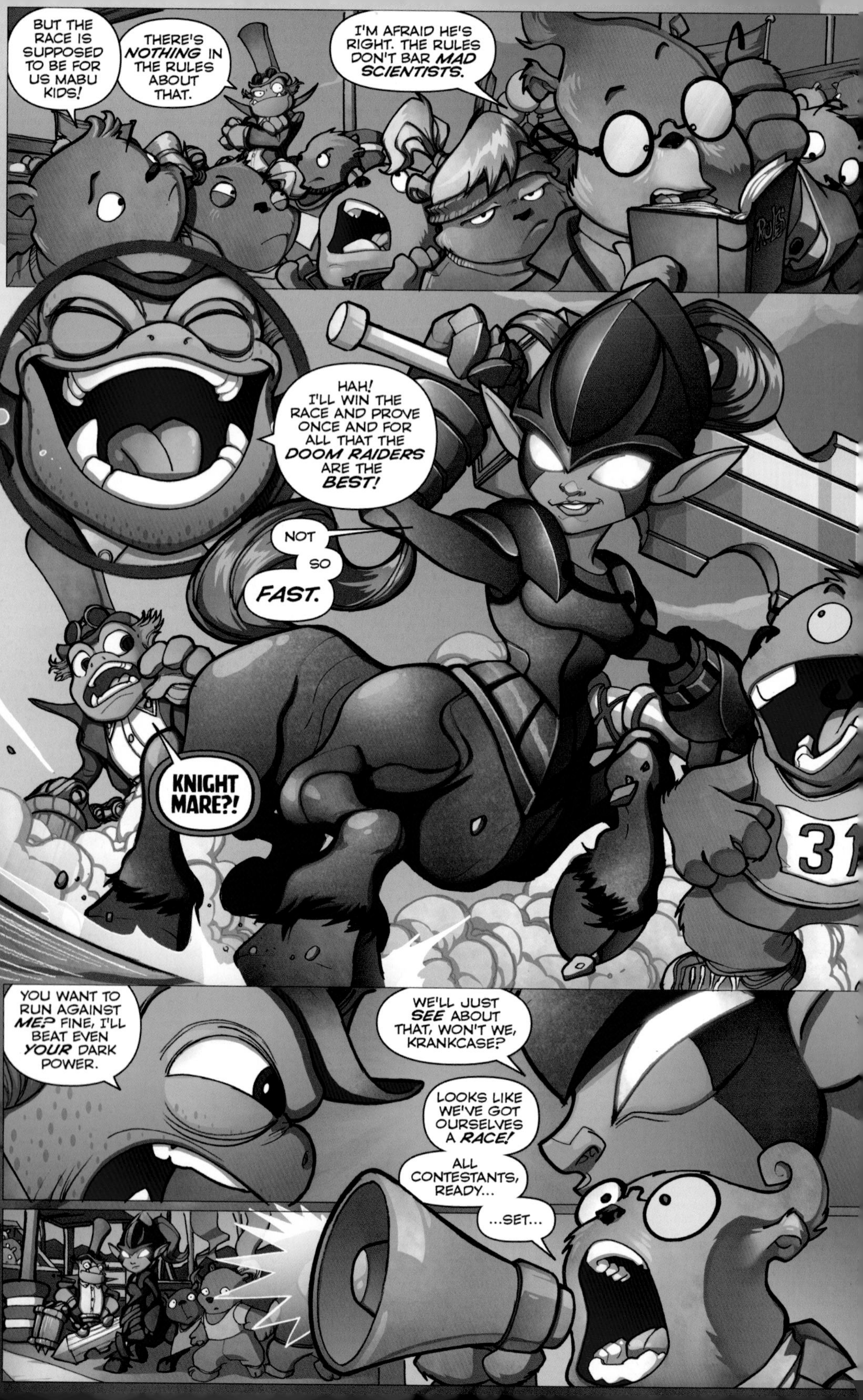
BUT THE RACE IS SUPPOSED TO BE FOR US MABU KIDS!
THERE'S *NOTHING* IN THE RULES ABOUT THAT.
I'M AFRAID HE'S RIGHT. THE RULES DON'T BAR *MAD SCIENTISTS*.
RULES
HAH! I'LL WIN THE RACE AND PROVE ONCE AND FOR ALL THAT THE *DOOM RAIDERS* ARE THE *BEST!*
NOT SO *FAST.*
KNIGHT MARE?!
31
YOU WANT TO RUN AGAINST *ME?* FINE, I'LL BEAT EVEN *YOUR* DARK POWER.
WE'LL JUST *SEE* ABOUT THAT, WON'T WE, KRANKCASE?
LOOKS LIKE WE'VE GOT OURSELVES A *RACE!*
ALL CONTESTANTS, READY...
...SET...

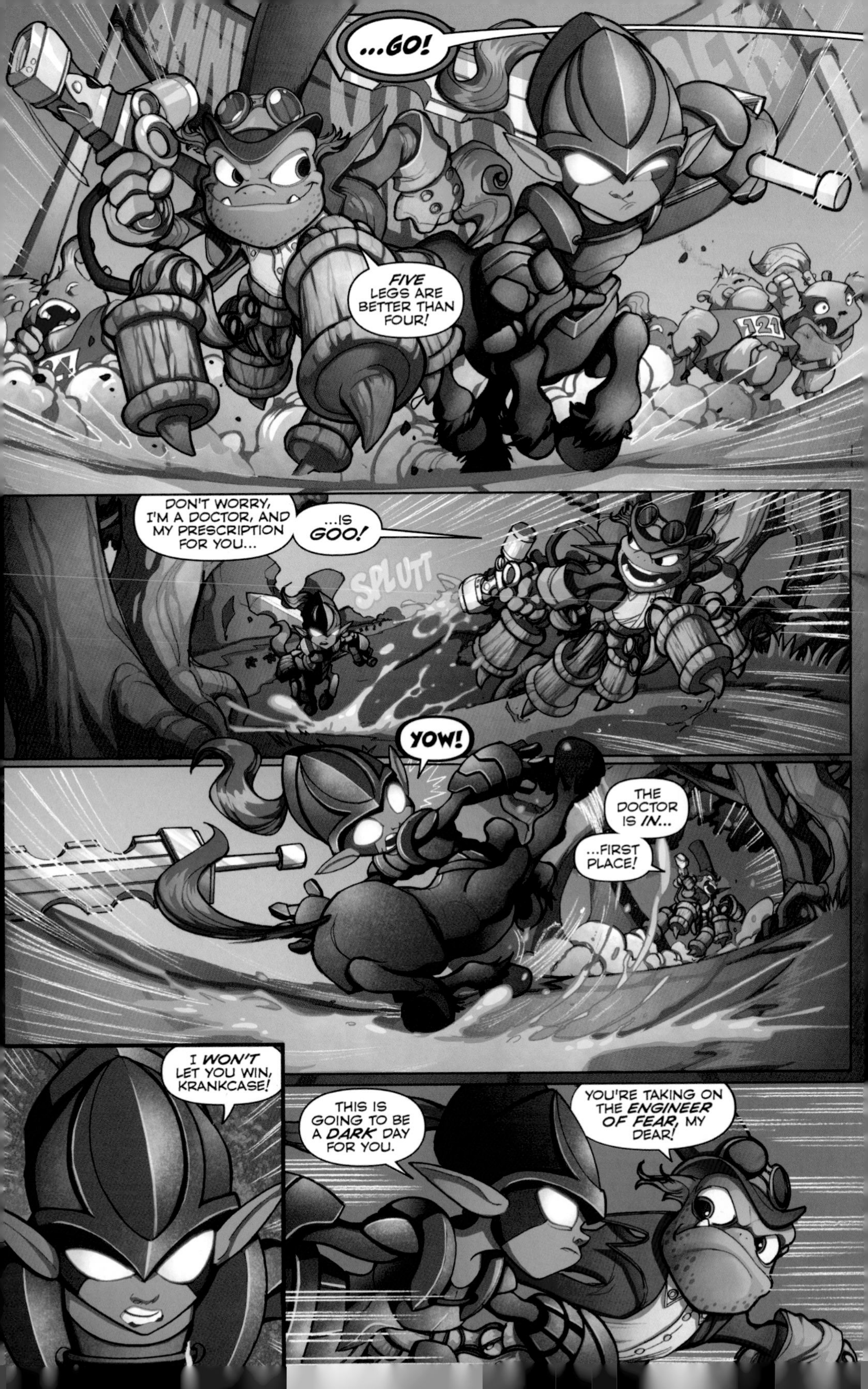

...GO!
FIVE LEGS ARE BETTER THAN FOUR!
121
DON'T WORRY, I'M A DOCTOR, AND MY PRESCRIPTION FOR YOU...
...IS GOO!
SPLUT!
YOW!
THE DOCTOR IS IN...
...FIRST PLACE!
I WON'T LET YOU WIN, KRANKCASE!
THIS IS GOING TO BE A DARK DAY FOR YOU.
YOU'RE TAKING ON THE ENGINEER OF FEAR, MY DEAR!

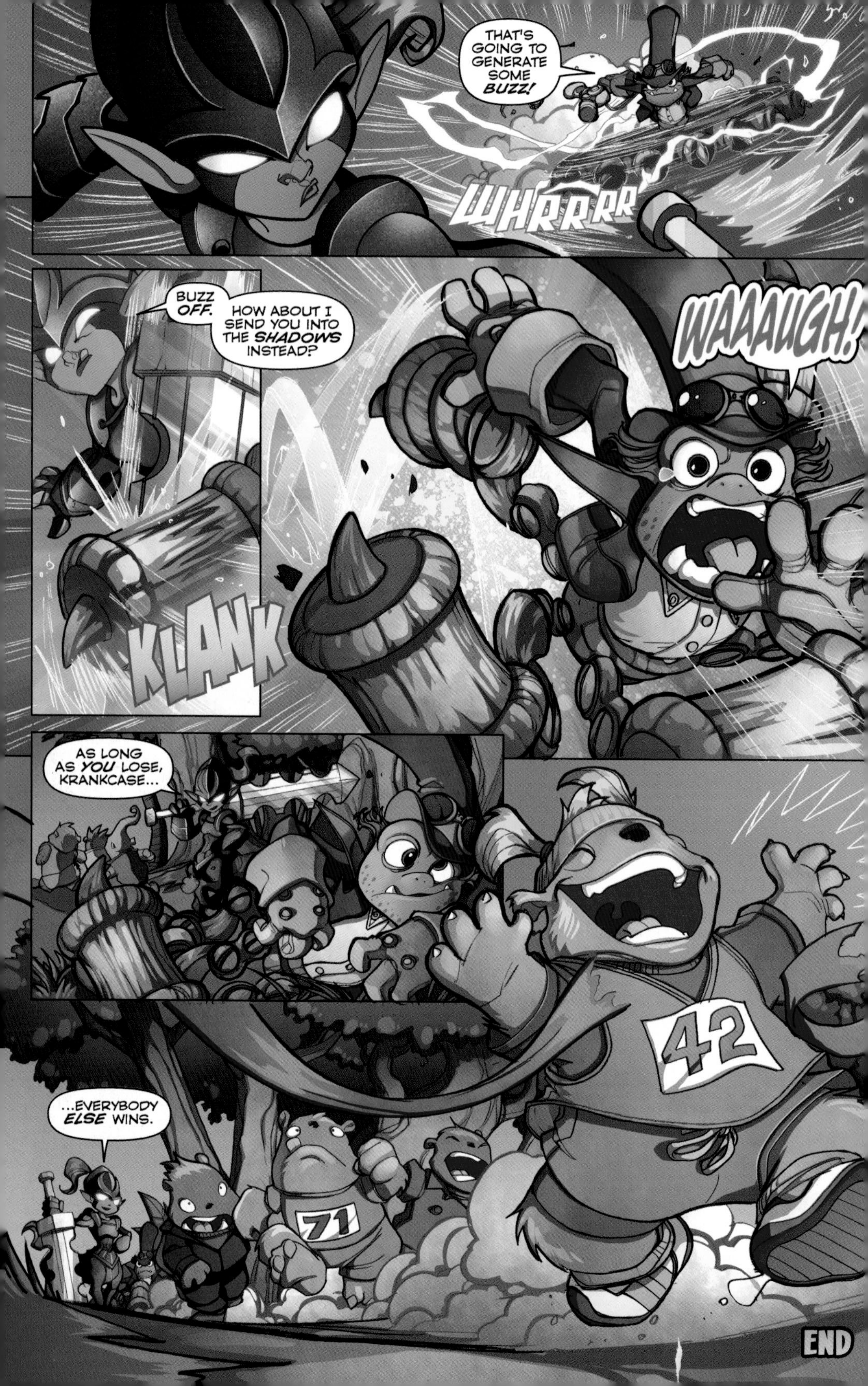
THAT'S GOING TO GENERATE SOME BUZZ!
WHRRRRR
BUZZ OFF.
HOW ABOUT I SEND YOU INTO THE SHADOWS INSTEAD?
KLANK
WAAAUGH!
AS LONG AS YOU LOSE, KRANKCASE...
42
...EVERYBODY ELSE WINS.
71
END

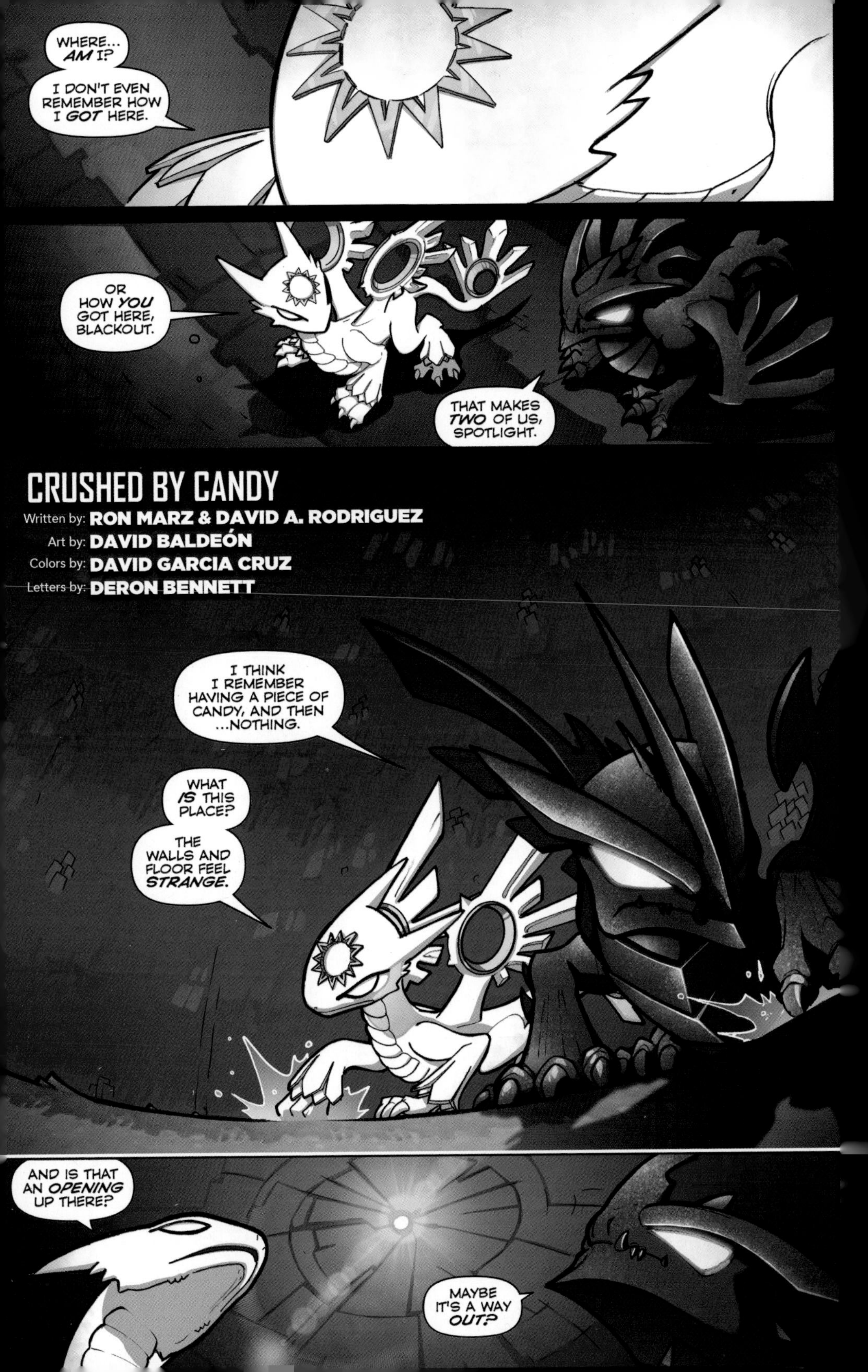

WHERE... AM I?
I DON'T EVEN REMEMBER HOW I GOT HERE.
OR HOW YOU GOT HERE, BLACKOUT.
THAT MAKES TWO OF US, SPOTLIGHT.
CRUSHED BY CANDY
Written by: RON MARZ & DAVID A. RODRIGUEZ
Art by: DAVID BALDEÓN
Colors by: DAVID GARCIA CRUZ
Letters by: DERON BENNETT
I THINK I REMEMBER HAVING A PIECE OF CANDY, AND THEN ...NOTHING.
WHAT IS THIS PLACE?
THE WALLS AND FLOOR FEEL STRANGE.
AND IS THAT AN OPENING UP THERE?
MAYBE IT'S A WAY OUT?

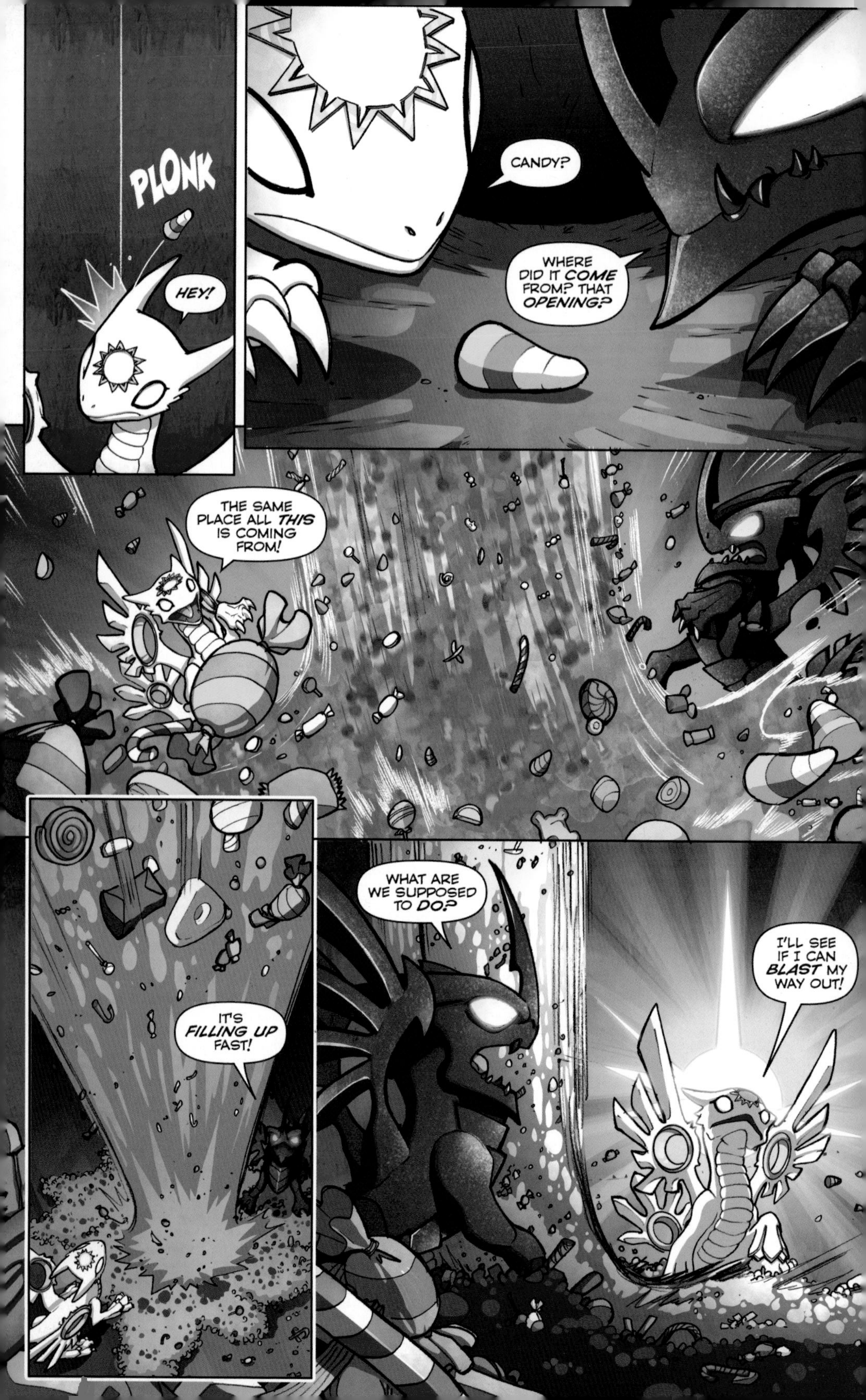
PLONK
HEY!
CANDY?
WHERE DID IT COME FROM? THAT OPENING?
THE SAME PLACE ALL THIS IS COMING FROM!
IT'S FILLING UP FAST!
WHAT ARE WE SUPPOSED TO DO?
I'LL SEE IF I CAN BLAST MY WAY OUT!

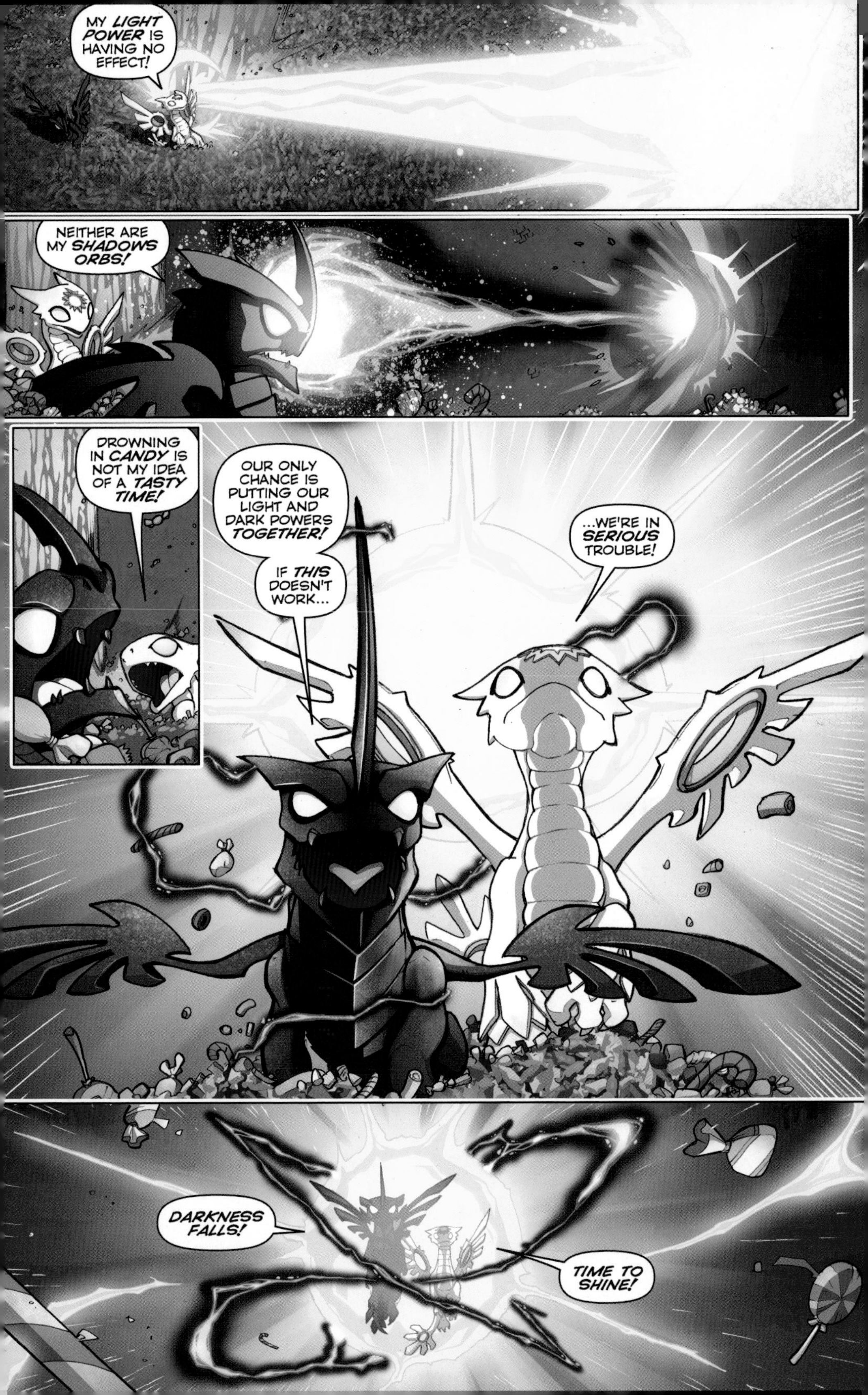
MY LIGHT POWER IS HAVING NO EFFECT!
NEITHER ARE MY SHADOWS ORBS!
DROWNING IN CANDY IS NOT MY IDEA OF A TASTY TIME!
OUR ONLY CHANCE IS PUTTING OUR LIGHT AND DARK POWERS TOGETHER!
IF THIS DOESN'T WORK...
...WE'RE IN SERIOUS TROUBLE!
DARKNESS FALLS!
TIME TO SHINE!

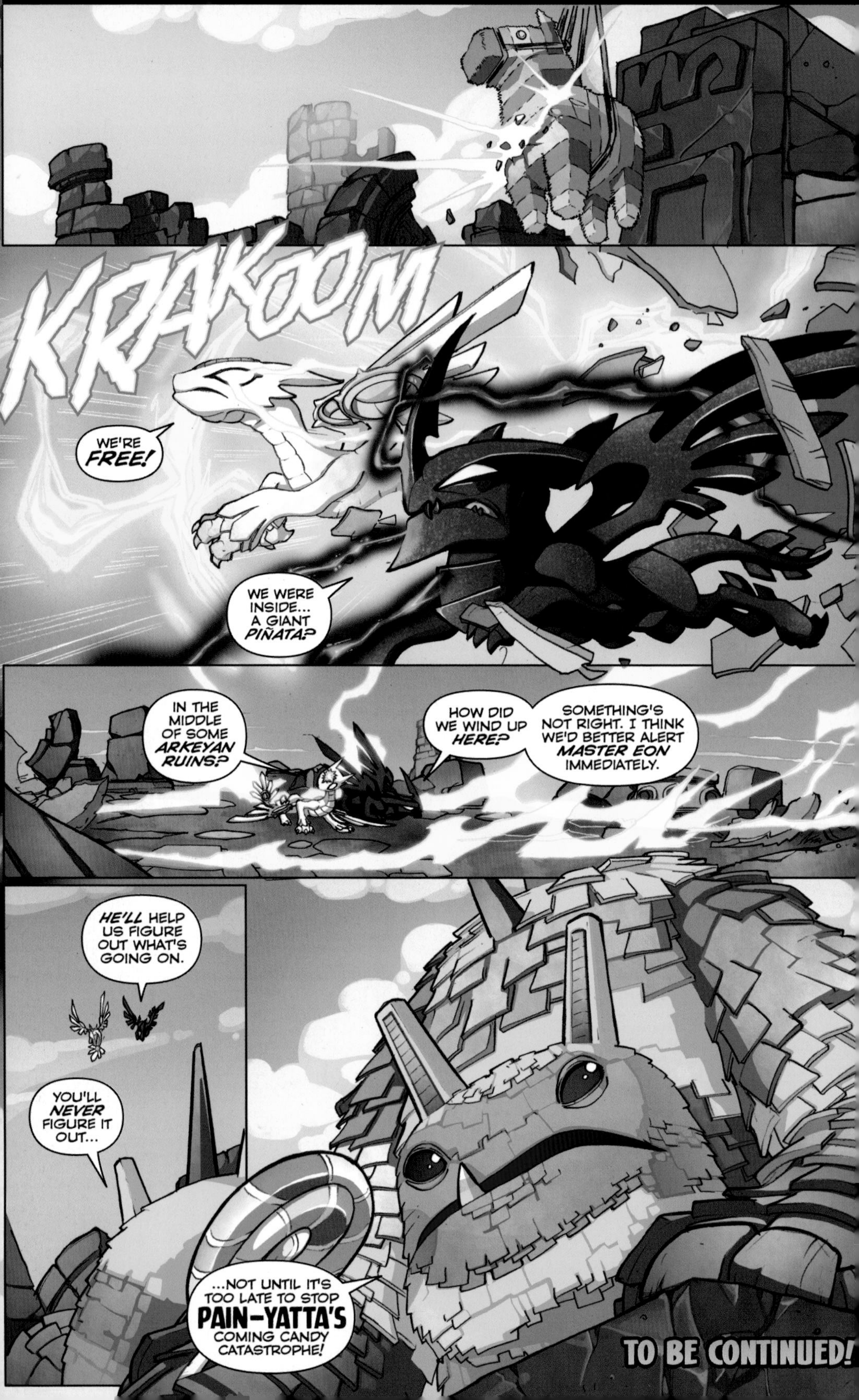
KRAKOOM
WE'RE *FREE!*
WE WERE INSIDE... A GIANT *PIÑATA?*
IN THE MIDDLE OF SOME *ARKEYAN RUINS?*
HOW DID WE WIND UP *HERE?*
SOMETHING'S NOT RIGHT. I THINK WE'D BETTER ALERT *MASTER EON* IMMEDIATELY.
HE'LL HELP US FIGURE OUT WHAT'S GOING ON.
YOU'LL *NEVER* FIGURE IT OUT...
...NOT UNTIL IT'S TOO LATE TO STOP **PAIN-YATTA'S** COMING CANDY CATASTROPHE!
TO BE CONTINUED!

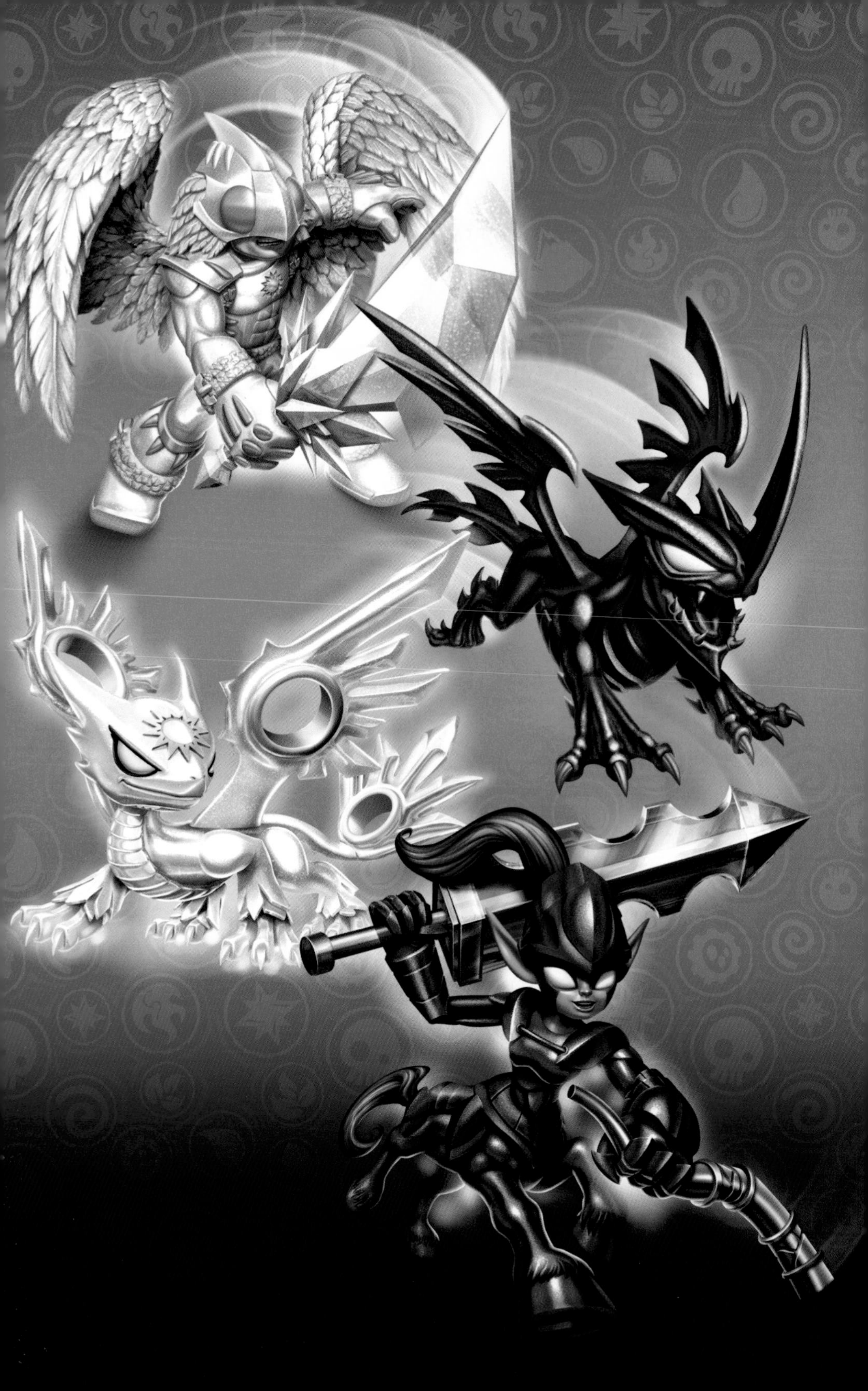

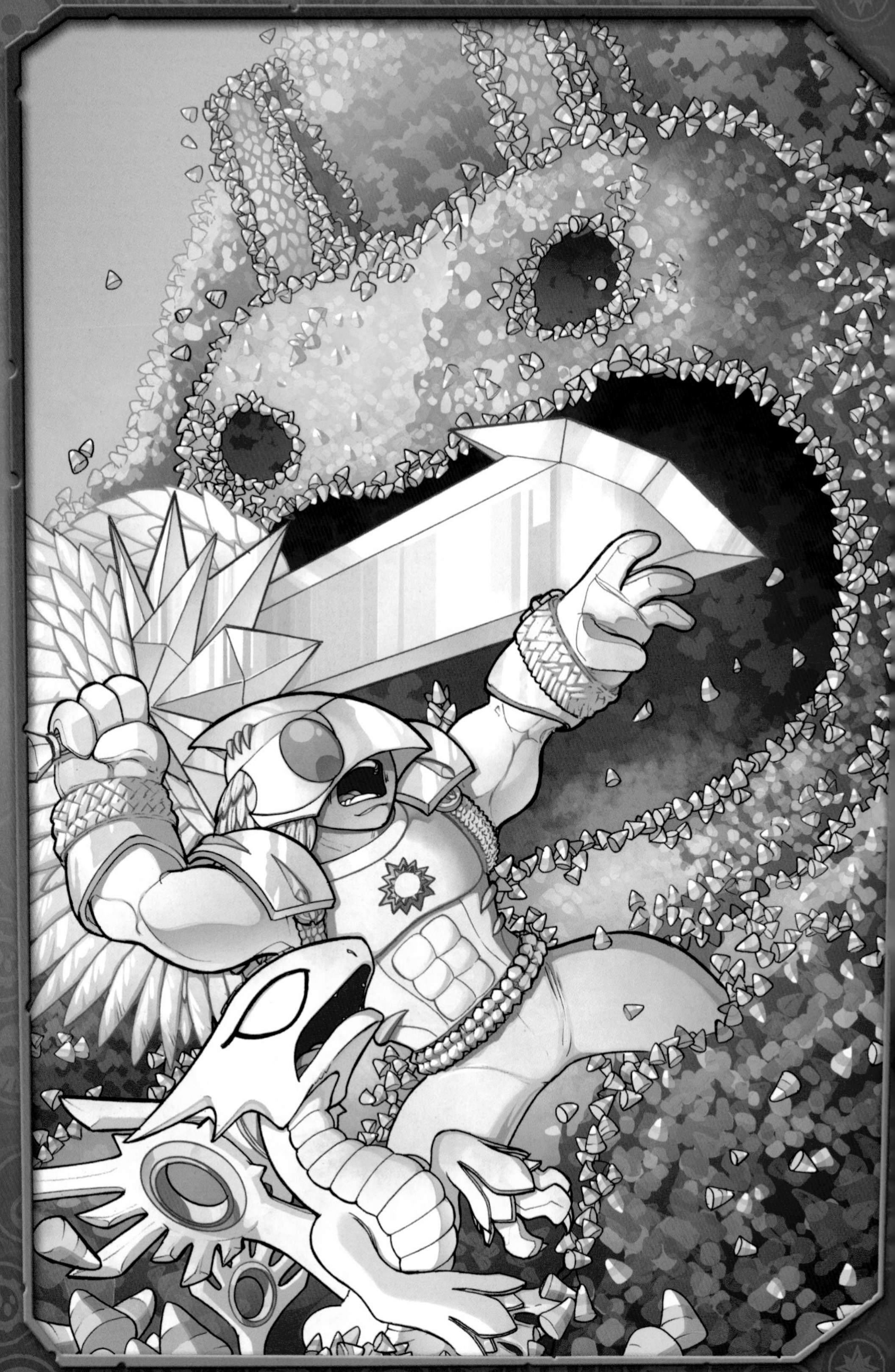

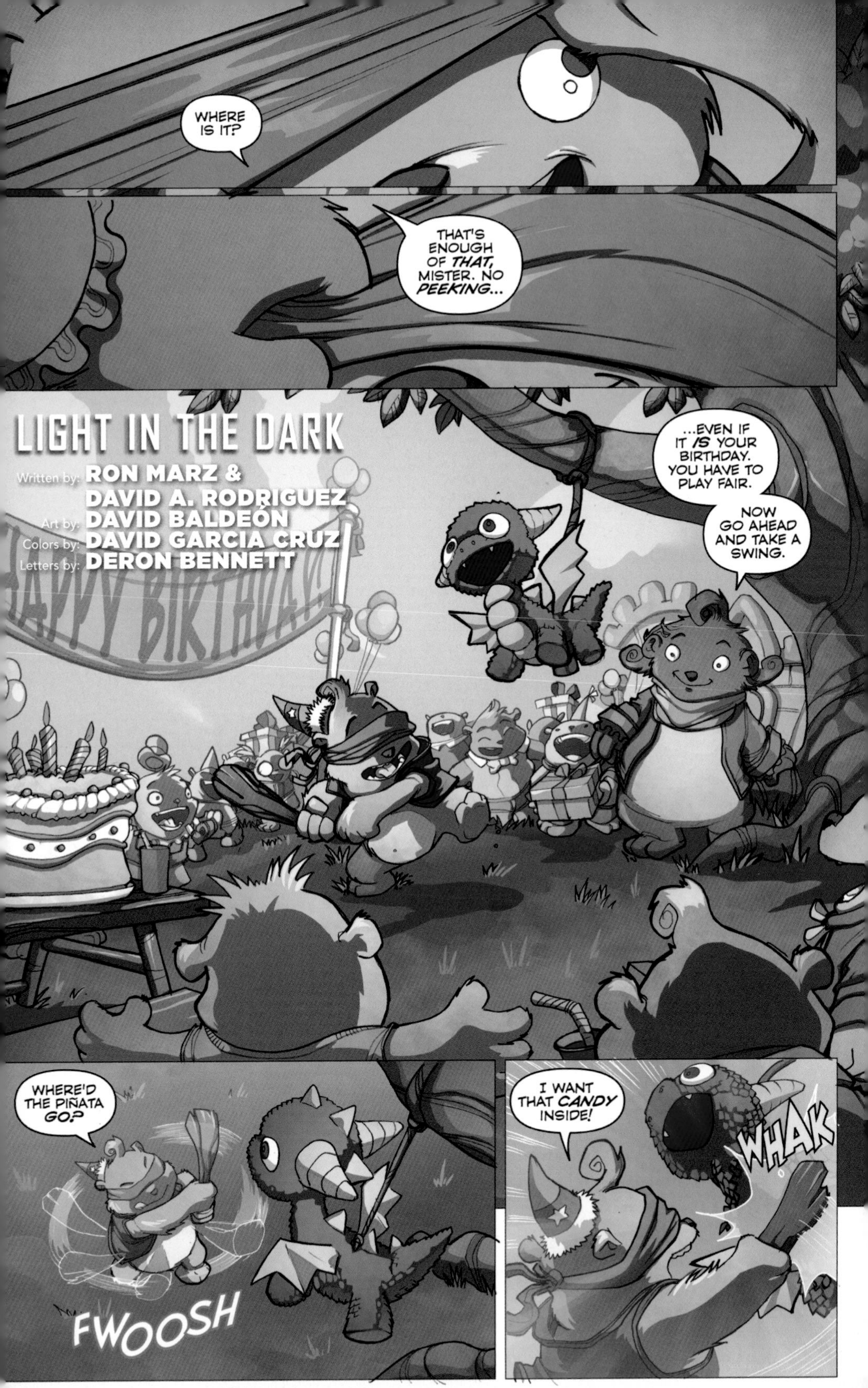
WHERE IS IT?
THAT'S ENOUGH OF *THAT*, MISTER. NO *PEEKING*...
LIGHT IN THE DARK
Written by: RON MARZ & DAVID A. RODRIGUEZ
Art by: DAVID BALDEÓN
Colors by: DAVID GARCIA CRUZ
Letters by: DERON BENNETT
HAPPY BIRTHDAY!
...EVEN IF IT *IS* YOUR BIRTHDAY. YOU HAVE TO PLAY FAIR.
NOW GO AHEAD AND TAKE A SWING.
WHERE'D THE PIÑATA GO?
FWOOSH
I WANT THAT *CANDY* INSIDE!
WHAK

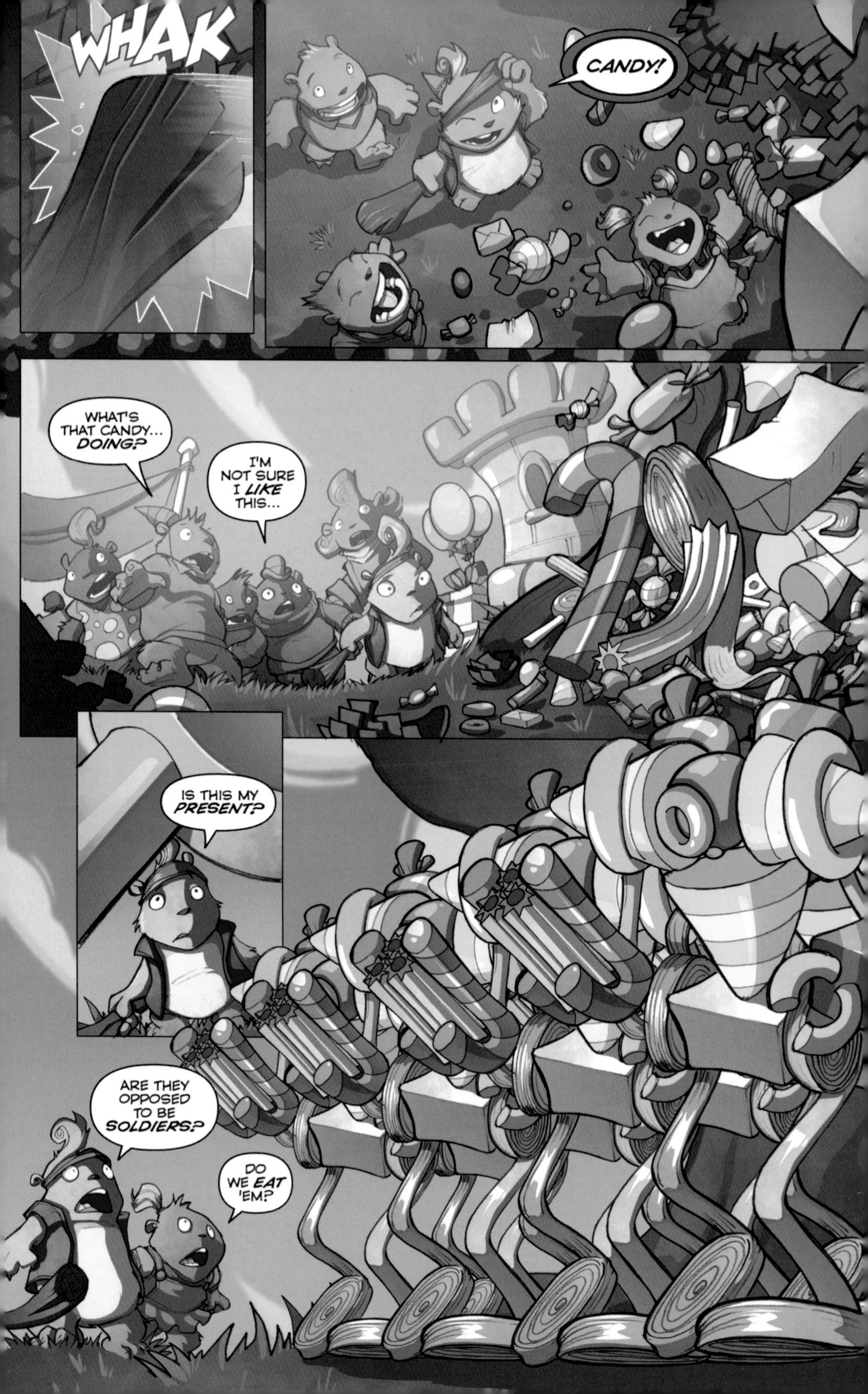
WHAK
CANDY!
WHAT'S THAT CANDY... DOING?
I'M NOT SURE I LIKE THIS...
IS THIS MY PRESENT?
ARE THEY OPPOSED TO BE SOLDIERS?
DO WE EAT 'EM?

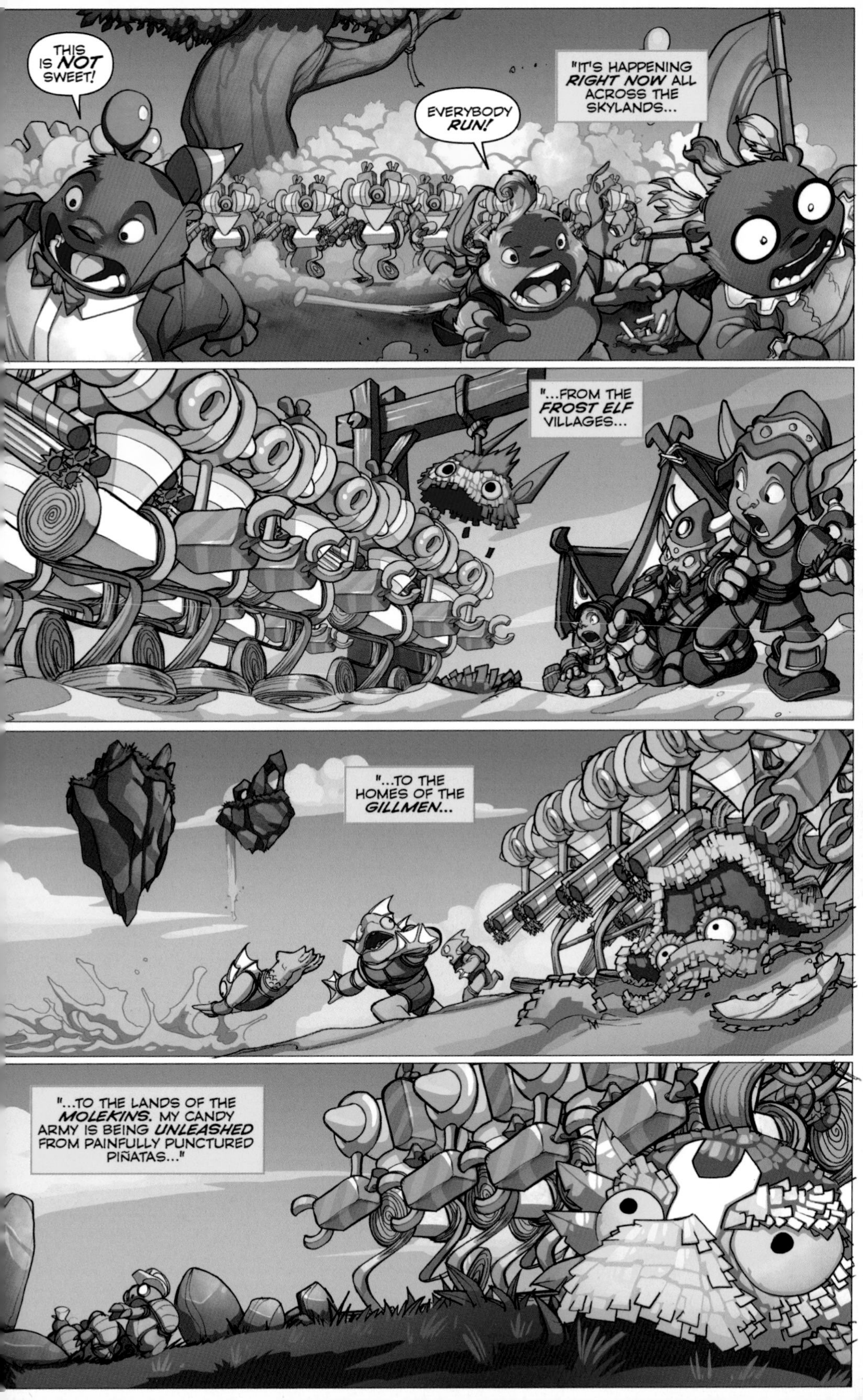
THIS IS NOT SWEET!
EVERYBODY RUN!
"IT'S HAPPENING RIGHT NOW ALL ACROSS THE SKYLANDS...
"...FROM THE FROST ELF VILLAGES...
"...TO THE HOMES OF THE GILLMEN...
"...TO THE LANDS OF THE MOLEKINS. MY CANDY ARMY IS BEING UNLEASHED FROM PAINFULLY PUNCTURED PIÑATAS..."

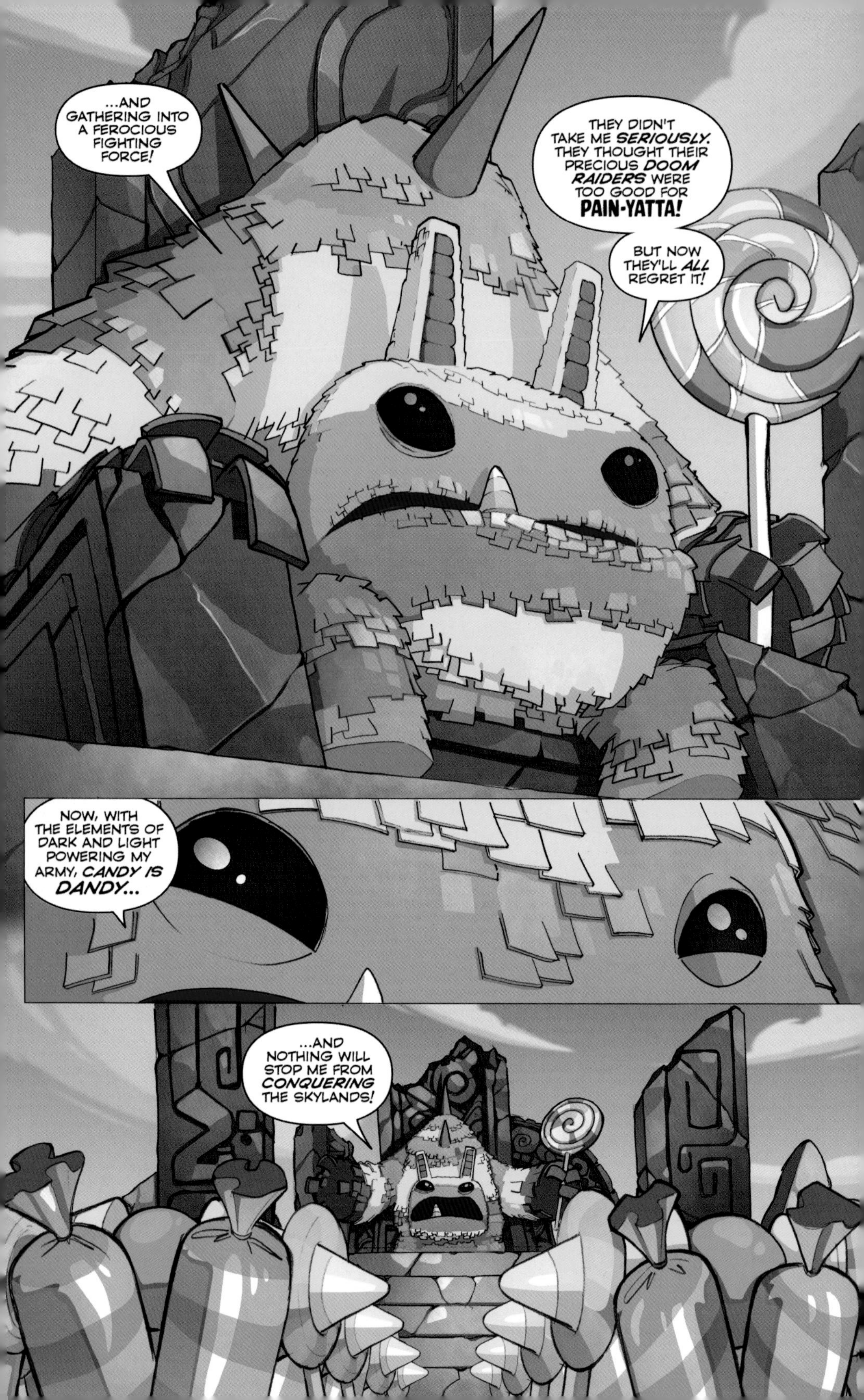
...AND GATHERING INTO A FEROCIOUS FIGHTING FORCE!
THEY DIDN'T TAKE ME *SERIOUSLY.* THEY THOUGHT THEIR PRECIOUS *DOOM RAIDERS* WERE TOO GOOD FOR **PAIN-YATTA!**
BUT NOW THEY'LL *ALL* REGRET IT!
NOW, WITH THE ELEMENTS OF DARK AND LIGHT POWERING MY ARMY, *CANDY IS DANDY...*
...AND NOTHING WILL STOP ME FROM *CONQUERING* THE SKYLANDS!

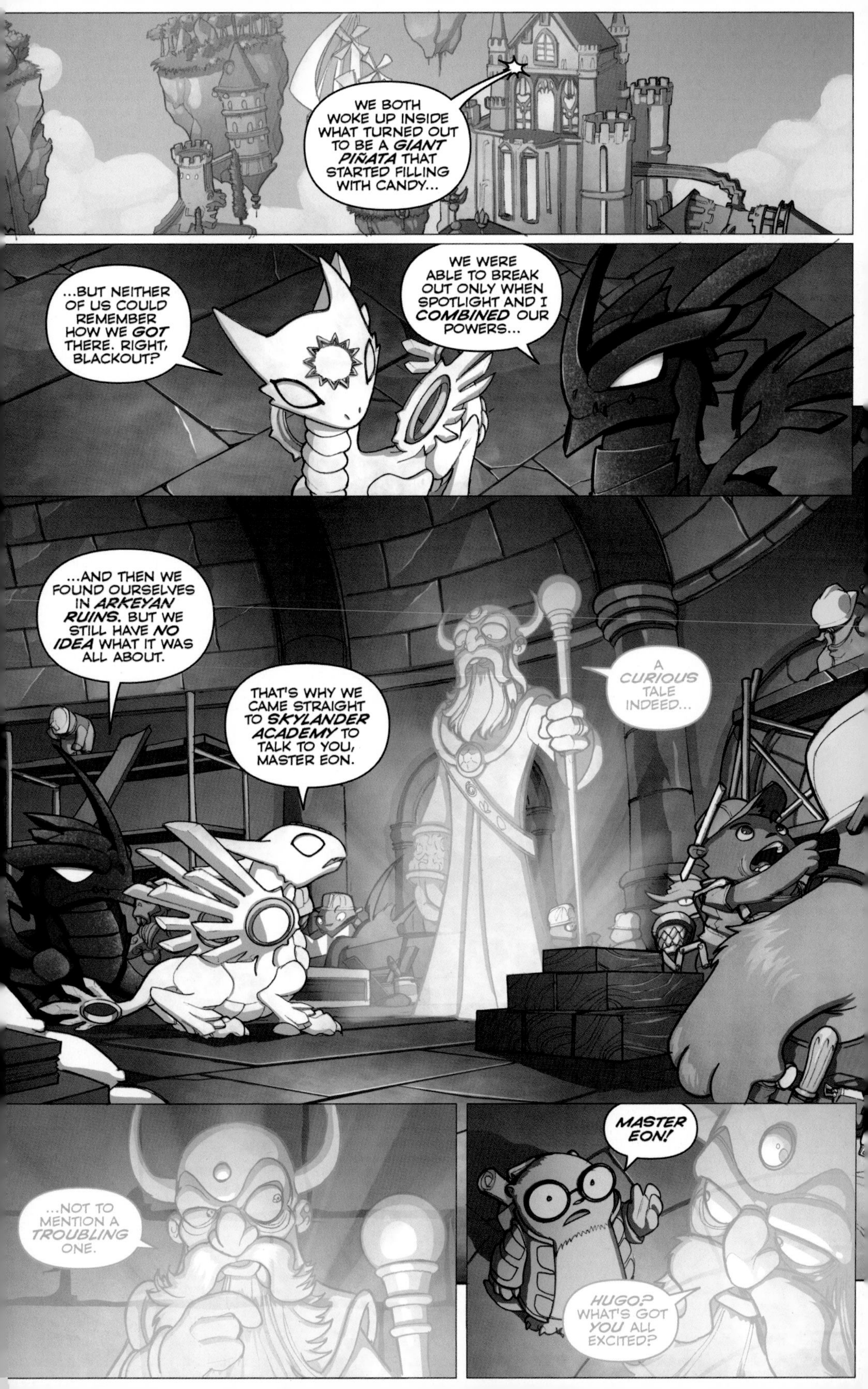
WE BOTH WOKE UP INSIDE WHAT TURNED OUT TO BE A *GIANT PIÑATA* THAT STARTED FILLING WITH CANDY...
...BUT NEITHER OF US COULD REMEMBER HOW WE *GOT* THERE. RIGHT, BLACKOUT?
WE WERE ABLE TO BREAK OUT ONLY WHEN SPOTLIGHT AND I *COMBINED* OUR POWERS...
...AND THEN WE FOUND OURSELVES IN *ARKEYAN RUINS*. BUT WE STILL HAVE *NO IDEA* WHAT IT WAS ALL ABOUT.
THAT'S WHY WE CAME STRAIGHT TO *SKYLANDER ACADEMY* TO TALK TO YOU, MASTER EON.
A *CURIOUS* TALE INDEED...
...NOT TO MENTION A *TROUBLING* ONE.
MASTER EON!
HUGO? WHAT'S GOT *YOU* ALL EXCITED?

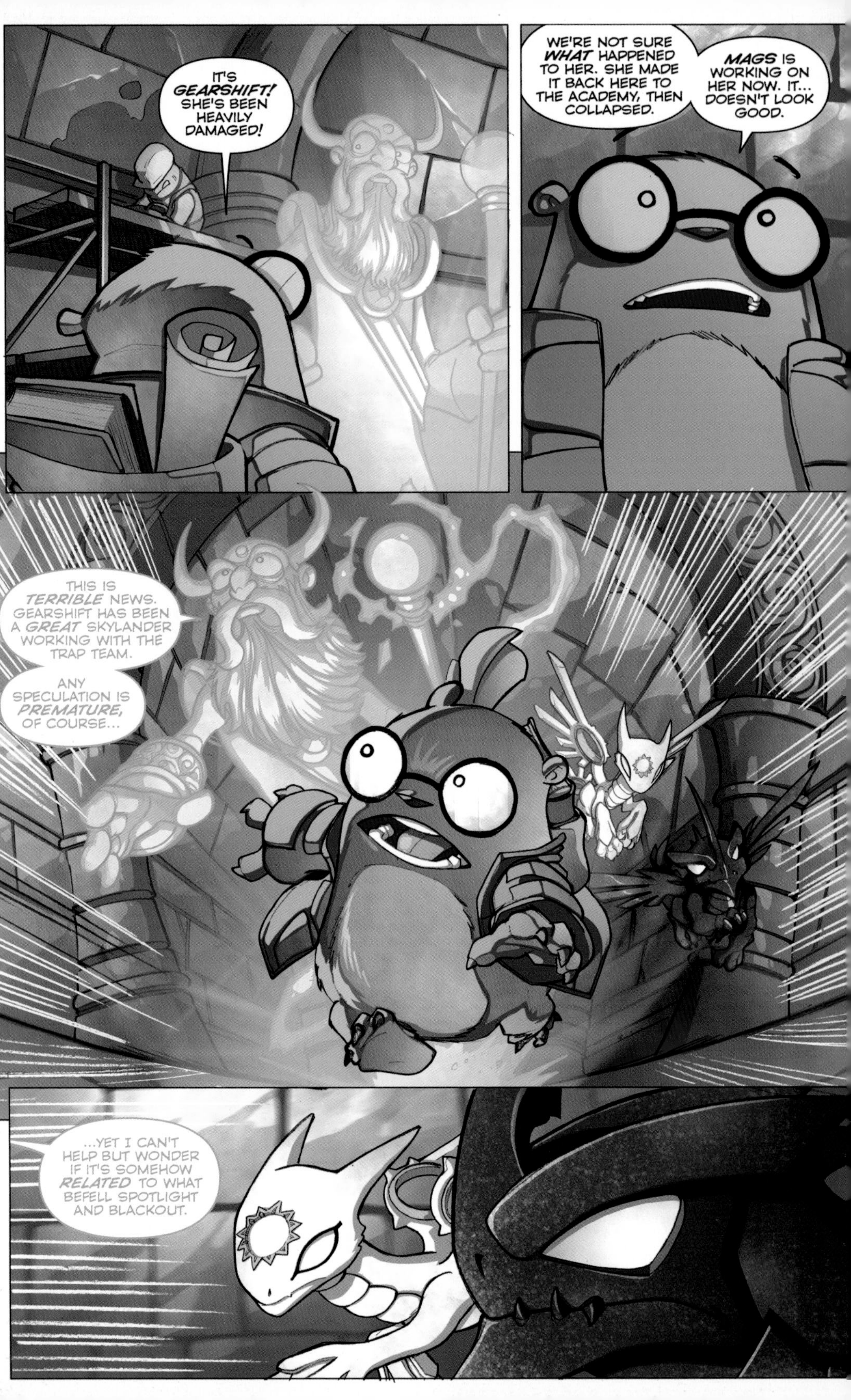
IT'S GEARSHIFT! SHE'S BEEN HEAVILY DAMAGED!
WE'RE NOT SURE WHAT HAPPENED TO HER. SHE MADE IT BACK HERE TO THE ACADEMY, THEN COLLAPSED.
MAGS IS WORKING ON HER NOW. IT... DOESN'T LOOK GOOD.
THIS IS TERRIBLE NEWS. GEARSHIFT HAS BEEN A GREAT SKYLANDER WORKING WITH THE TRAP TEAM.
ANY SPECULATION IS PREMATURE, OF COURSE...
...YET I CAN'T HELP BUT WONDER IF IT'S SOMEHOW RELATED TO WHAT BEFELL SPOTLIGHT AND BLACKOUT.

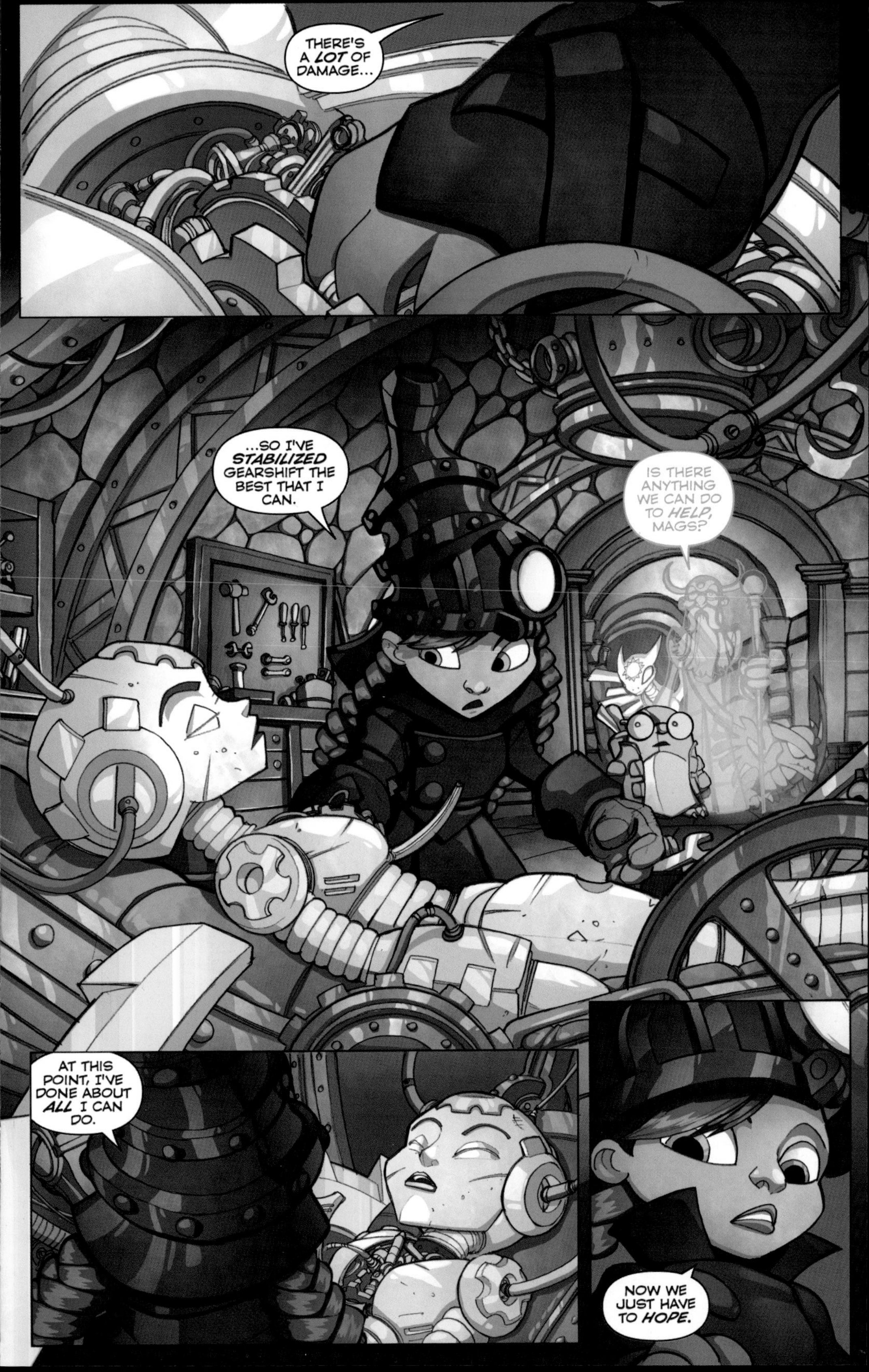
THERE'S A *LOT* OF DAMAGE...
...SO I'VE *STABILIZED* GEARSHIFT THE BEST THAT I CAN.
IS THERE ANYTHING WE CAN DO TO *HELP,* MAGS?
AT THIS POINT, I'VE DONE ABOUT *ALL* I CAN DO.
NOW WE JUST HAVE TO *HOPE.*

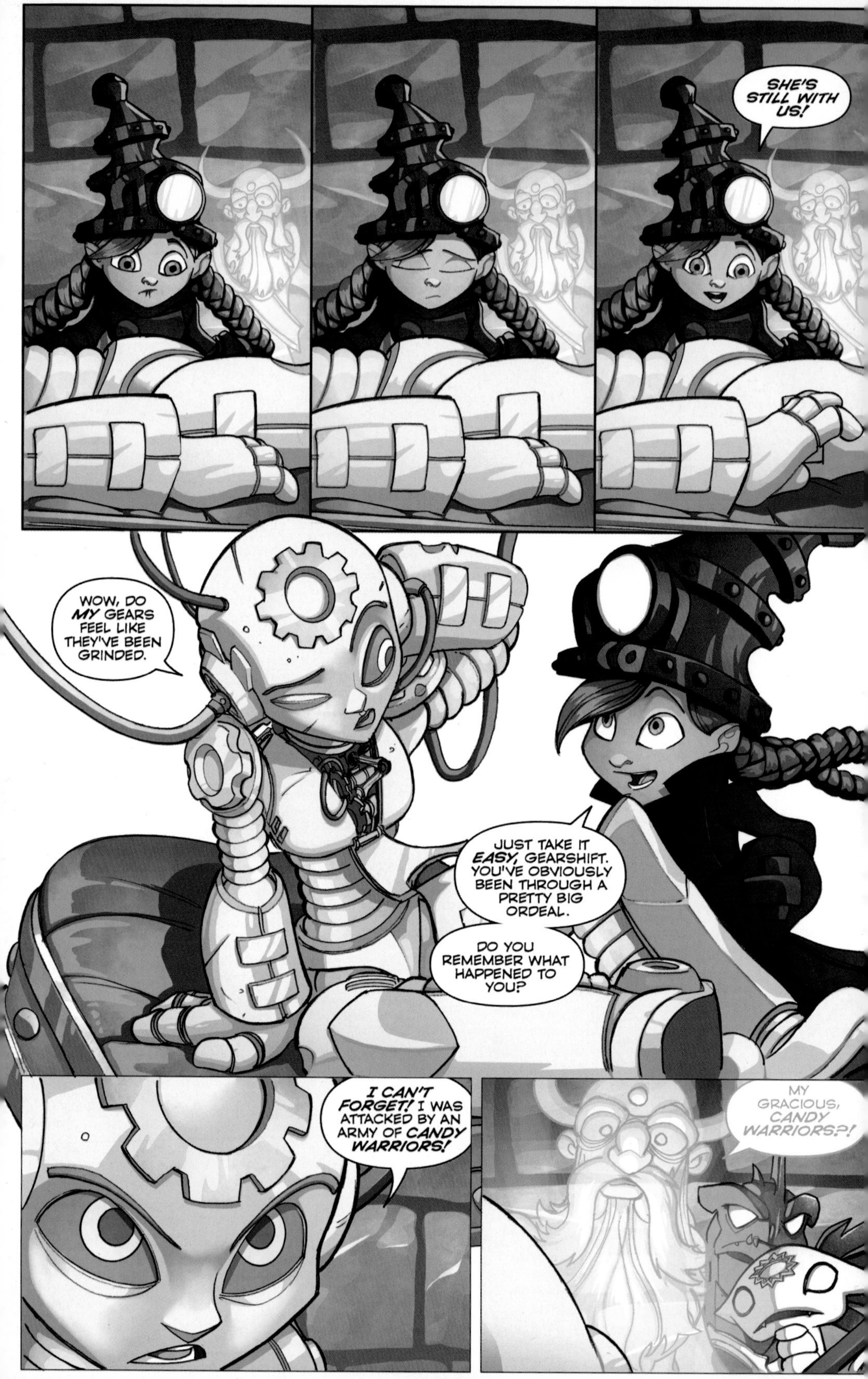
SHE'S STILL WITH US!
WOW, DO MY GEARS FEEL LIKE THEY'VE BEEN GRINDED.
JUST TAKE IT EASY, GEARSHIFT. YOU'VE OBVIOUSLY BEEN THROUGH A PRETTY BIG ORDEAL.
DO YOU REMEMBER WHAT HAPPENED TO YOU?
I CAN'T FORGET! I WAS ATTACKED BY AN ARMY OF CANDY WARRIORS!
MY GRACIOUS, CANDY WARRIORS?!

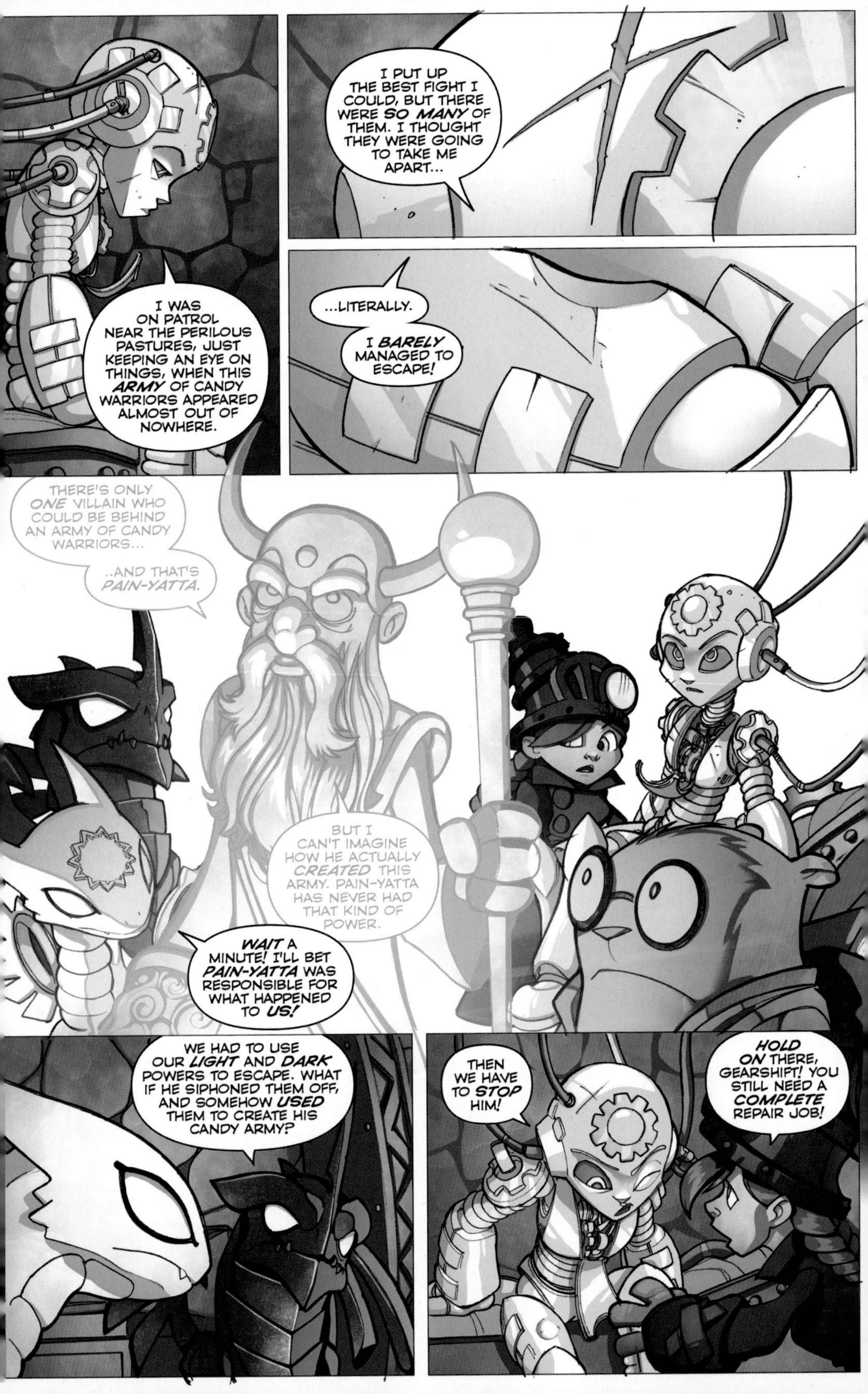
I WAS ON PATROL NEAR THE PERILOUS PASTURES, JUST KEEPING AN EYE ON THINGS, WHEN THIS ARMY OF CANDY WARRIORS APPEARED ALMOST OUT OF NOWHERE.
I PUT UP THE BEST FIGHT I COULD, BUT THERE WERE SO MANY OF THEM. I THOUGHT THEY WERE GOING TO TAKE ME APART...
...LITERALLY.
I BARELY MANAGED TO ESCAPE!
THERE'S ONLY ONE VILLAIN WHO COULD BE BEHIND AN ARMY OF CANDY WARRIORS...
..AND THAT'S PAIN-YATTA.
BUT I CAN'T IMAGINE HOW HE ACTUALLY CREATED THIS ARMY. PAIN-YATTA HAS NEVER HAD THAT KIND OF POWER.
WAIT A MINUTE! I'LL BET PAIN-YATTA WAS RESPONSIBLE FOR WHAT HAPPENED TO US!
WE HAD TO USE OUR LIGHT AND DARK POWERS TO ESCAPE. WHAT IF HE SIPHONED THEM OFF, AND SOMEHOW USED THEM TO CREATE HIS CANDY ARMY?
THEN WE HAVE TO STOP HIM!
HOLD ON THERE, GEARSHIFT! YOU STILL NEED A COMPLETE REPAIR JOB!

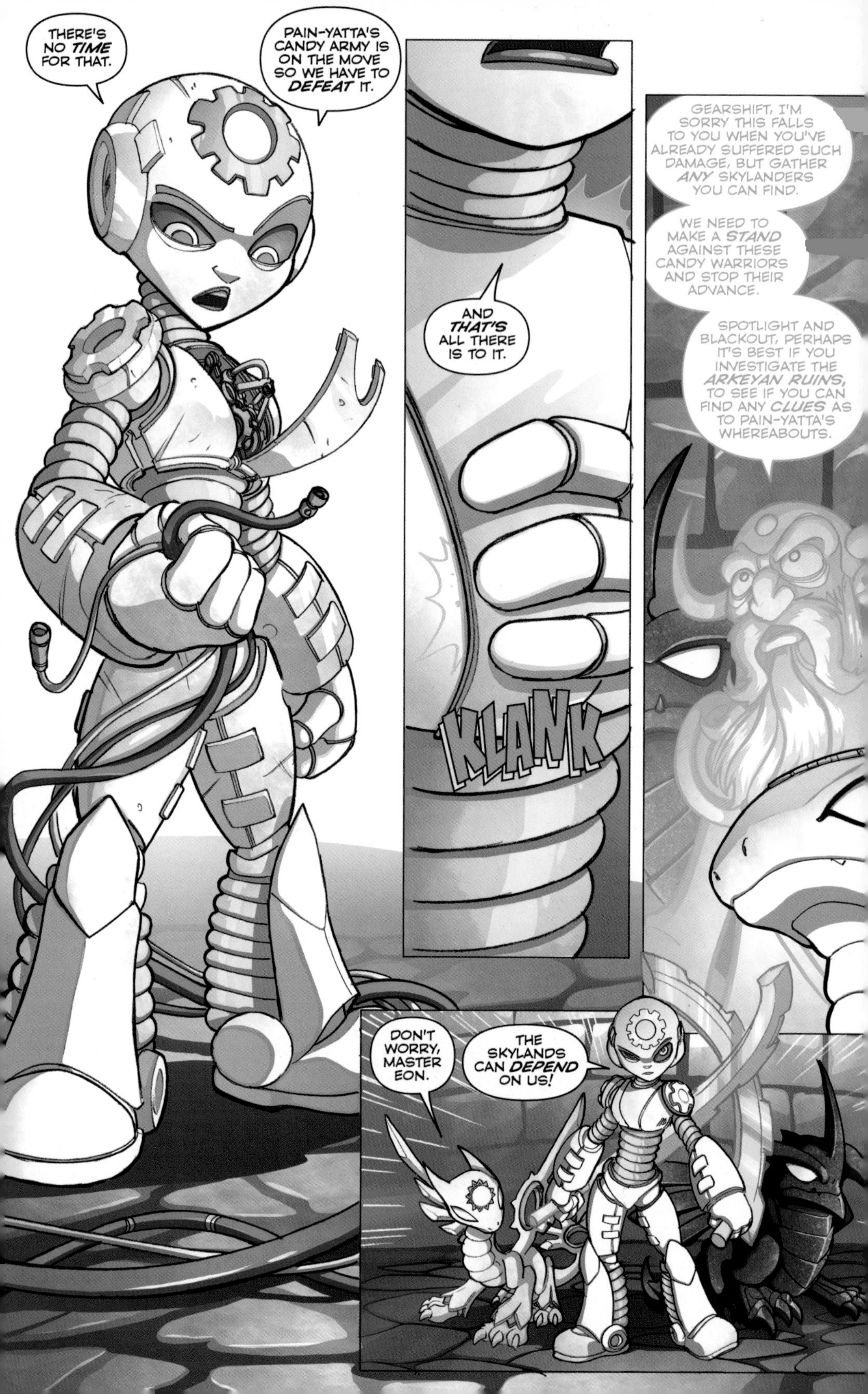
THERE'S NO TIME FOR THAT.
PAIN-YATTA'S CANDY ARMY IS ON THE MOVE SO WE HAVE TO DEFEAT IT.
AND THAT'S ALL THERE IS TO IT.
KLANK
GEARSHIFT, I'M SORRY THIS FALLS TO YOU WHEN YOU'VE ALREADY SUFFERED SUCH DAMAGE, BUT GATHER ANY SKYLANDERS YOU CAN FIND.
WE NEED TO MAKE A STAND AGAINST THESE CANDY WARRIORS AND STOP THEIR ADVANCE.
SPOTLIGHT AND BLACKOUT, PERHAPS IT'S BEST IF YOU INVESTIGATE THE ARKEYAN RUINS, TO SEE IF YOU CAN FIND ANY CLUES AS TO PAIN-YATTA'S WHEREABOUTS.
DON'T WORRY, MASTER EON.
THE SKYLANDS CAN DEPEND ON US!

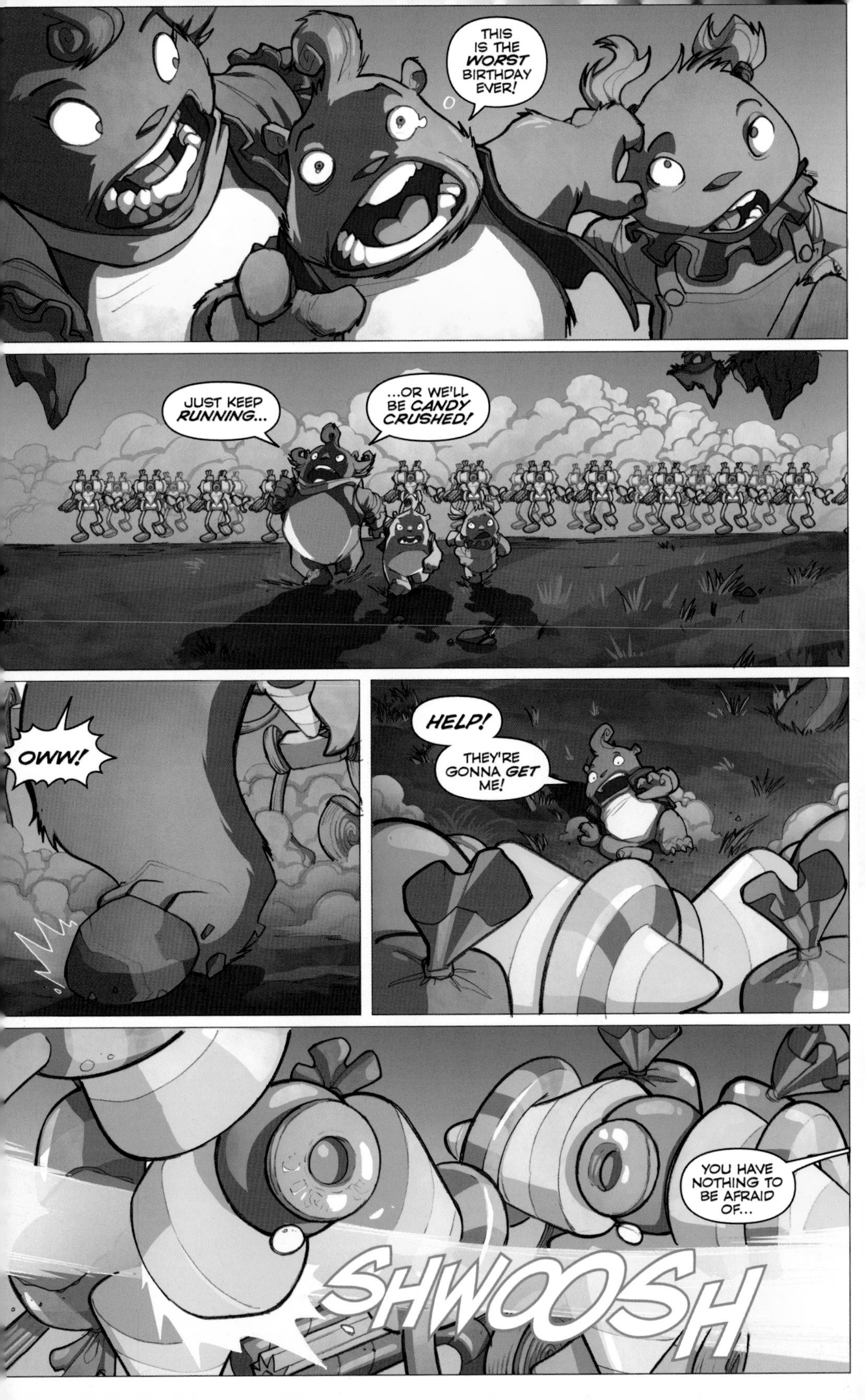
THIS IS THE WORST BIRTHDAY EVER!
JUST KEEP RUNNING...
...OR WE'LL BE CANDY CRUSHED!
OWW!
HELP!
THEY'RE GONNA GET ME!
YOU HAVE NOTHING TO BE AFRAID OF...
SHWOOSH

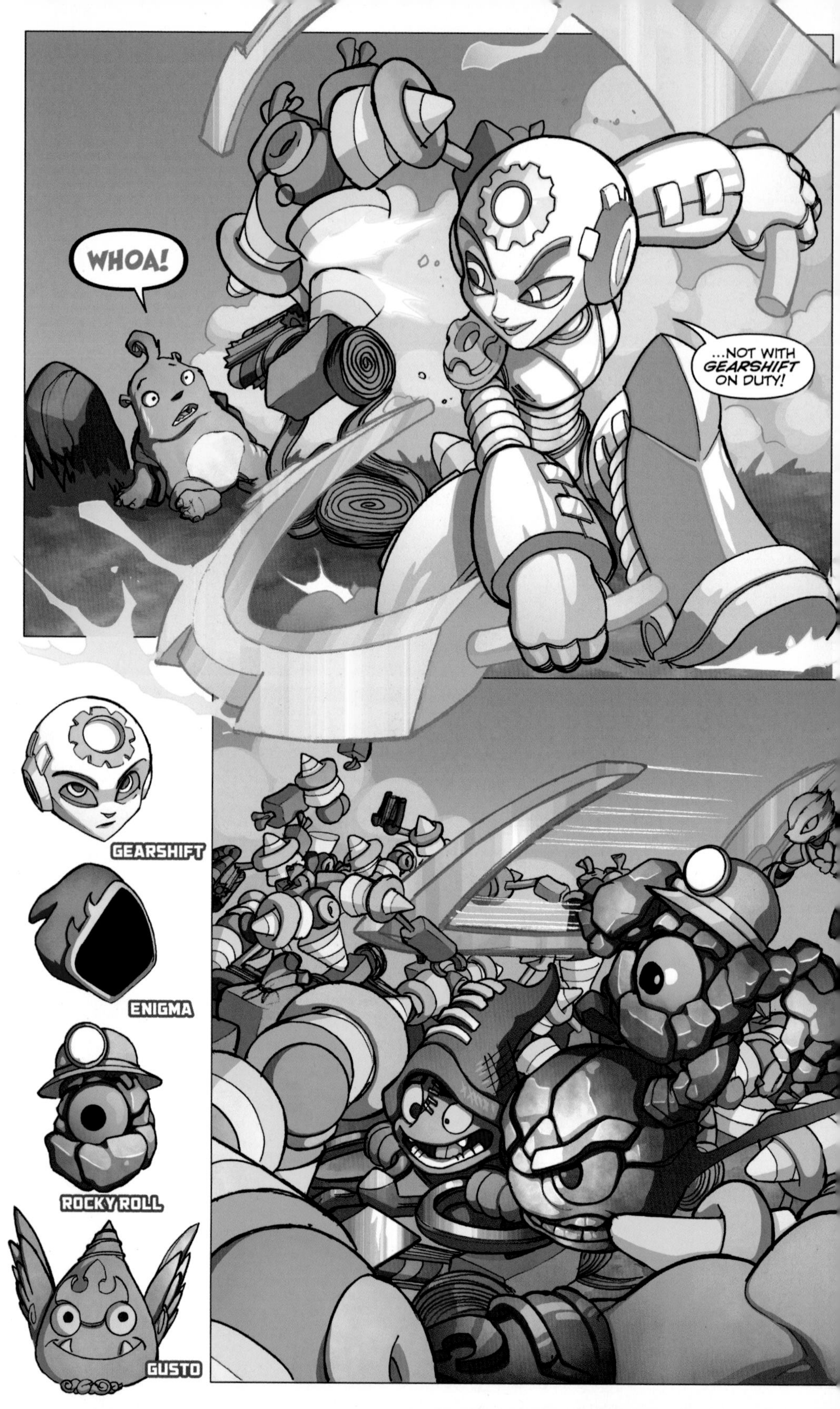
WHOA!
...NOT WITH GEARSHIFT ON DUTY!
GEARSHIFT
ENIGMA
ROCKY ROLL
GUSTO

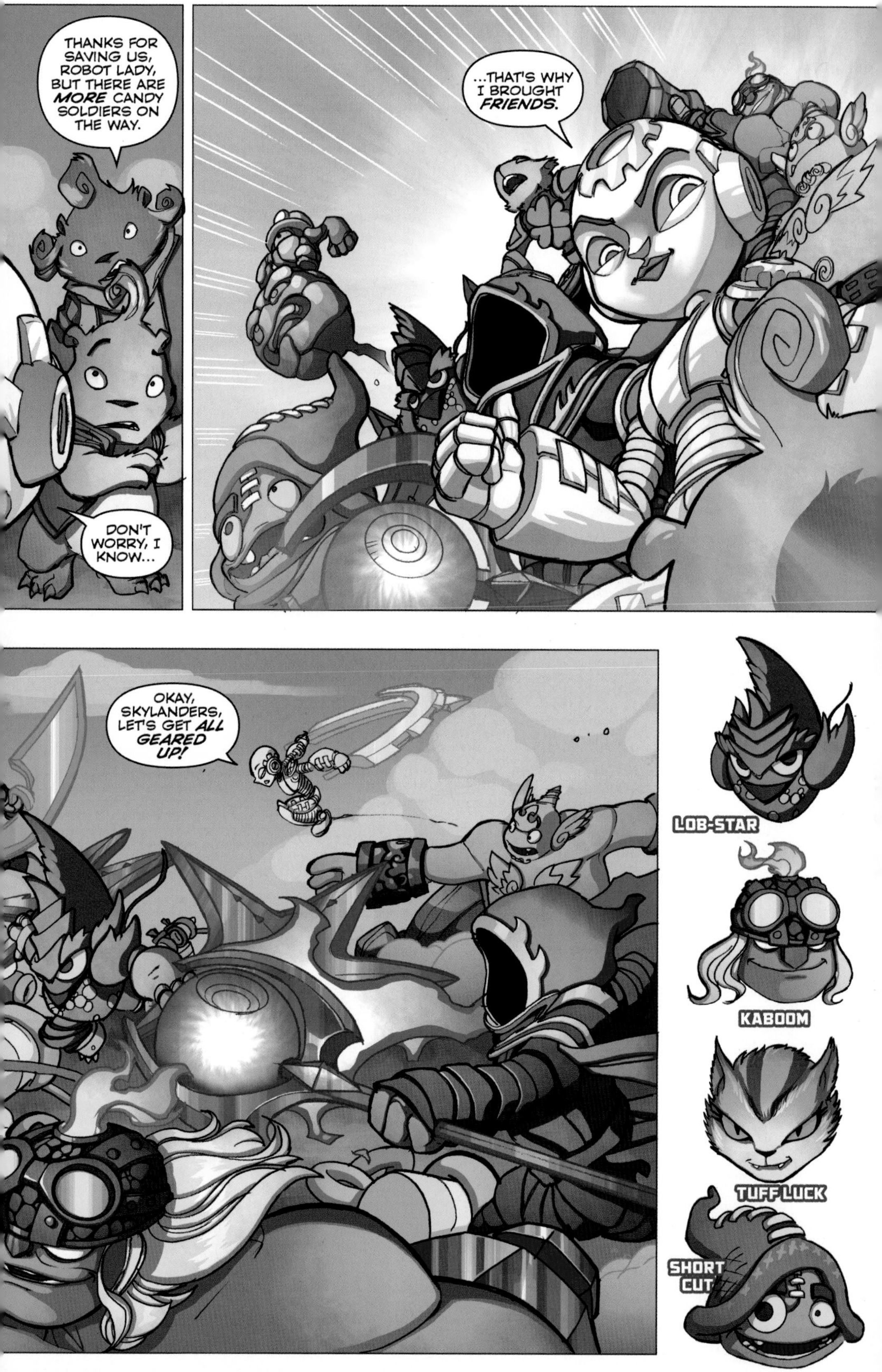
THANKS FOR SAVING US, ROBOT LADY, BUT THERE ARE *MORE* CANDY SOLDIERS ON THE WAY.
DON'T WORRY, I KNOW...
...THAT'S WHY I BROUGHT *FRIENDS*.
OKAY, SKYLANDERS, LET'S GET *ALL GEARED UP!*
LOB-STAR
KABOOM
TUFF LUCK
SHORT CUT

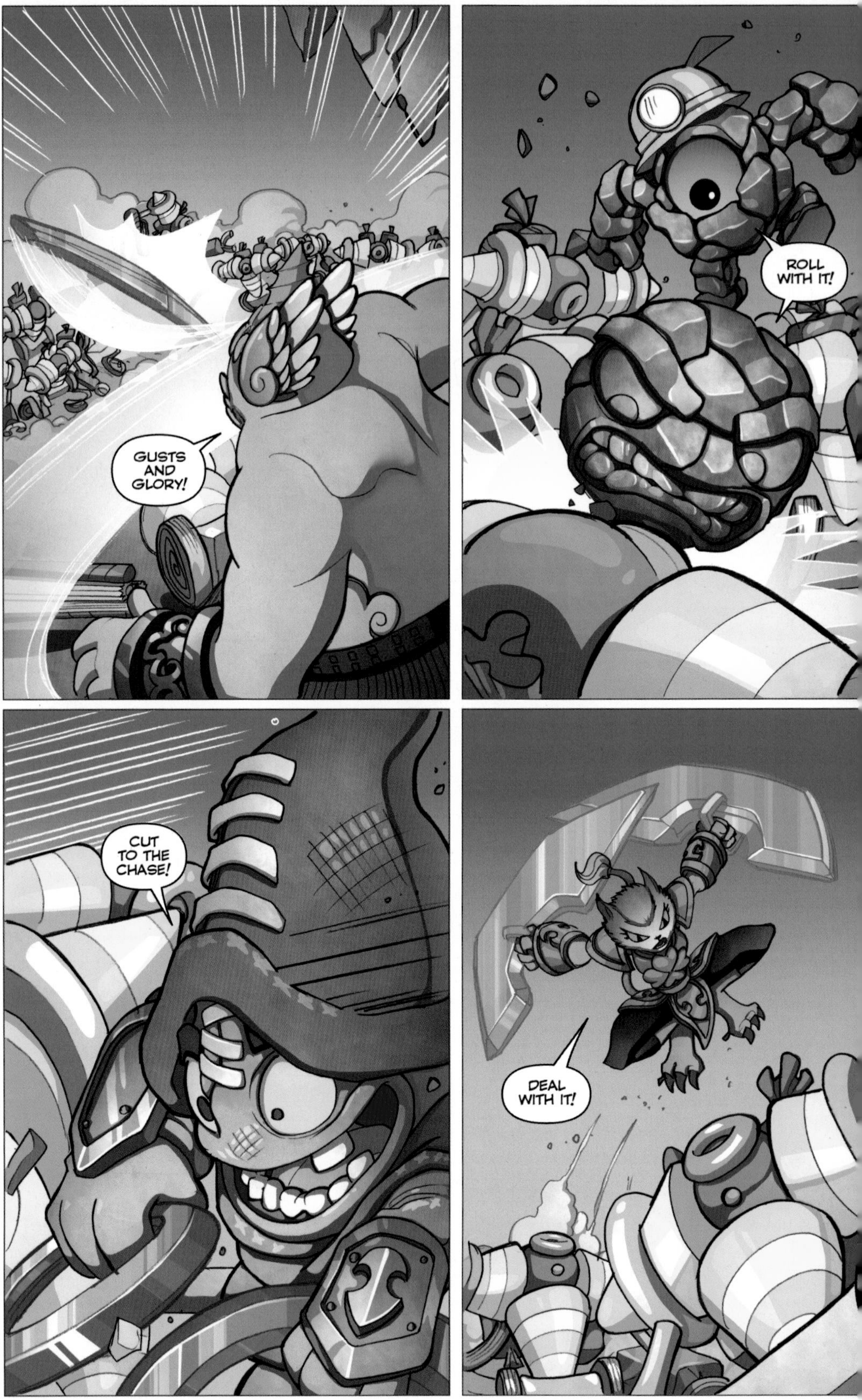
GUSTS AND GLORY!
ROLL WITH IT!
CUT TO THE CHASE!
DEAL WITH IT!

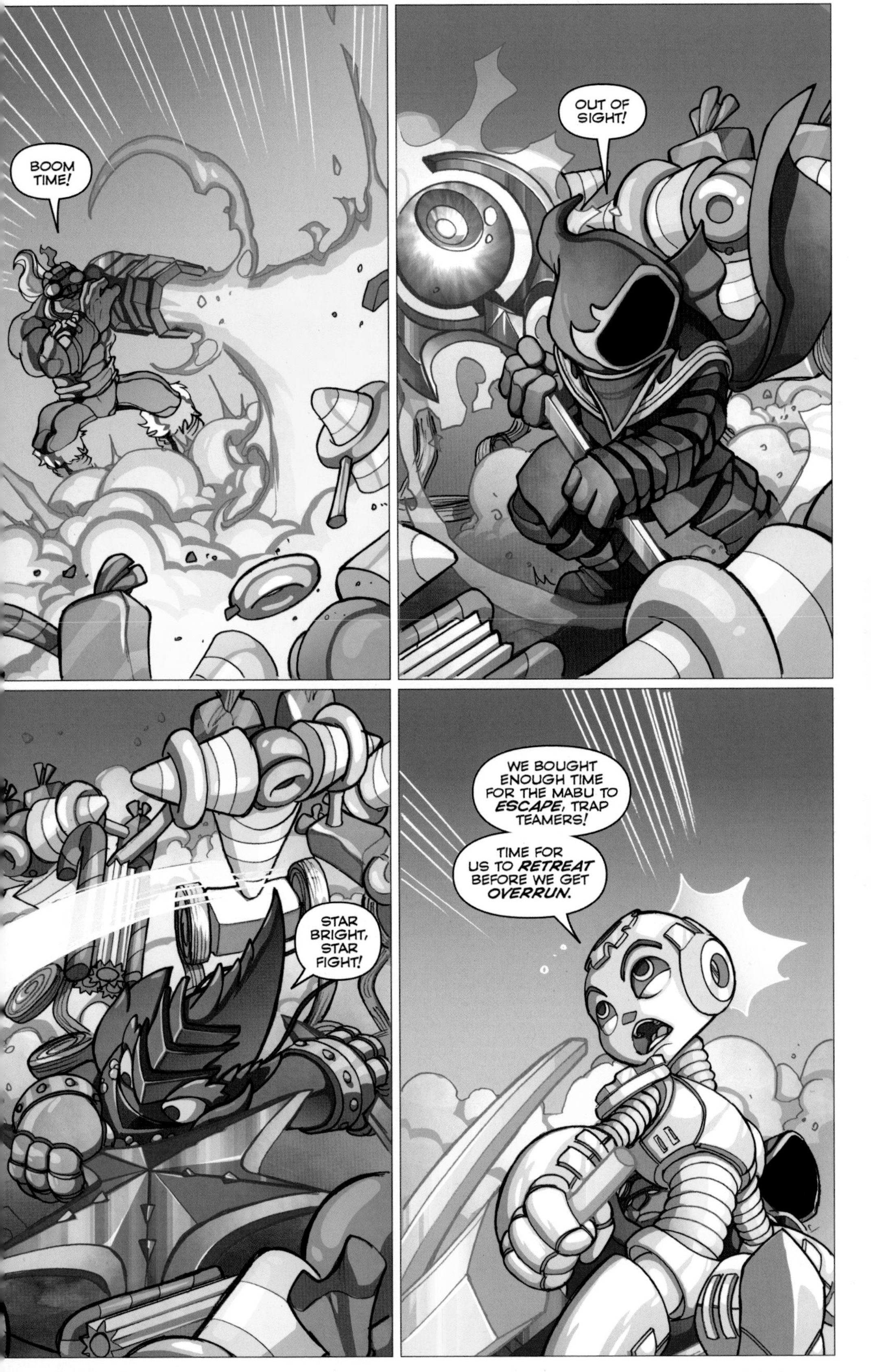
BOOM TIME!
OUT OF SIGHT!
STAR BRIGHT, STAR FIGHT!
WE BOUGHT ENOUGH TIME FOR THE MABU TO ESCAPE, TRAP TEAMERS!
TIME FOR US TO RETREAT BEFORE WE GET OVERRUN.

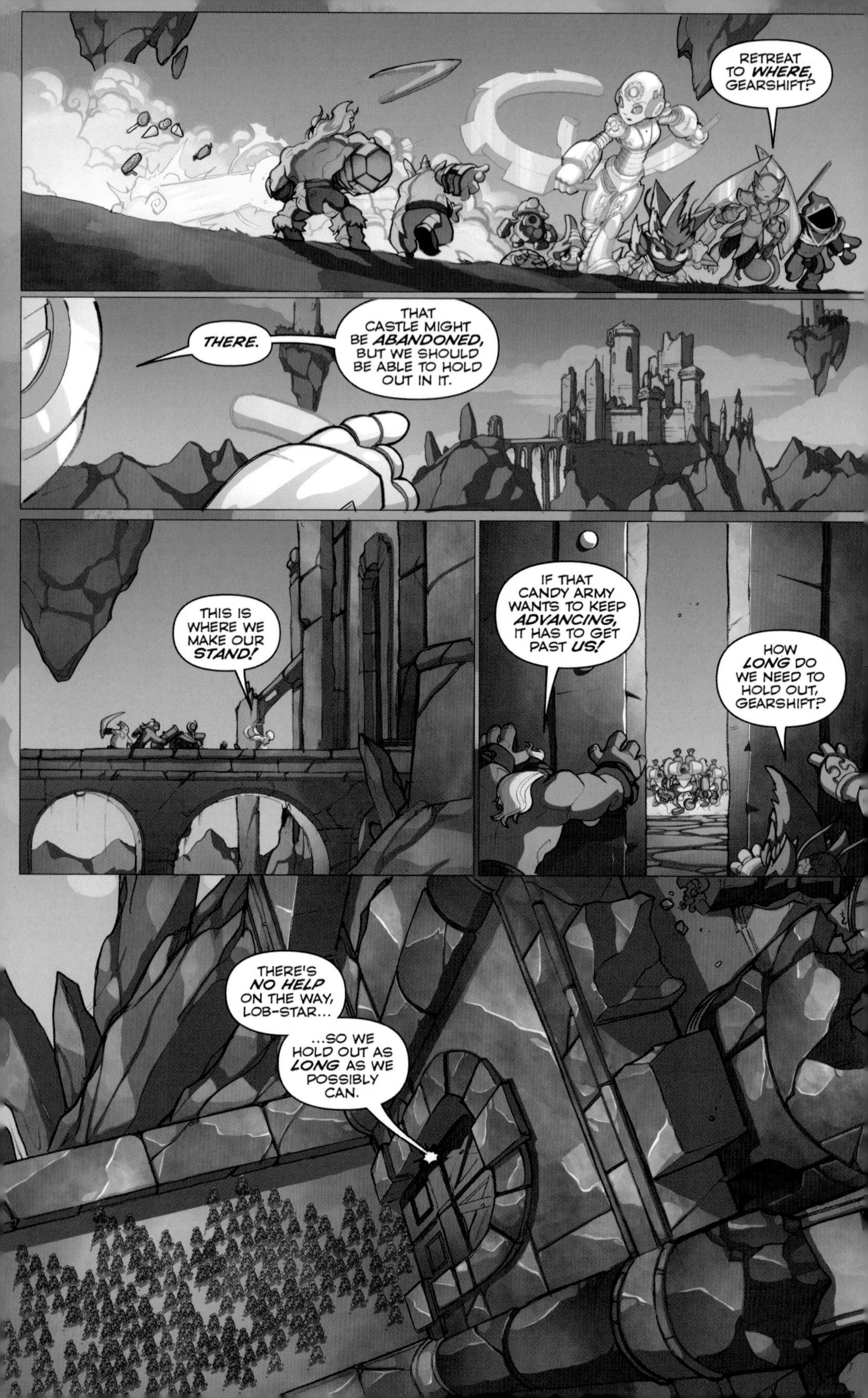
RETREAT TO WHERE, GEARSHIFT?
THERE.
THAT CASTLE MIGHT BE ABANDONED, BUT WE SHOULD BE ABLE TO HOLD OUT IN IT.
THIS IS WHERE WE MAKE OUR STAND!
IF THAT CANDY ARMY WANTS TO KEEP ADVANCING, IT HAS TO GET PAST US!
HOW LONG DO WE NEED TO HOLD OUT, GEARSHIFT?
THERE'S NO HELP ON THE WAY, LOB-STAR...
...SO WE HOLD OUT AS LONG AS WE POSSIBLY CAN.

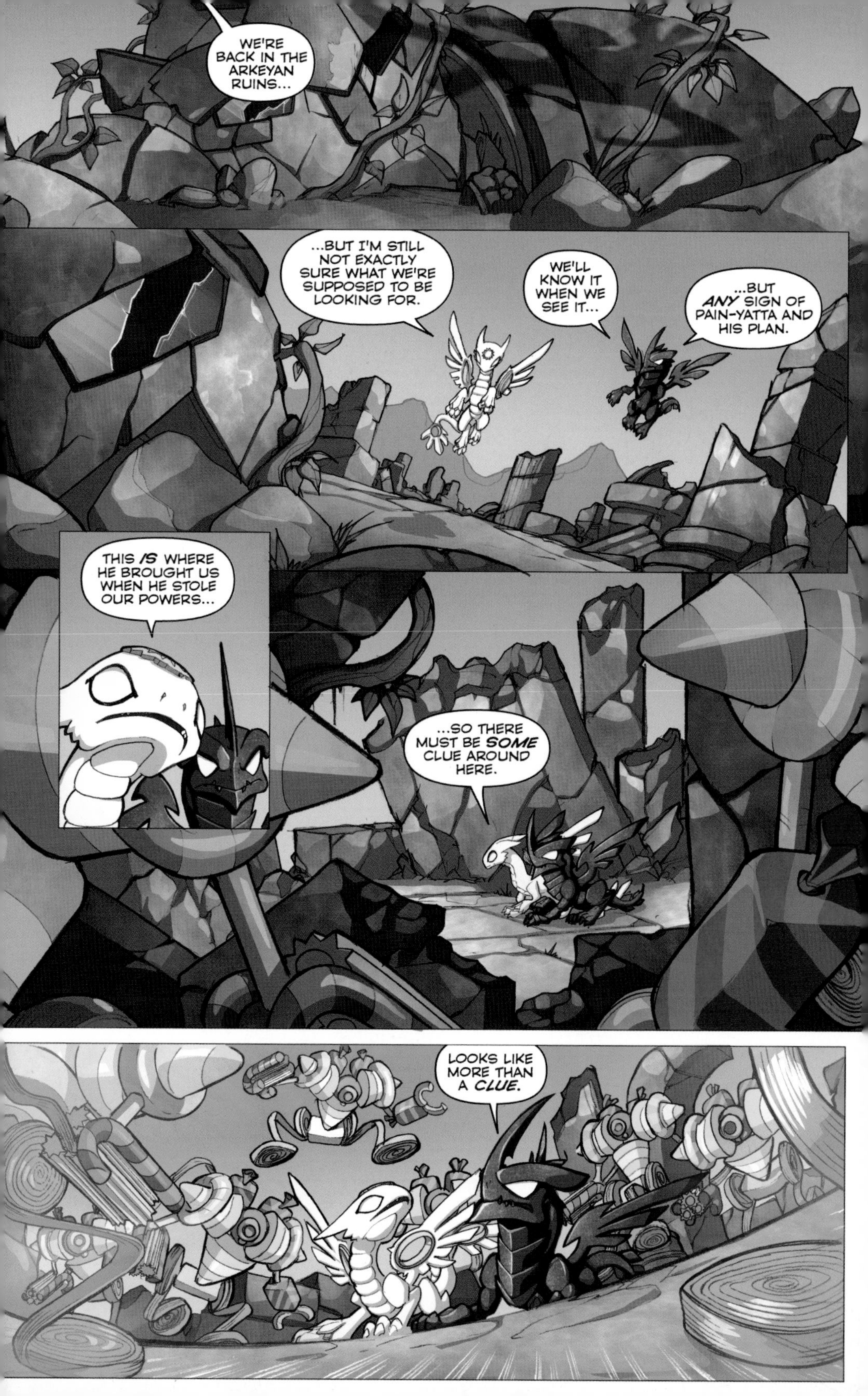
WE'RE BACK IN THE ARKEYAN RUINS...
...BUT I'M STILL NOT EXACTLY SURE WHAT WE'RE SUPPOSED TO BE LOOKING FOR.
WE'LL KNOW IT WHEN WE SEE IT...
...BUT ANY SIGN OF PAIN-YATTA AND HIS PLAN.
THIS IS WHERE HE BROUGHT US WHEN HE STOLE OUR POWERS...
...SO THERE MUST BE SOME CLUE AROUND HERE.
LOOKS LIKE MORE THAN A CLUE.

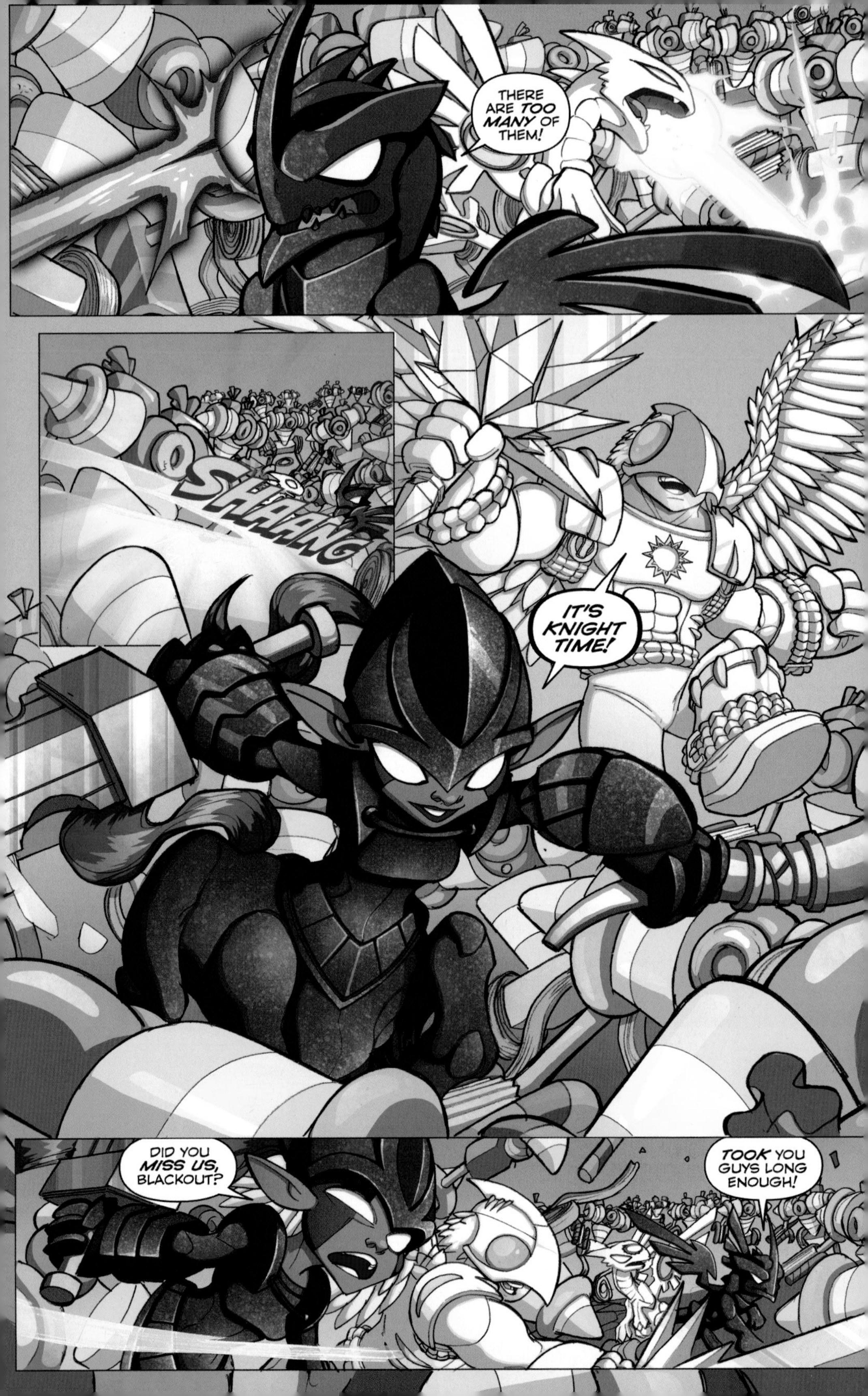
THERE ARE TOO MANY OF THEM!
SHAAANG
IT'S KNIGHT TIME!
DID YOU MISS US, BLACKOUT?
TOOK YOU GUYS LONG ENOUGH!

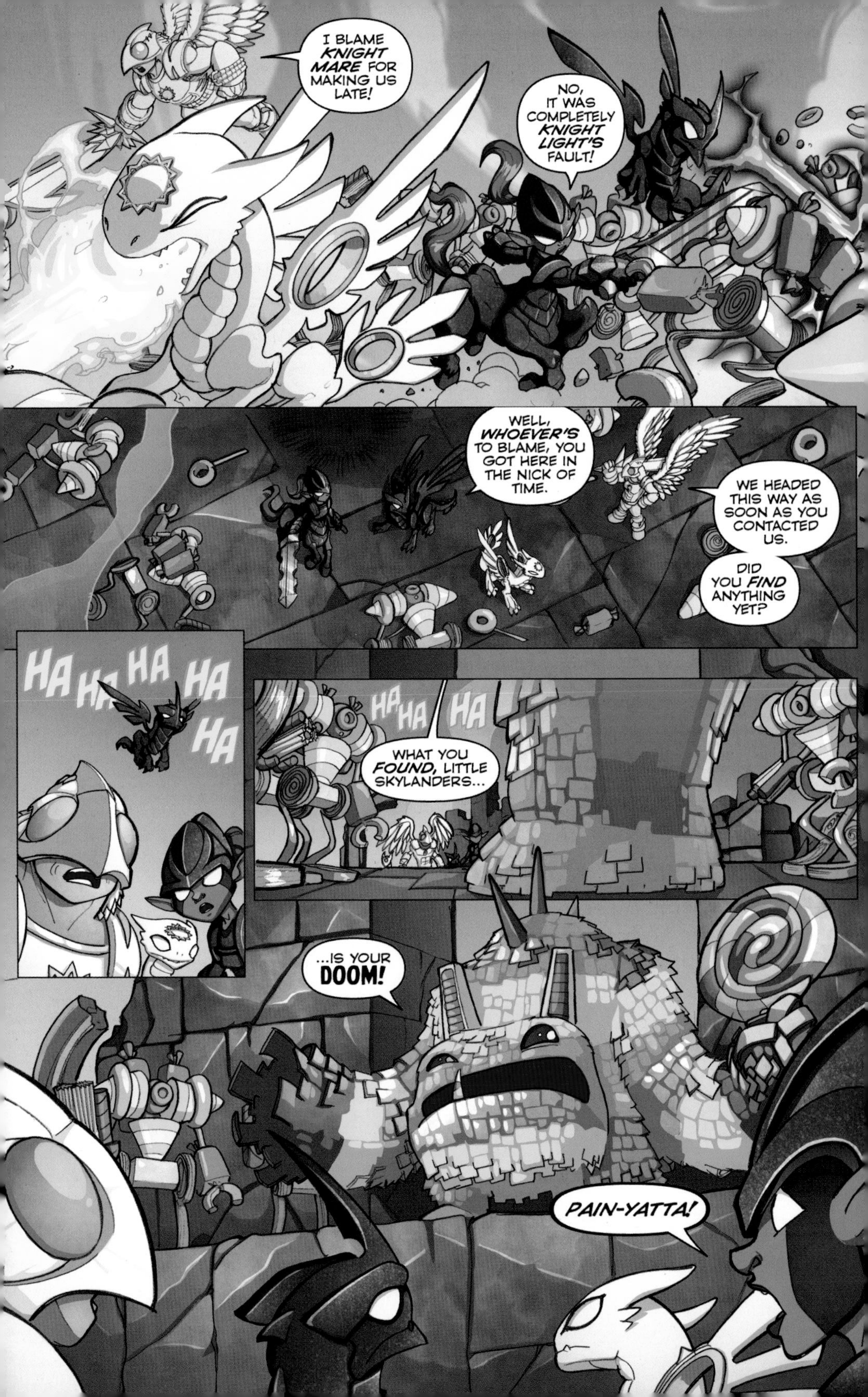
I BLAME KNIGHT MARE FOR MAKING US LATE!
NO, IT WAS COMPLETELY KNIGHT LIGHT'S FAULT!
WELL, WHOEVER'S TO BLAME, YOU GOT HERE IN THE NICK OF TIME.
WE HEADED THIS WAY AS SOON AS YOU CONTACTED US.
DID YOU FIND ANYTHING YET?
HA HA HA HA HA
HA HA HA
WHAT YOU FOUND, LITTLE SKYLANDERS...
...IS YOUR DOOM!
PAIN-YATTA!

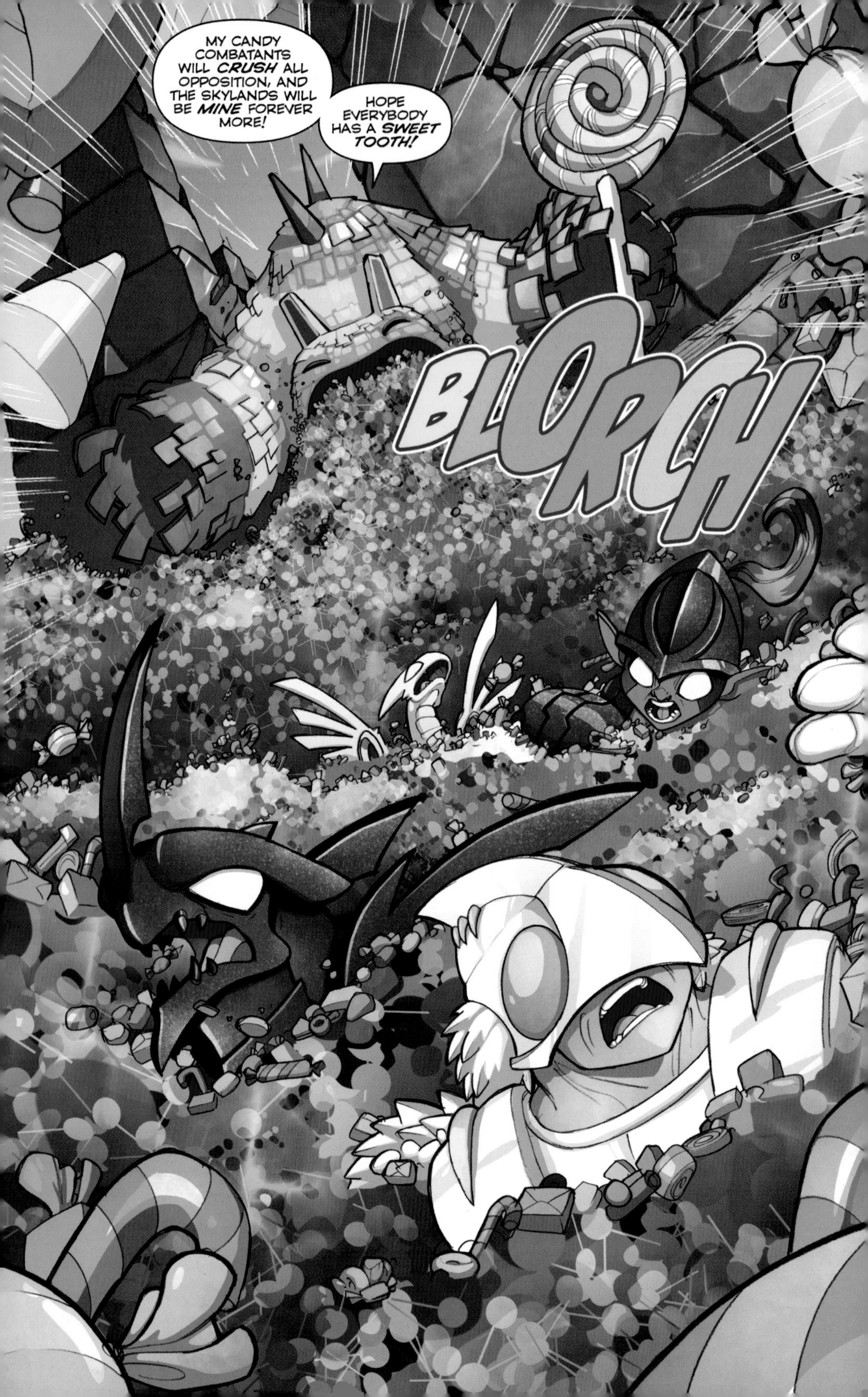
MY CANDY COMBATANTS WILL *CRUSH* ALL OPPOSITION, AND THE SKYLANDS WILL BE *MINE* FOREVER MORE!
HOPE EVERYBODY HAS A *SWEET TOOTH!*
BLORCH

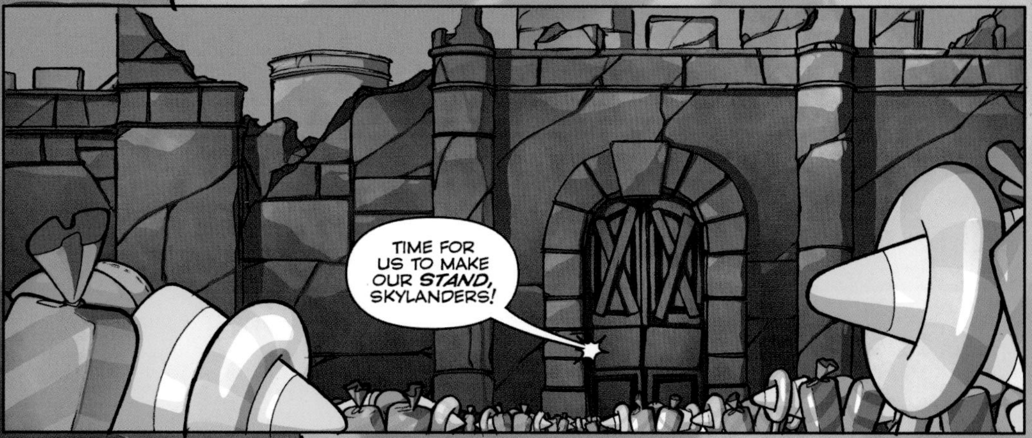
TIME FOR US TO MAKE OUR **STAND,** SKYLANDERS!

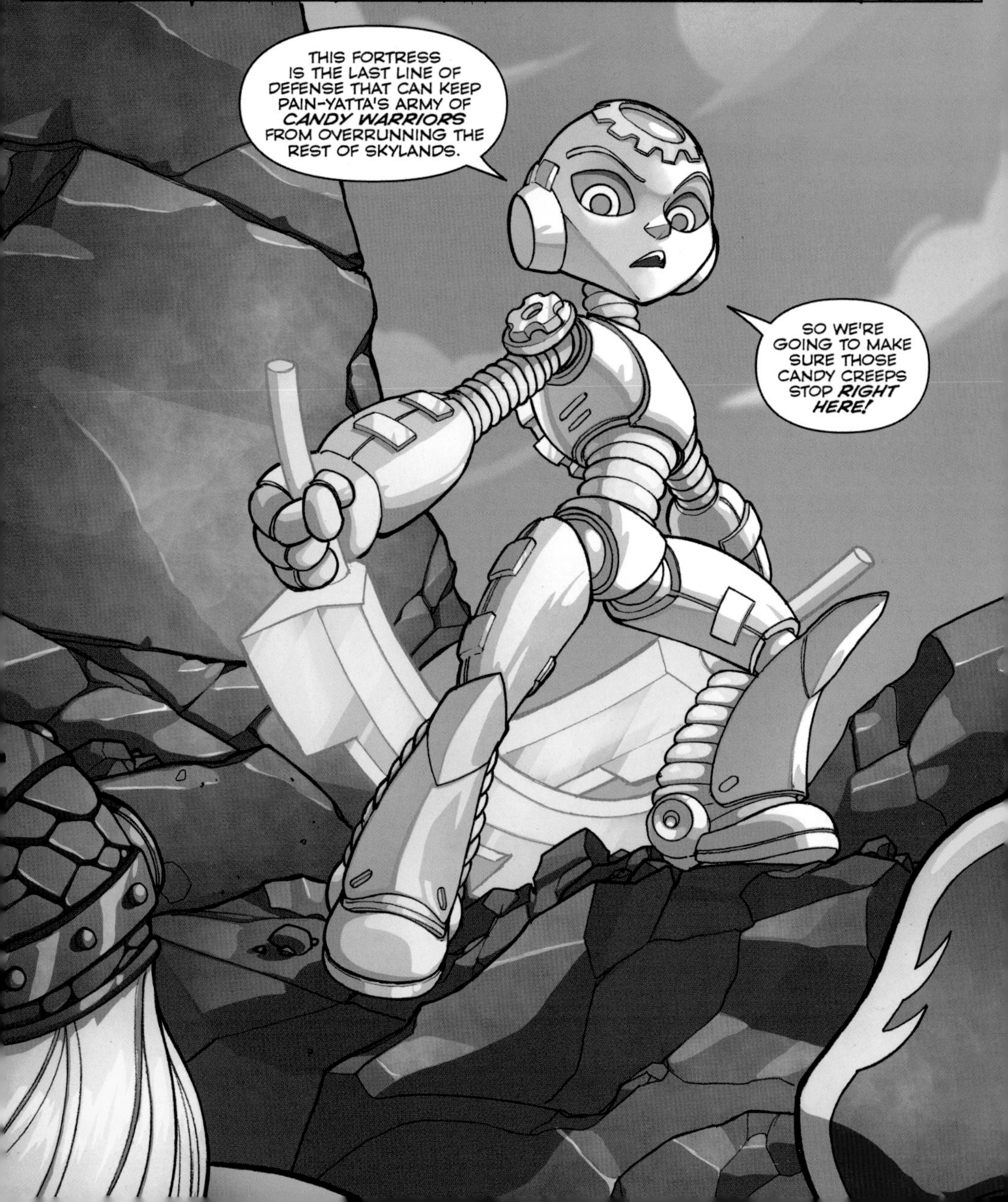
THIS FORTRESS IS THE LAST LINE OF DEFENSE THAT CAN KEEP PAIN-YATTA'S ARMY OF **CANDY WARRIORS** FROM OVERRUNNING THE REST OF SKYLANDS.
SO WE'RE GOING TO MAKE SURE THOSE CANDY CREEPS STOP **RIGHT HERE!**

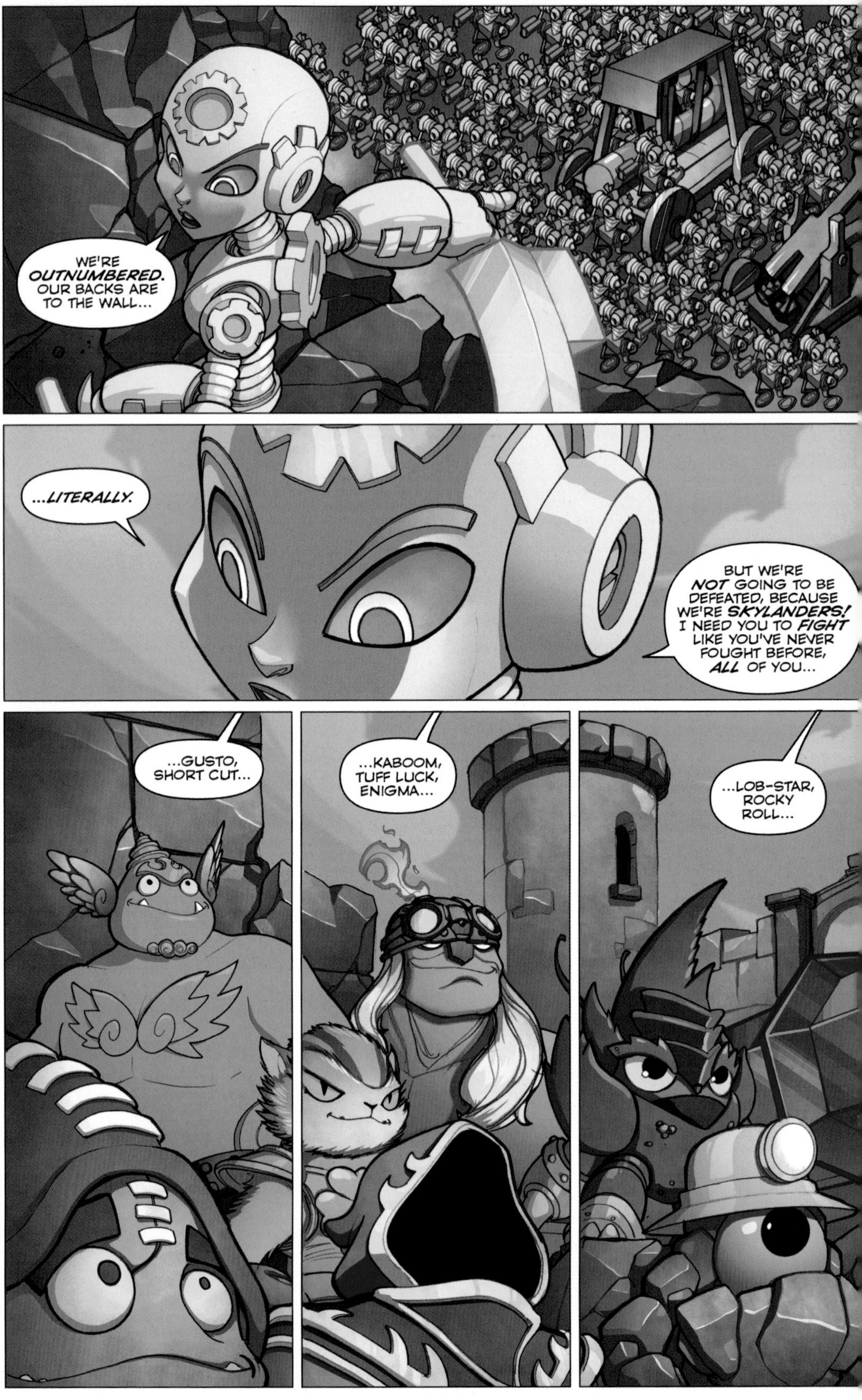
WE'RE OUTNUMBERED. OUR BACKS ARE TO THE WALL...
...LITERALLY.
BUT WE'RE NOT GOING TO BE DEFEATED, BECAUSE WE'RE SKYLANDERS! I NEED YOU TO FIGHT LIKE YOU'VE NEVER FOUGHT BEFORE, ALL OF YOU...
...GUSTO, SHORT CUT...
...KABOOM, TUFF LUCK, ENIGMA...
...LOB-STAR, ROCKY ROLL...

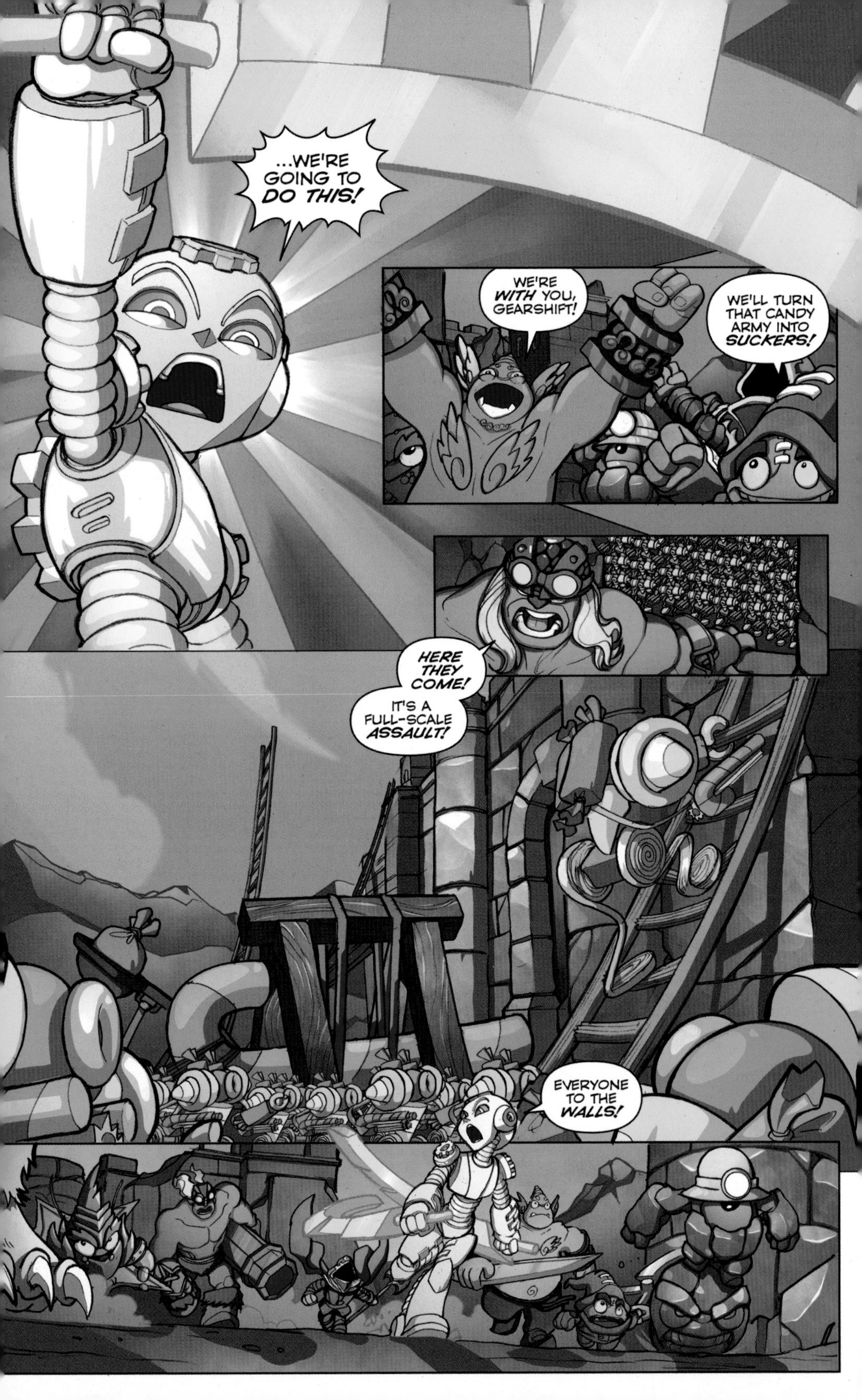
...WE'RE GOING TO *DO THIS!*
WE'RE *WITH* YOU, GEARSHIFT!
WE'LL TURN THAT CANDY ARMY INTO *SUCKERS!*
HERE THEY COME!
IT'S A FULL-SCALE *ASSAULT!*
EVERYONE TO THE *WALLS!*

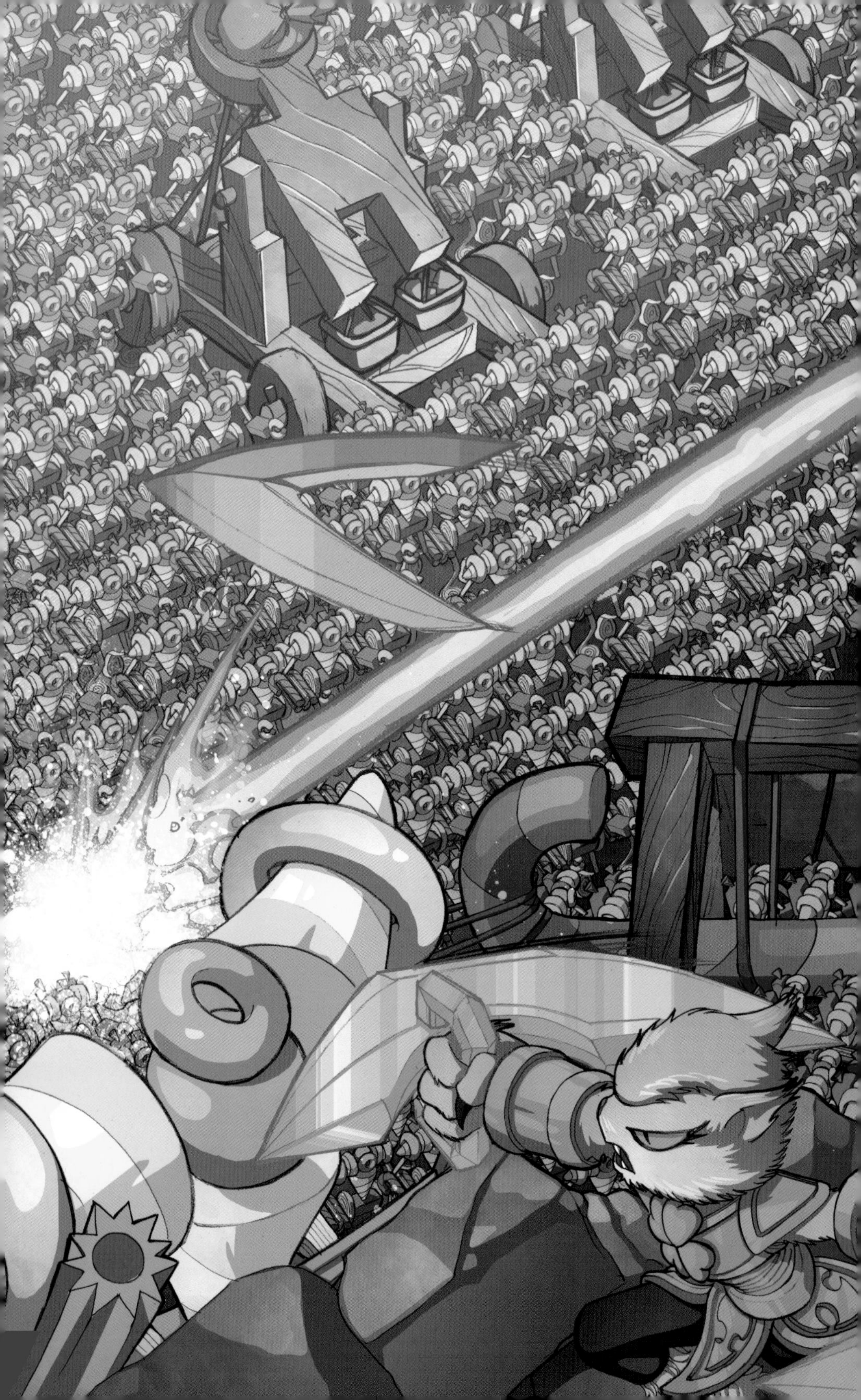

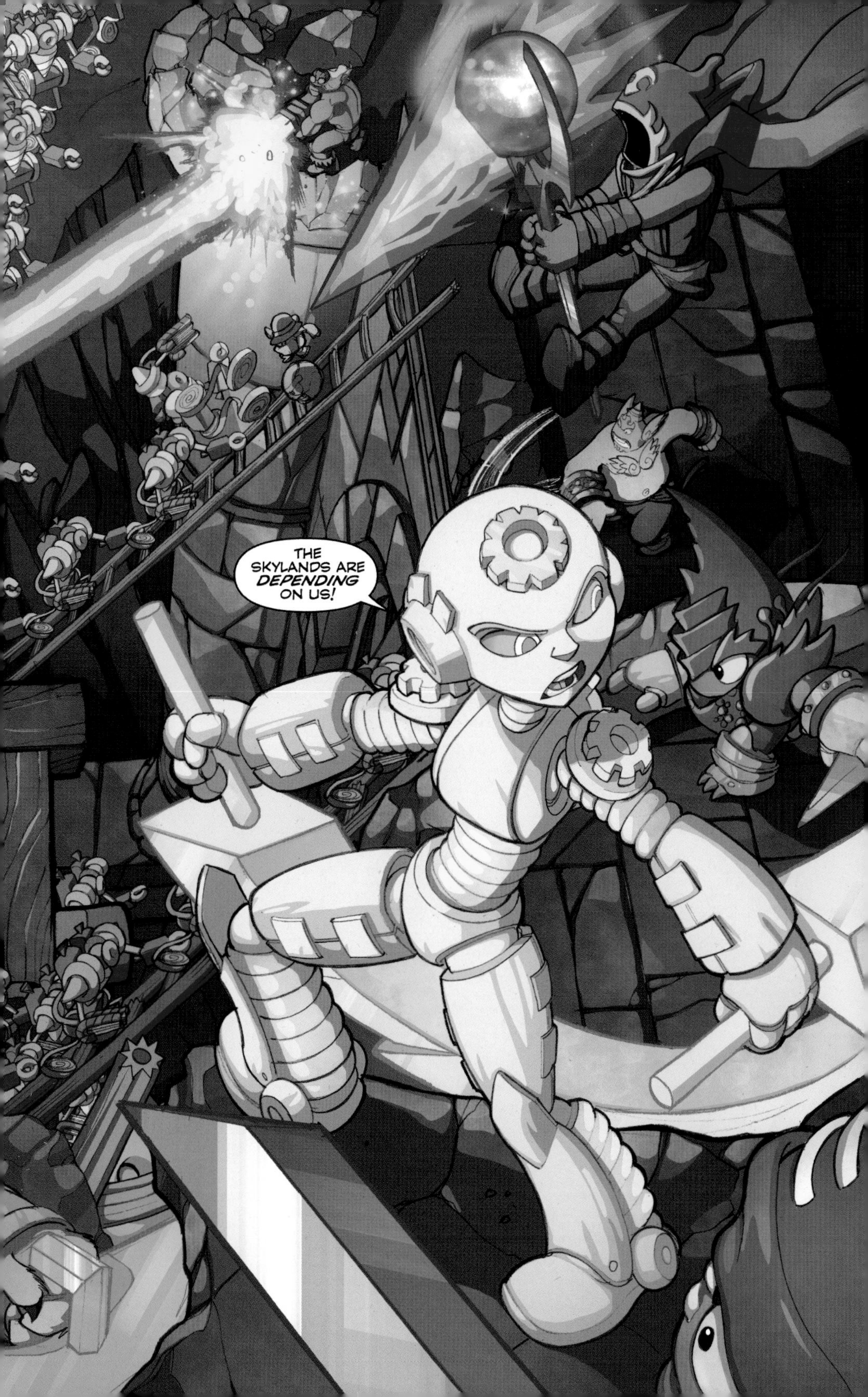
THE SKYLANDS ARE *DEPENDING* ON US!

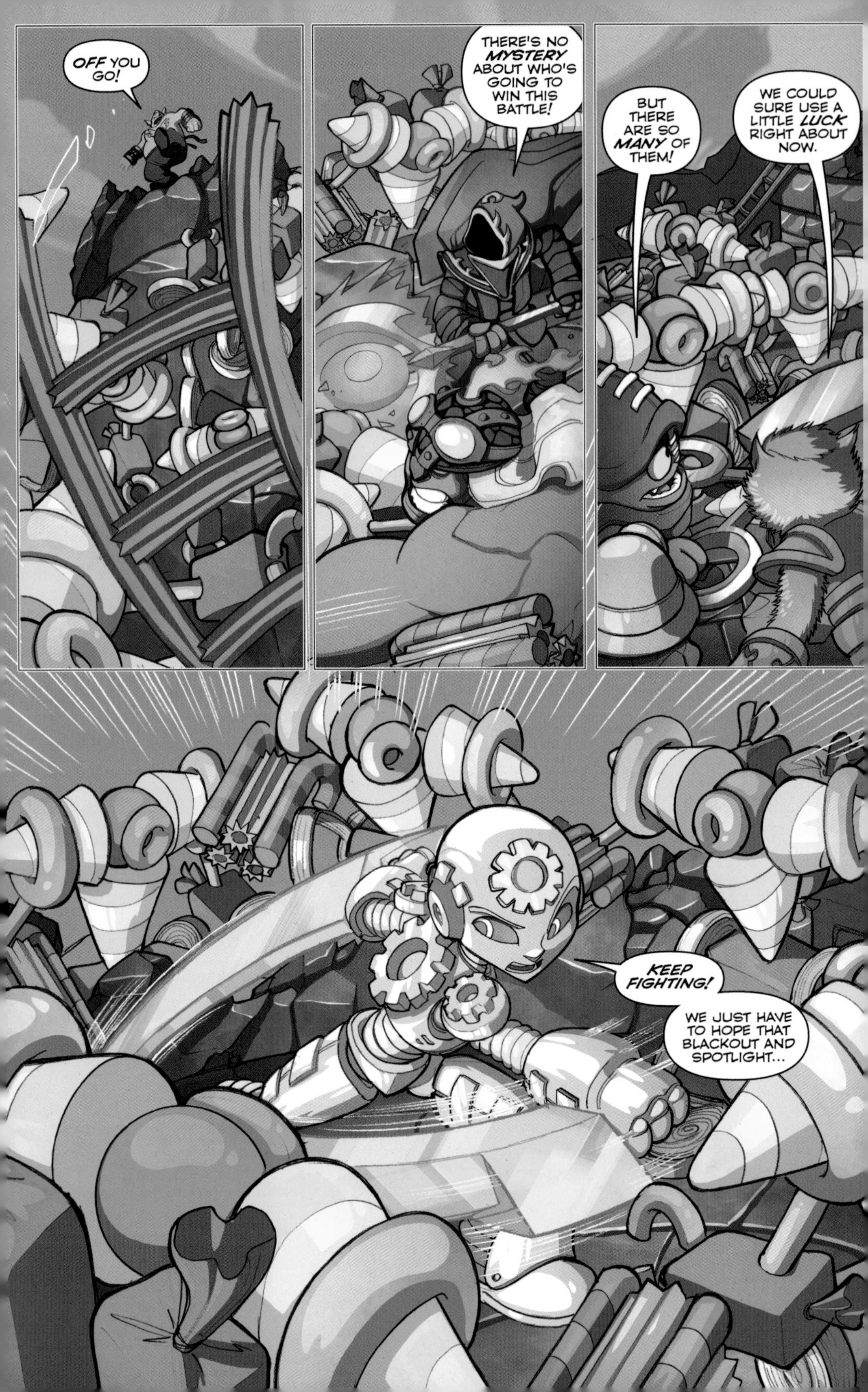
OFF YOU GO!
THERE'S NO MYSTERY ABOUT WHO'S GOING TO WIN THIS BATTLE!
BUT THERE ARE SO MANY OF THEM!
WE COULD SURE USE A LITTLE LUCK RIGHT ABOUT NOW.
KEEP FIGHTING!
WE JUST HAVE TO HOPE THAT BLACKOUT AND SPOTLIGHT...

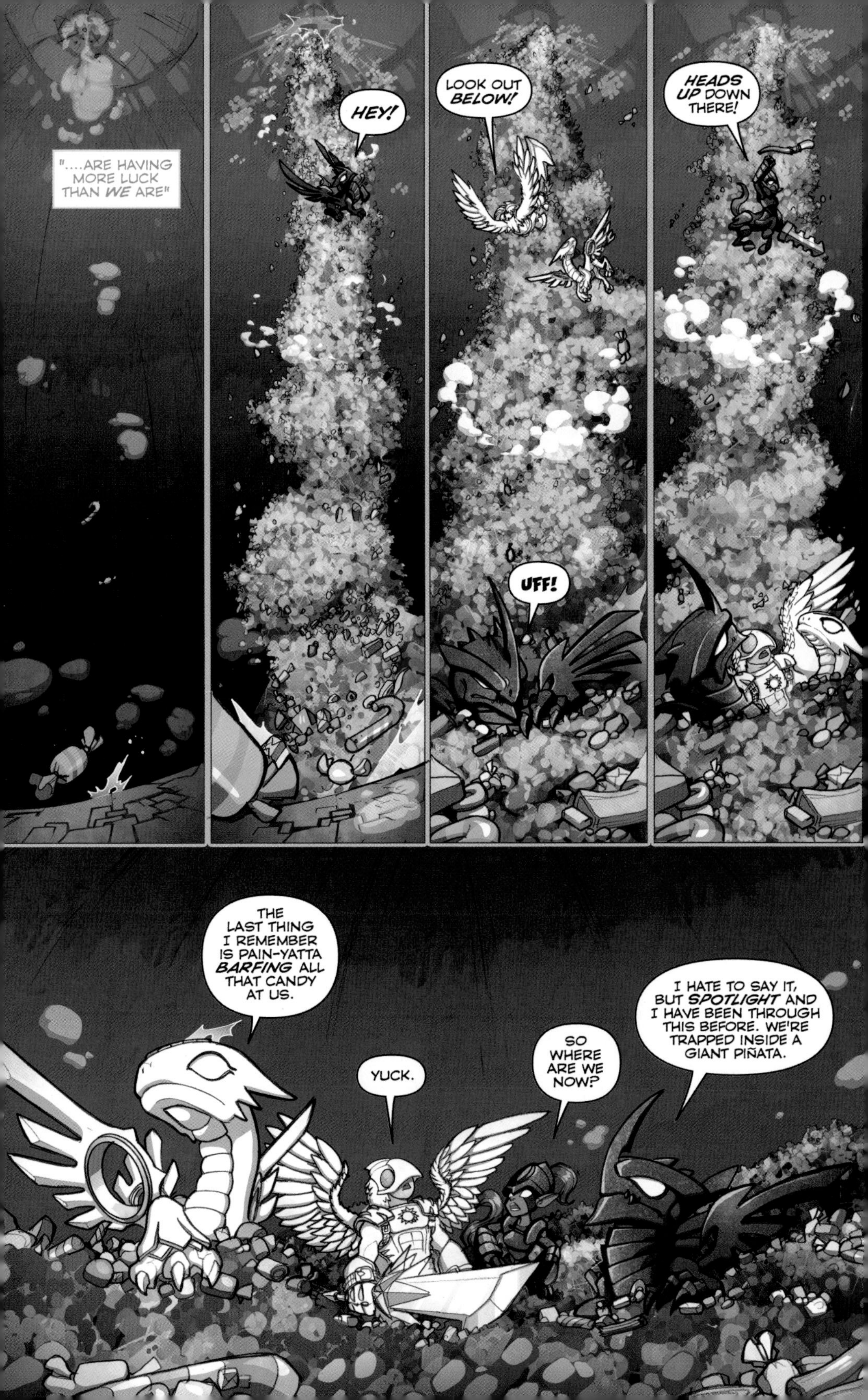
"....ARE HAVING MORE LUCK THAN WE ARE"
HEY!
LOOK OUT BELOW!
UFF!
HEADS UP DOWN THERE!
THE LAST THING I REMEMBER IS PAIN-YATTA BARFING ALL THAT CANDY AT US.
YUCK.
SO WHERE ARE WE NOW?
I HATE TO SAY IT, BUT SPOTLIGHT AND I HAVE BEEN THROUGH THIS BEFORE. WE'RE TRAPPED INSIDE A GIANT PIÑATA.

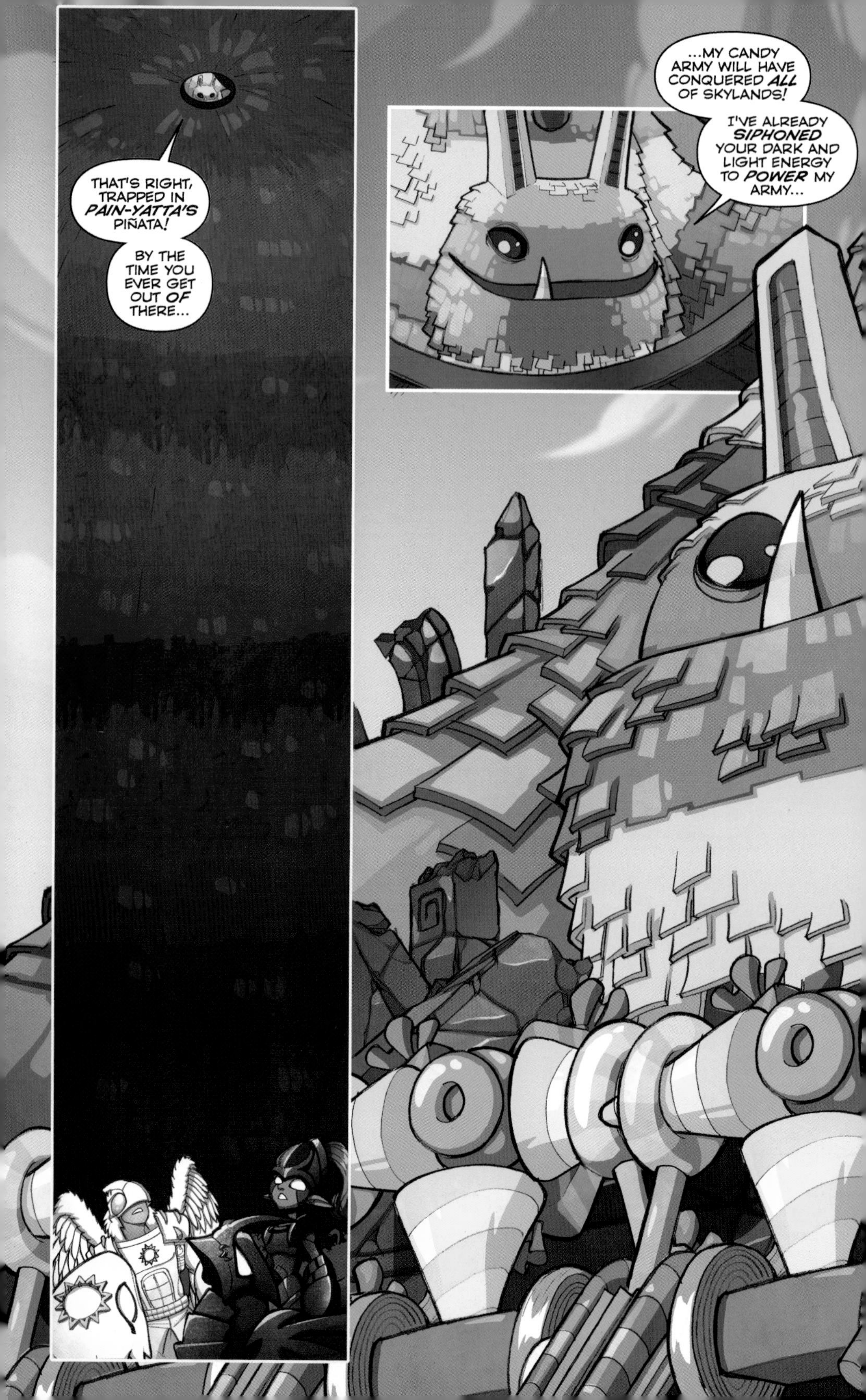
THAT'S RIGHT, TRAPPED IN PAIN-YATTA'S PIÑATA!
BY THE TIME YOU EVER GET OUT OF THERE...
...MY CANDY ARMY WILL HAVE CONQUERED ALL OF SKYLANDS!
I'VE ALREADY SIPHONED YOUR DARK AND LIGHT ENERGY TO POWER MY ARMY...

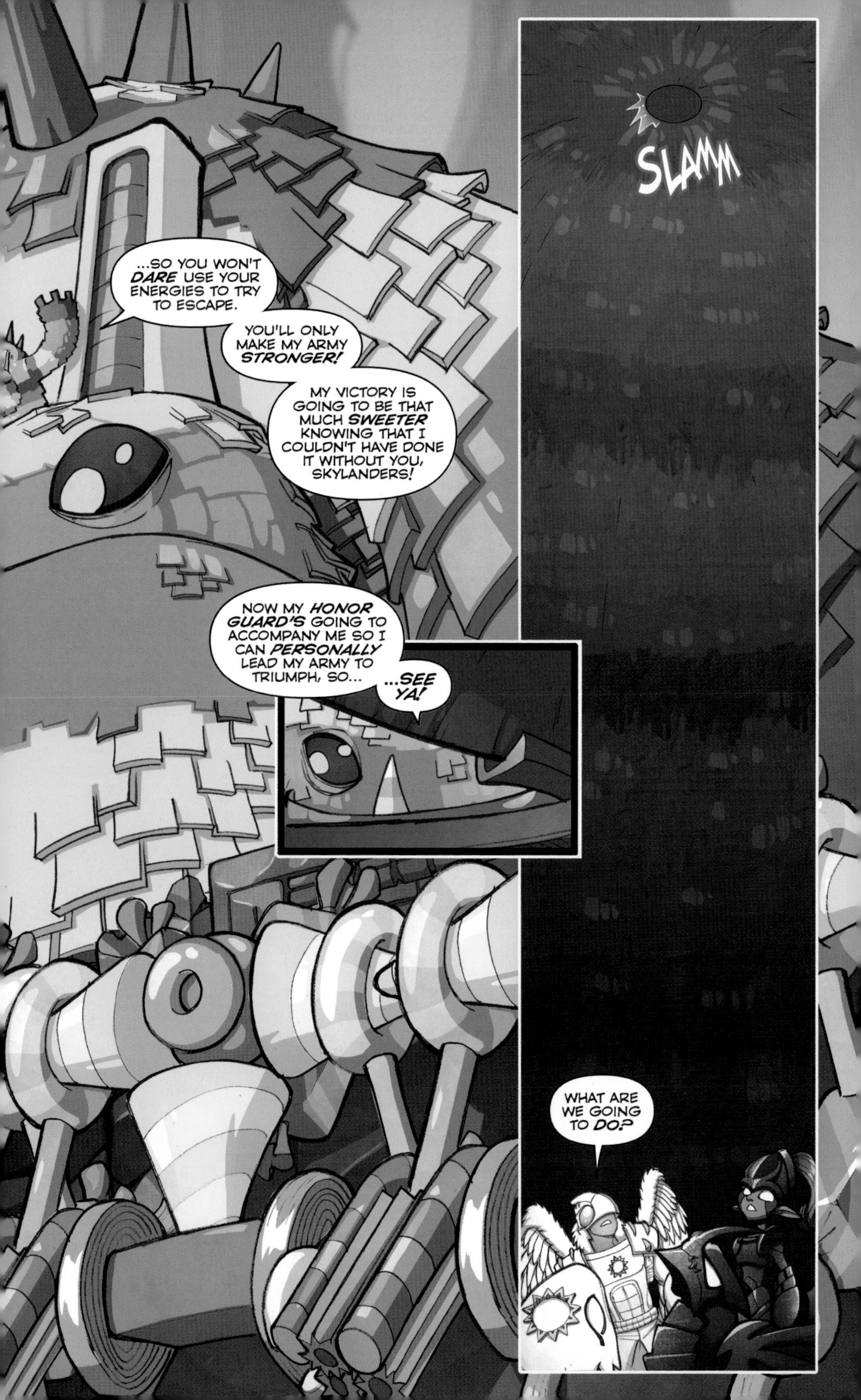
...SO YOU WON'T DARE USE YOUR ENERGIES TO TRY TO ESCAPE.
YOU'LL ONLY MAKE MY ARMY STRONGER!
MY VICTORY IS GOING TO BE THAT MUCH SWEETER KNOWING THAT I COULDN'T HAVE DONE IT WITHOUT YOU, SKYLANDERS!
NOW MY HONOR GUARD'S GOING TO ACCOMPANY ME SO I CAN PERSONALLY LEAD MY ARMY TO TRIUMPH, SO...
...SEE YA!
SLAMM
WHAT ARE WE GOING TO DO?

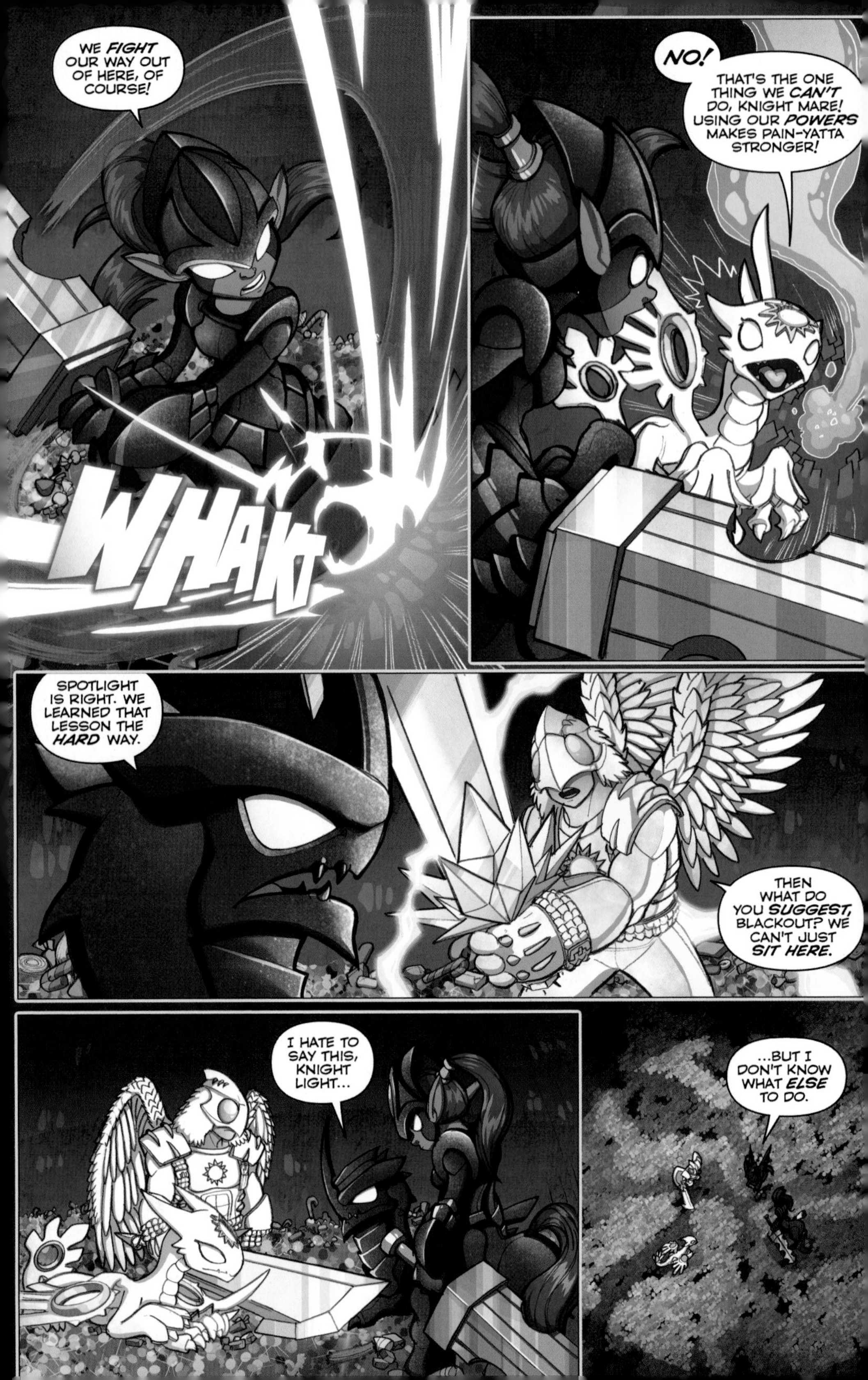
WE FIGHT OUR WAY OUT OF HERE, OF COURSE!
WHAK!
NO!
THAT'S THE ONE THING WE CAN'T DO, KNIGHT MARE! USING OUR POWERS MAKES PAIN-YATTA STRONGER!
SPOTLIGHT IS RIGHT. WE LEARNED THAT LESSON THE HARD WAY.
THEN WHAT DO YOU SUGGEST, BLACKOUT? WE CAN'T JUST SIT HERE.
I HATE TO SAY THIS, KNIGHT LIGHT...
...BUT I DON'T KNOW WHAT ELSE TO DO.

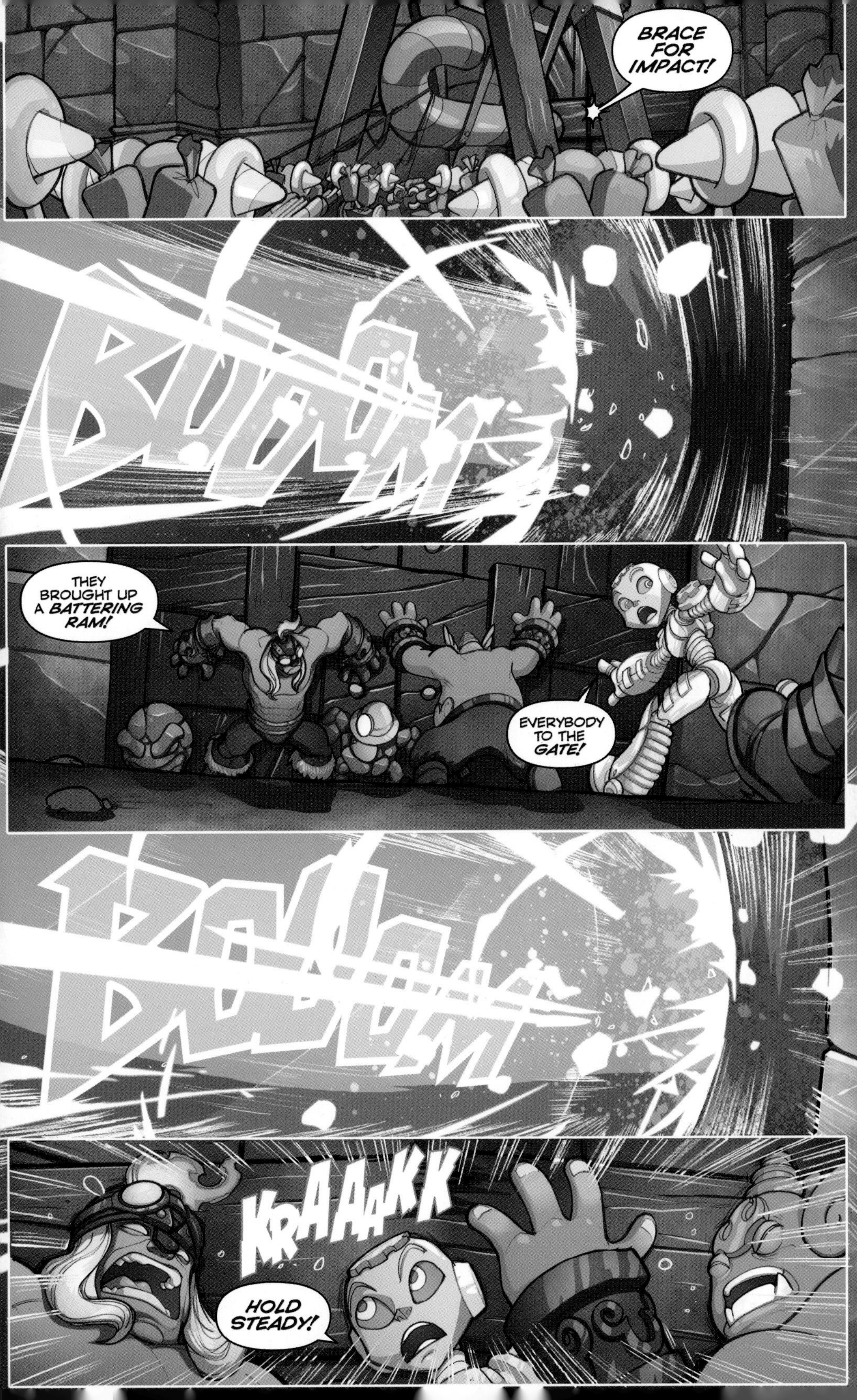
BRACE FOR IMPACT!
THEY BROUGHT UP A BATTERING RAM!
EVERYBODY TO THE GATE!
KRAAAKK
HOLD STEADY!

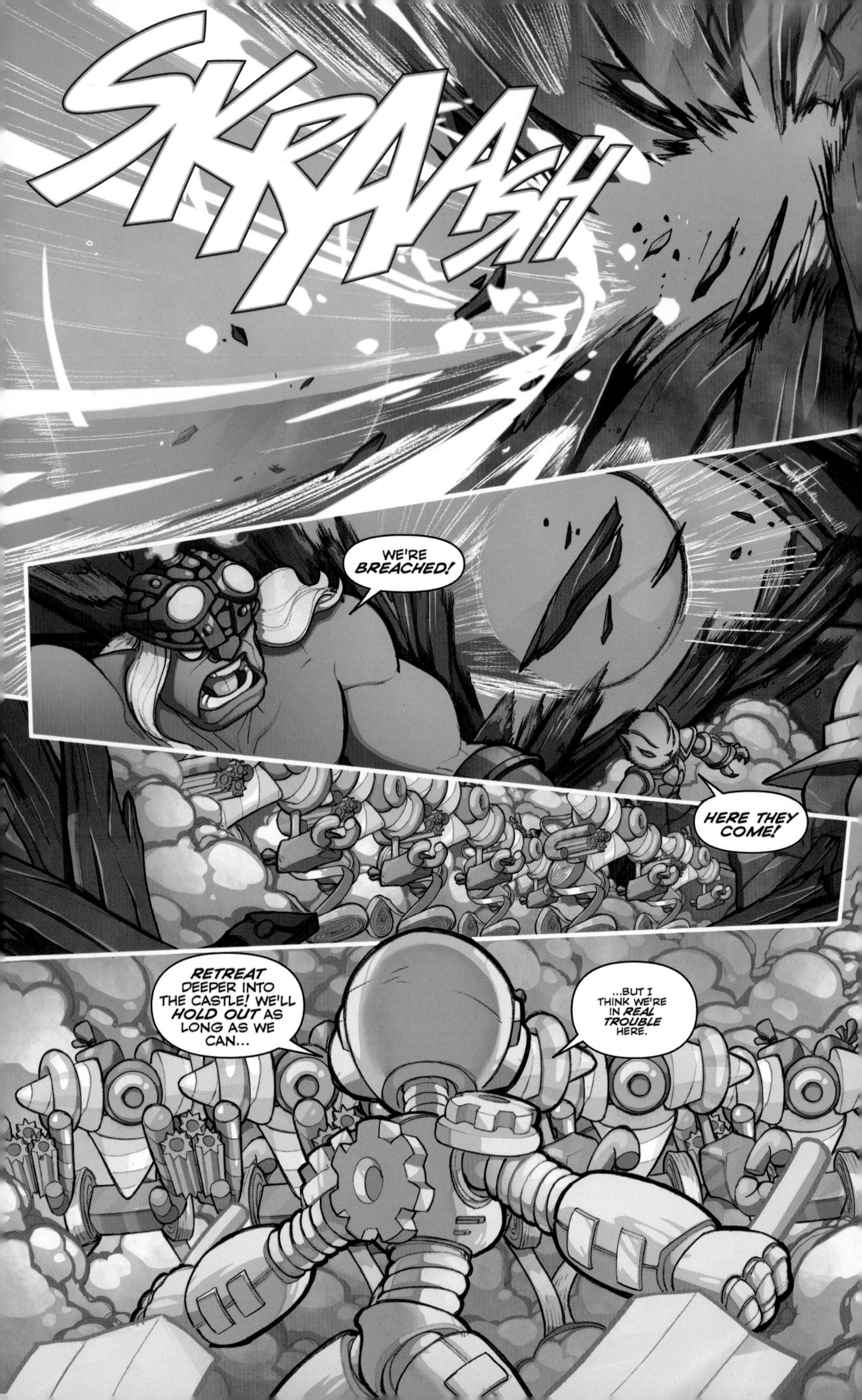
SKRAASH
WE'RE BREACHED!
HERE THEY COME!
RETREAT DEEPER INTO THE CASTLE! WE'LL HOLD OUT AS LONG AS WE CAN...
...BUT I THINK WE'RE IN REAL TROUBLE HERE.

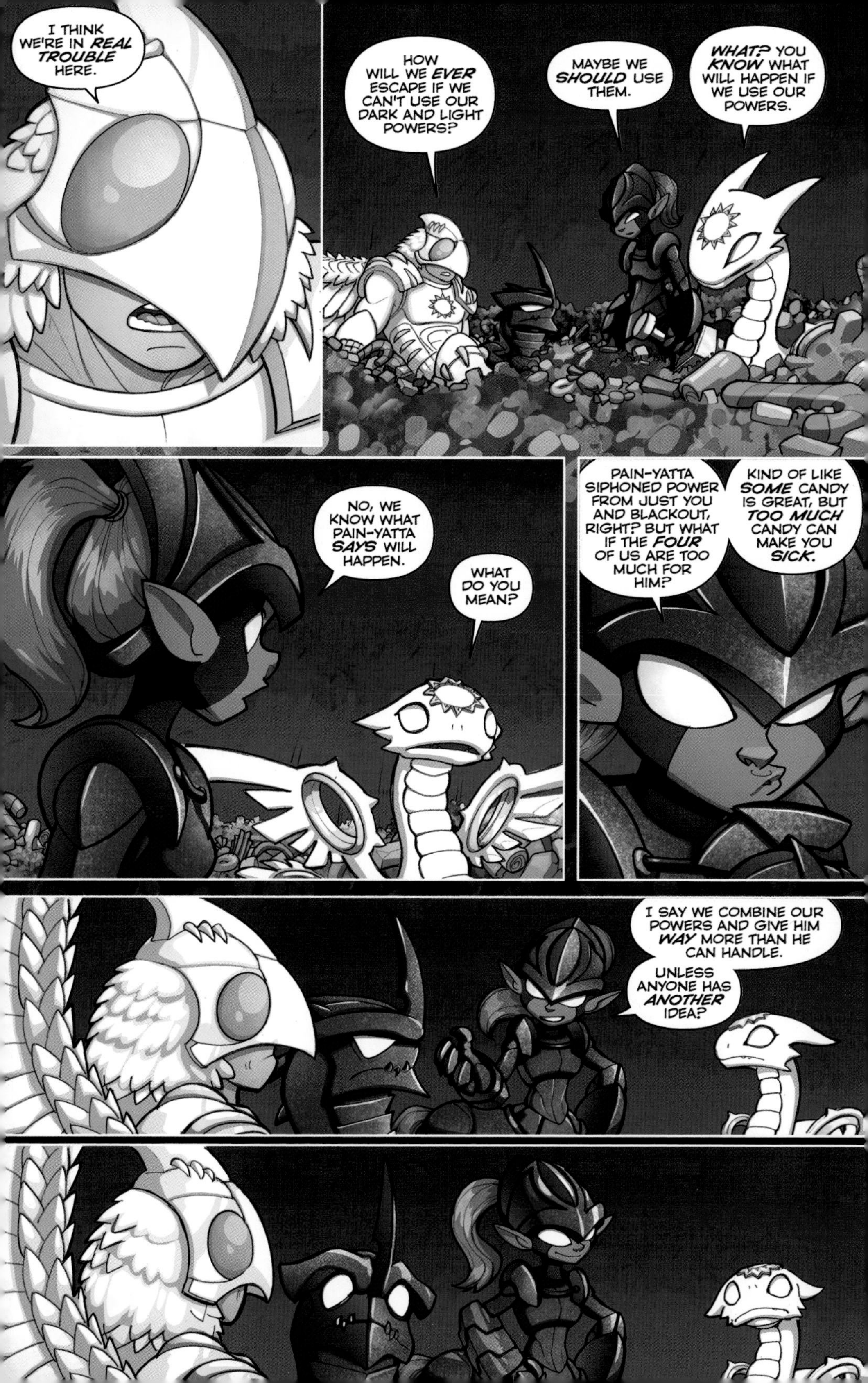
I THINK WE'RE IN REAL TROUBLE HERE.
HOW WILL WE EVER ESCAPE IF WE CAN'T USE OUR DARK AND LIGHT POWERS?
MAYBE WE SHOULD USE THEM.
WHAT? YOU KNOW WHAT WILL HAPPEN IF WE USE OUR POWERS.
NO, WE KNOW WHAT PAIN-YATTA SAYS WILL HAPPEN.
WHAT DO YOU MEAN?
PAIN-YATTA SIPHONED POWER FROM JUST YOU AND BLACKOUT, RIGHT? BUT WHAT IF THE FOUR OF US ARE TOO MUCH FOR HIM?
KIND OF LIKE SOME CANDY IS GREAT, BUT TOO MUCH CANDY CAN MAKE YOU SICK.
I SAY WE COMBINE OUR POWERS AND GIVE HIM WAY MORE THAN HE CAN HANDLE.
UNLESS ANYONE HAS ANOTHER IDEA?

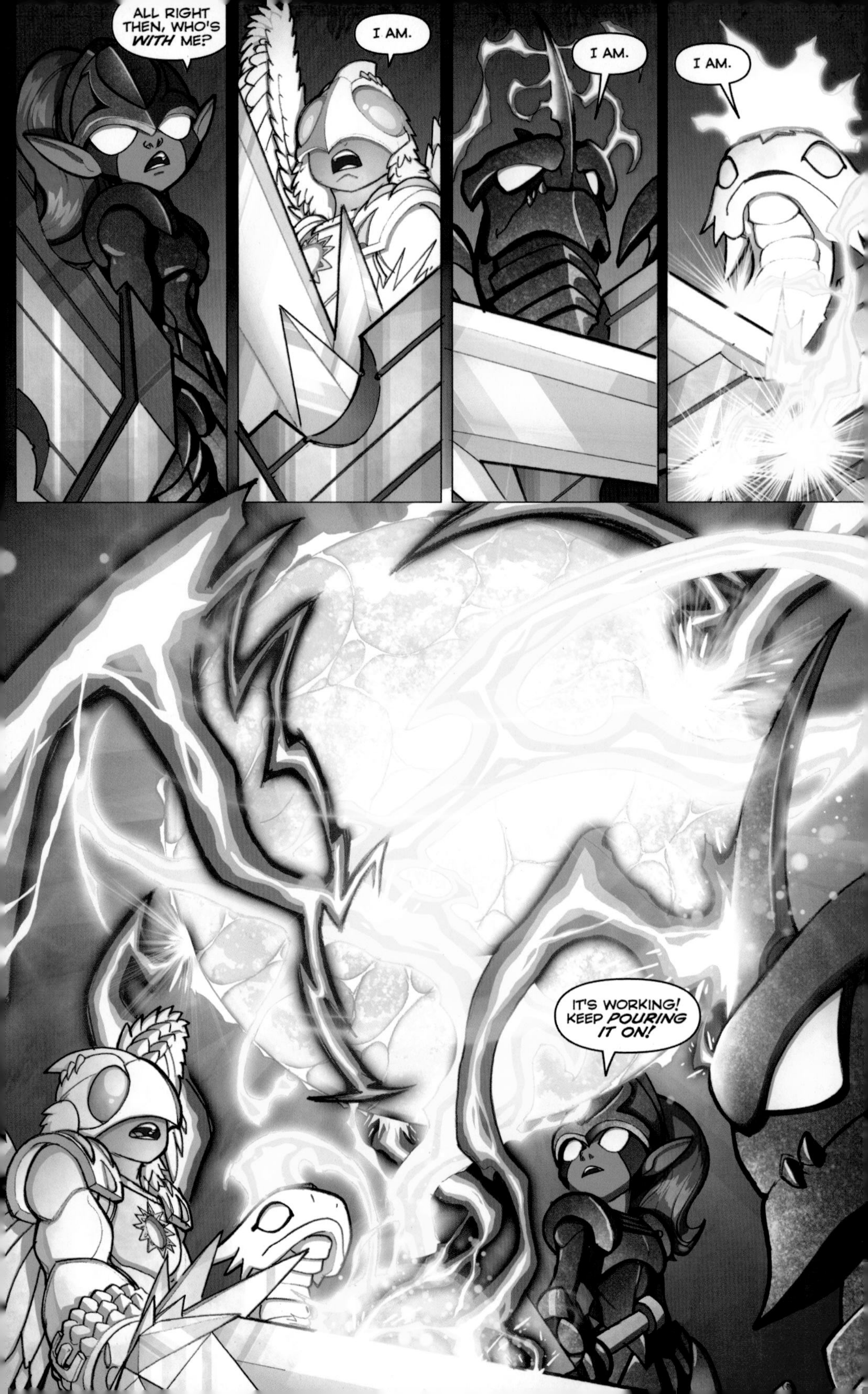
ALL RIGHT THEN, WHO'S *WITH* ME?
I AM.
I AM.
I AM.
IT'S WORKING! KEEP *POURING* IT ON!

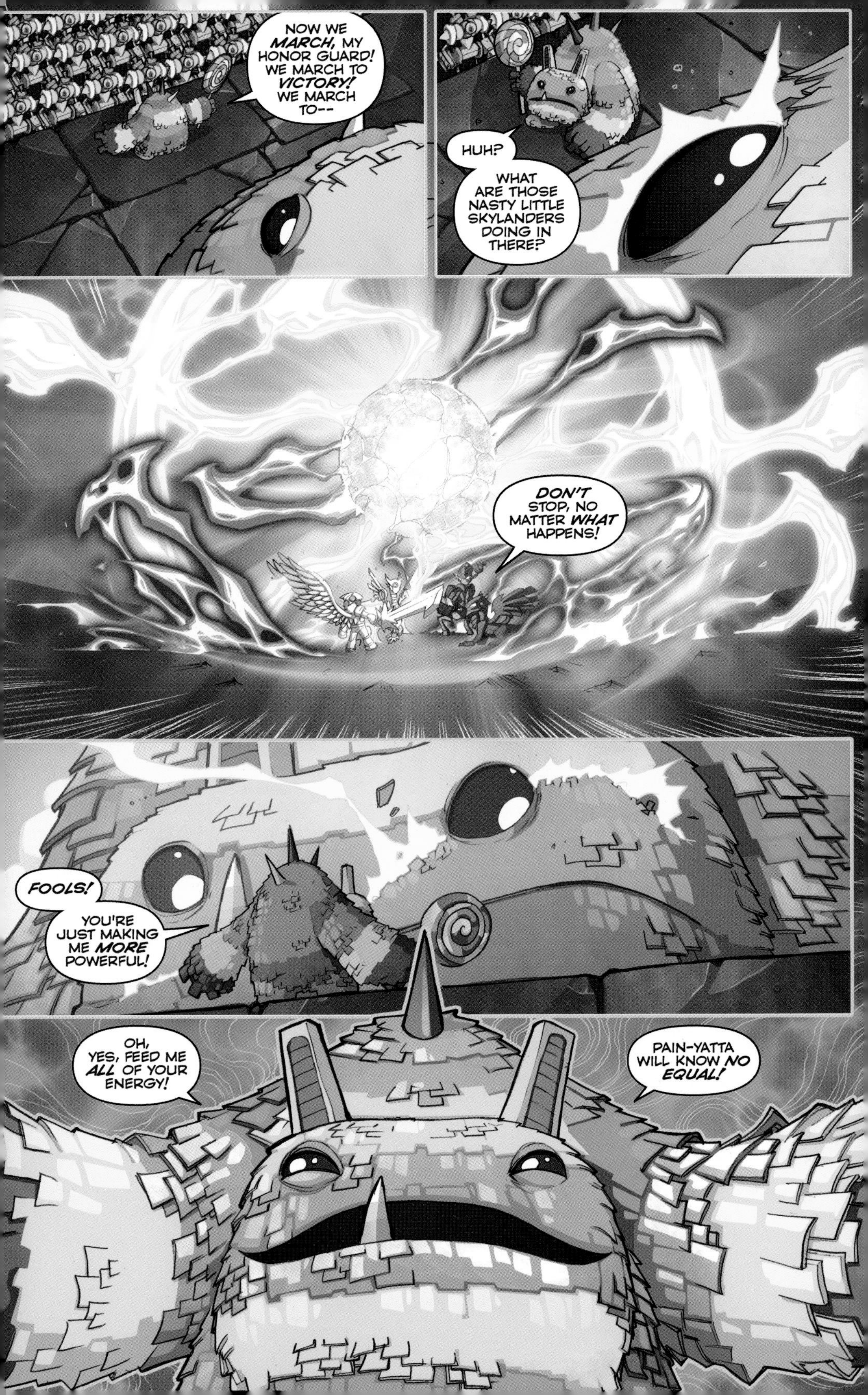
NOW WE MARCH, MY HONOR GUARD! WE MARCH TO VICTORY! WE MARCH TO--
HUH?
WHAT ARE THOSE NASTY LITTLE SKYLANDERS DOING IN THERE?
DON'T STOP, NO MATTER WHAT HAPPENS!
FOOLS!
YOU'RE JUST MAKING ME MORE POWERFUL!
OH, YES, FEED ME ALL OF YOUR ENERGY!
PAIN-YATTA WILL KNOW NO EQUAL!

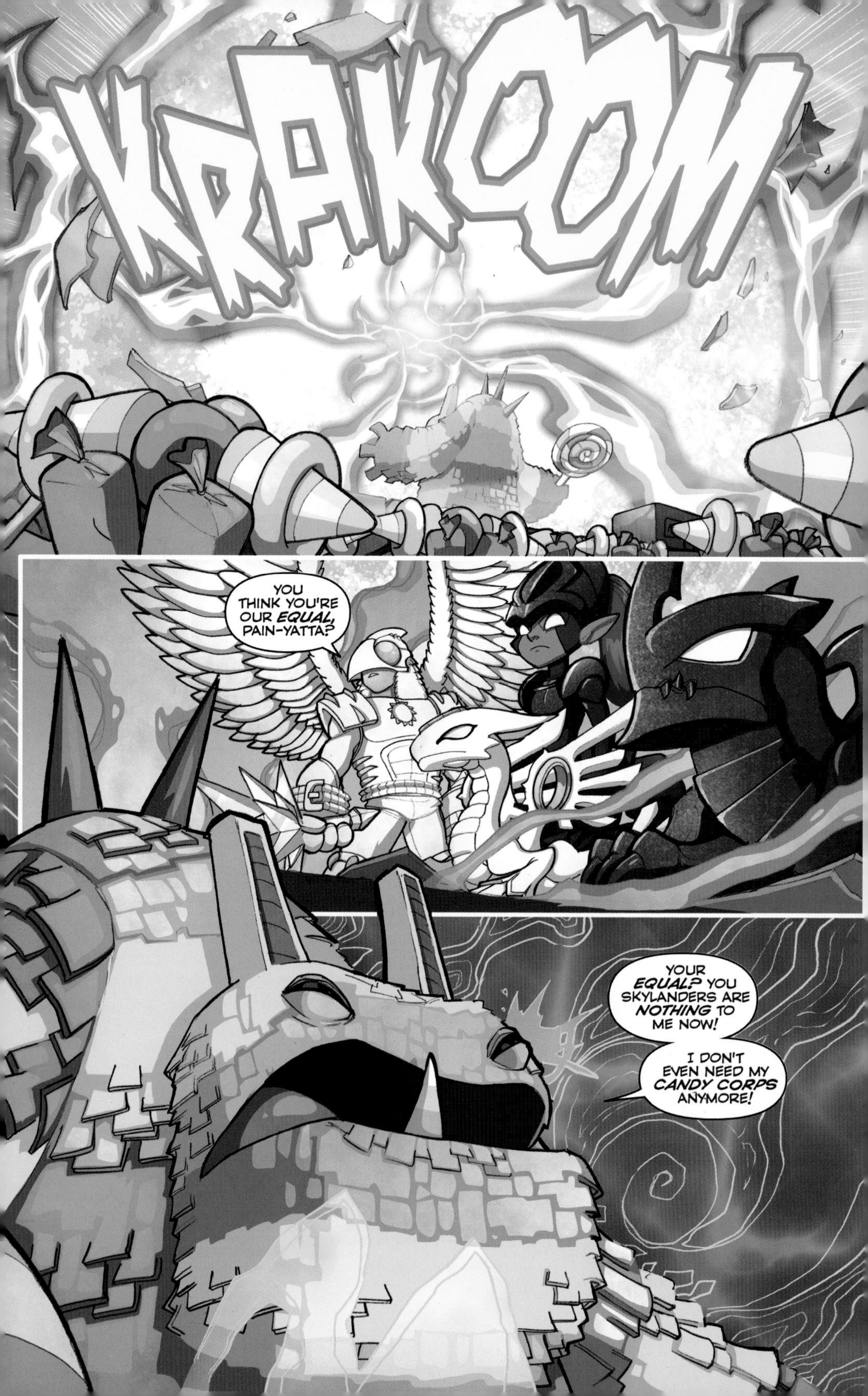
KRAKOOM
YOU THINK YOU'RE OUR EQUAL, PAIN-YATTA?
YOUR EQUAL? YOU SKYLANDERS ARE NOTHING TO ME NOW!
I DON'T EVEN NEED MY CANDY CORPS ANYMORE!

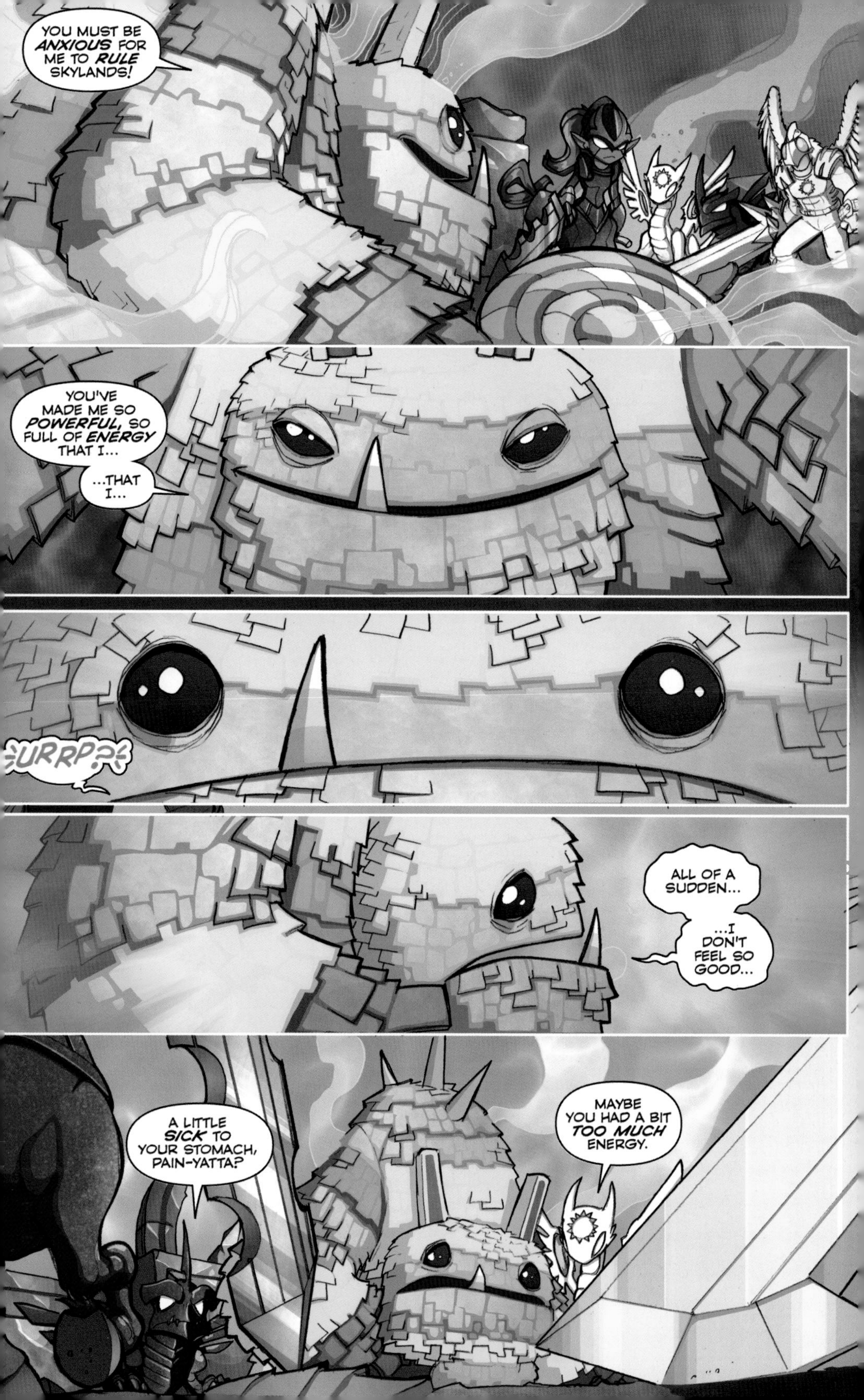
YOU MUST BE ANXIOUS FOR ME TO RULE SKYLANDS!
YOU'VE MADE ME SO POWERFUL, SO FULL OF ENERGY THAT I...
...THAT I...
URRP?
ALL OF A SUDDEN...
...I DON'T FEEL SO GOOD...
A LITTLE SICK TO YOUR STOMACH, PAIN-YATTA?
MAYBE YOU HAD A BIT TOO MUCH ENERGY.

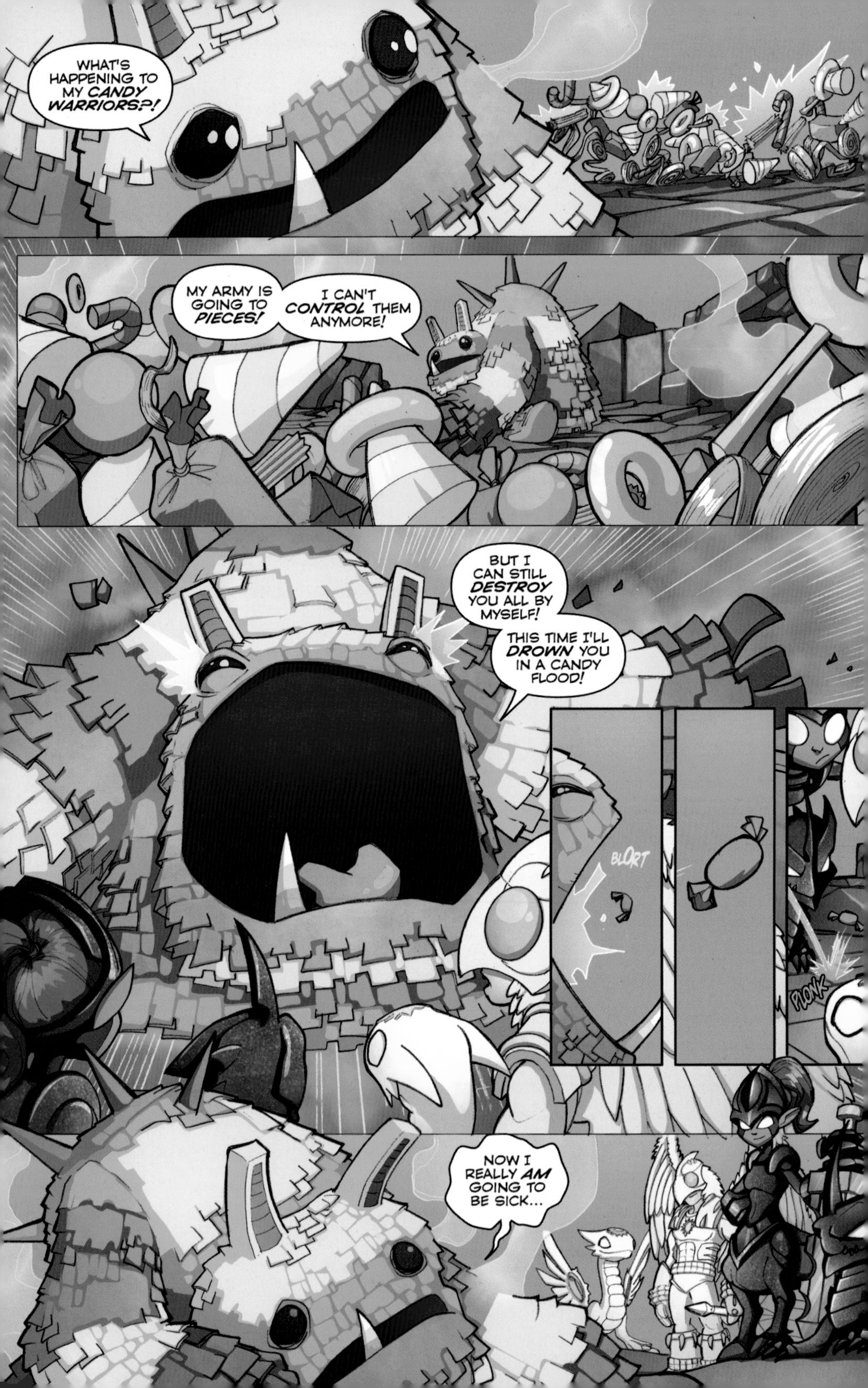

WHAT'S HAPPENING TO MY *CANDY WARRIORS?!*
MY ARMY IS GOING TO *PIECES!*
I CAN'T *CONTROL* THEM ANYMORE!
BUT I CAN STILL *DESTROY* YOU ALL BY MYSELF!
THIS TIME I'LL *DROWN* YOU IN A CANDY FLOOD!
BLORT
PLONK
NOW I REALLY *AM* GOING TO BE SICK...

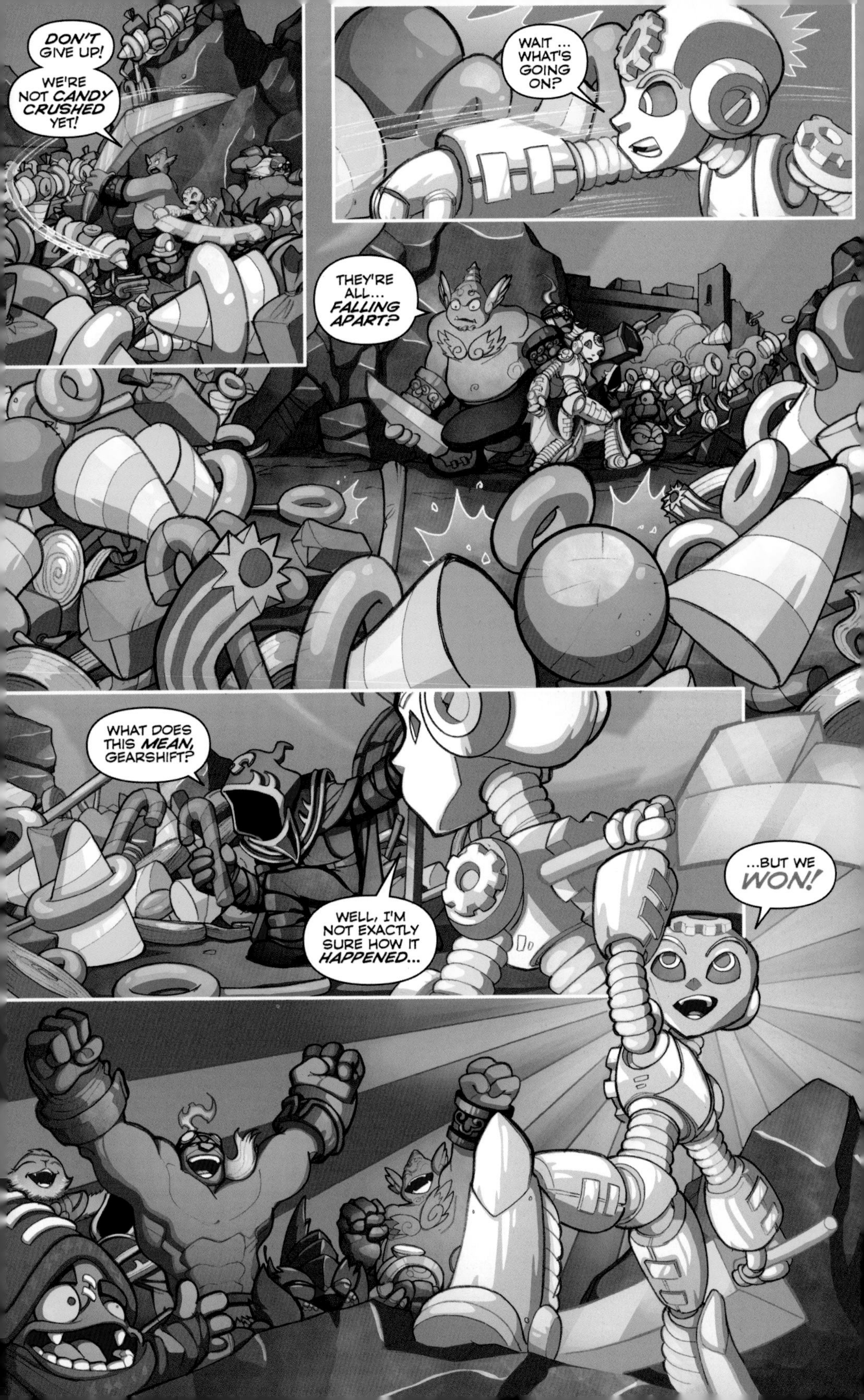
DON'T GIVE UP!
WE'RE NOT CANDY CRUSHED YET!
WAIT ... WHAT'S GOING ON?
THEY'RE ALL... FALLING APART?
WHAT DOES THIS MEAN, GEARSHIFT?
WELL, I'M NOT EXACTLY SURE HOW IT HAPPENED...
...BUT WE WON!

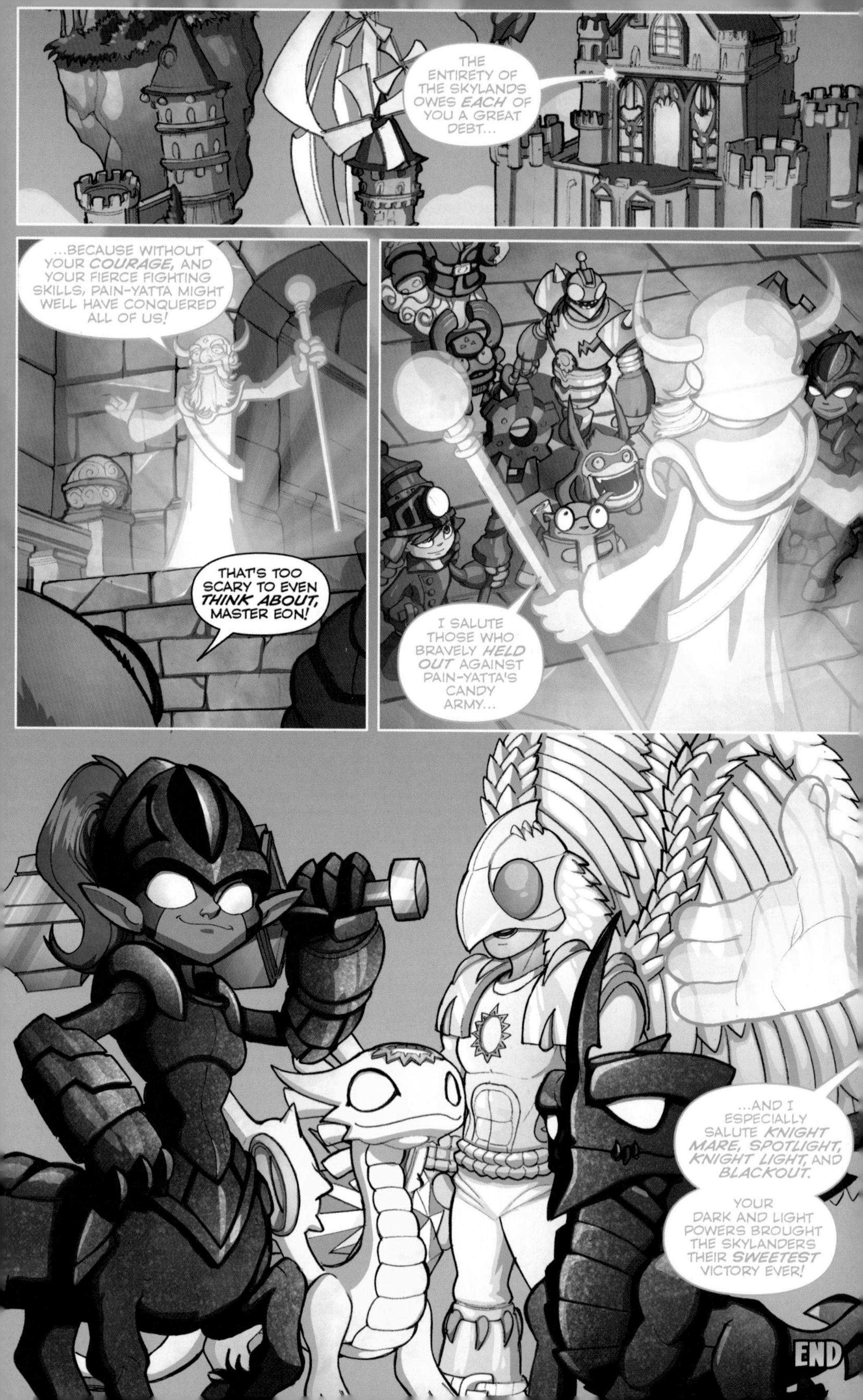
THE ENTIRETY OF THE SKYLANDS OWES EACH OF YOU A GREAT DEBT...
...BECAUSE WITHOUT YOUR COURAGE, AND YOUR FIERCE FIGHTING SKILLS, PAIN-YATTA MIGHT WELL HAVE CONQUERED ALL OF US!
THAT'S TOO SCARY TO EVEN THINK ABOUT, MASTER EON!
I SALUTE THOSE WHO BRAVELY HELD OUT AGAINST PAIN-YATTA'S CANDY ARMY...
...AND I ESPECIALLY SALUTE KNIGHT MARE, SPOTLIGHT, KNIGHT LIGHT, AND BLACKOUT.
YOUR DARK AND LIGHT POWERS BROUGHT THE SKYLANDERS THEIR SWEETEST VICTORY EVER!
END

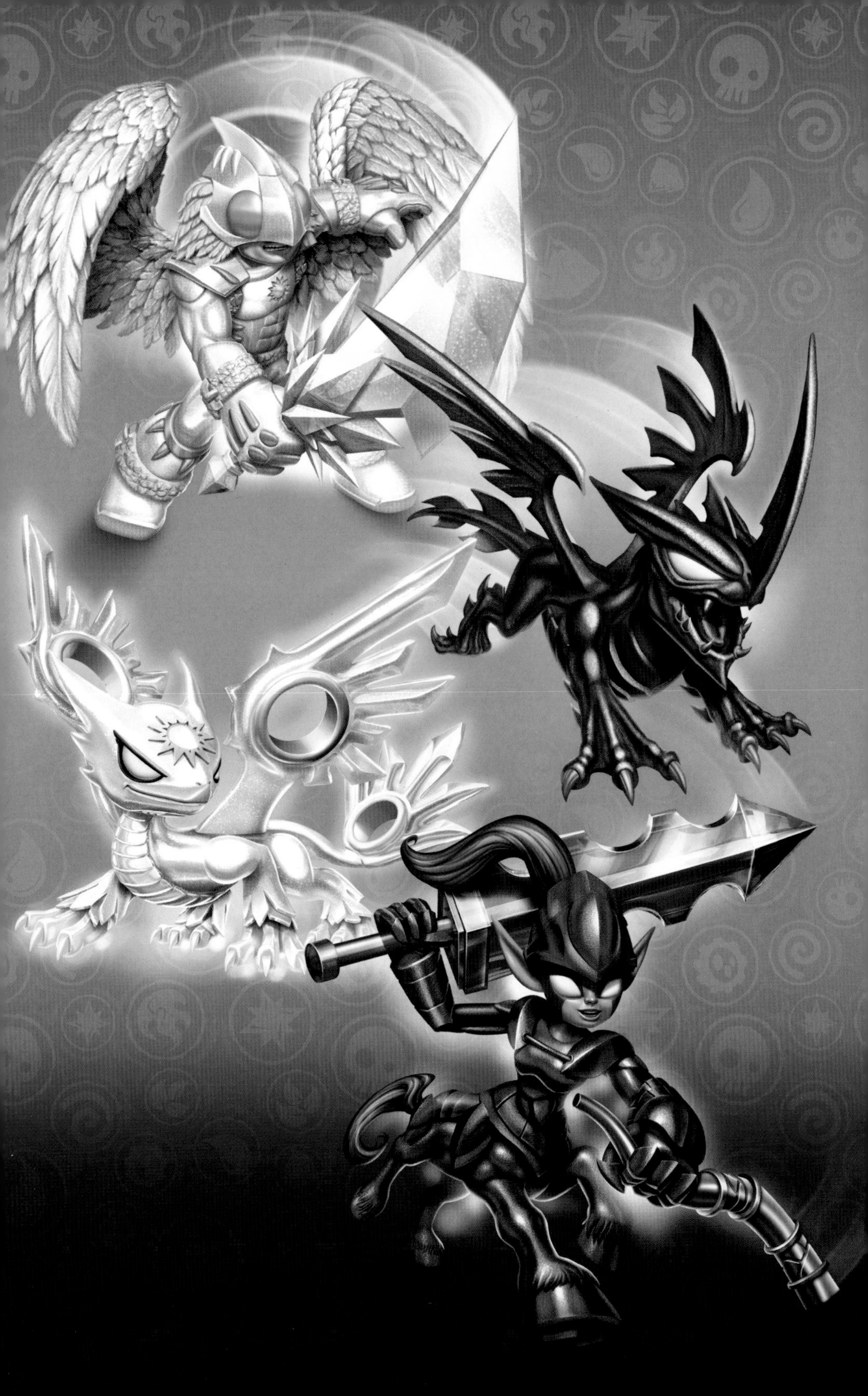

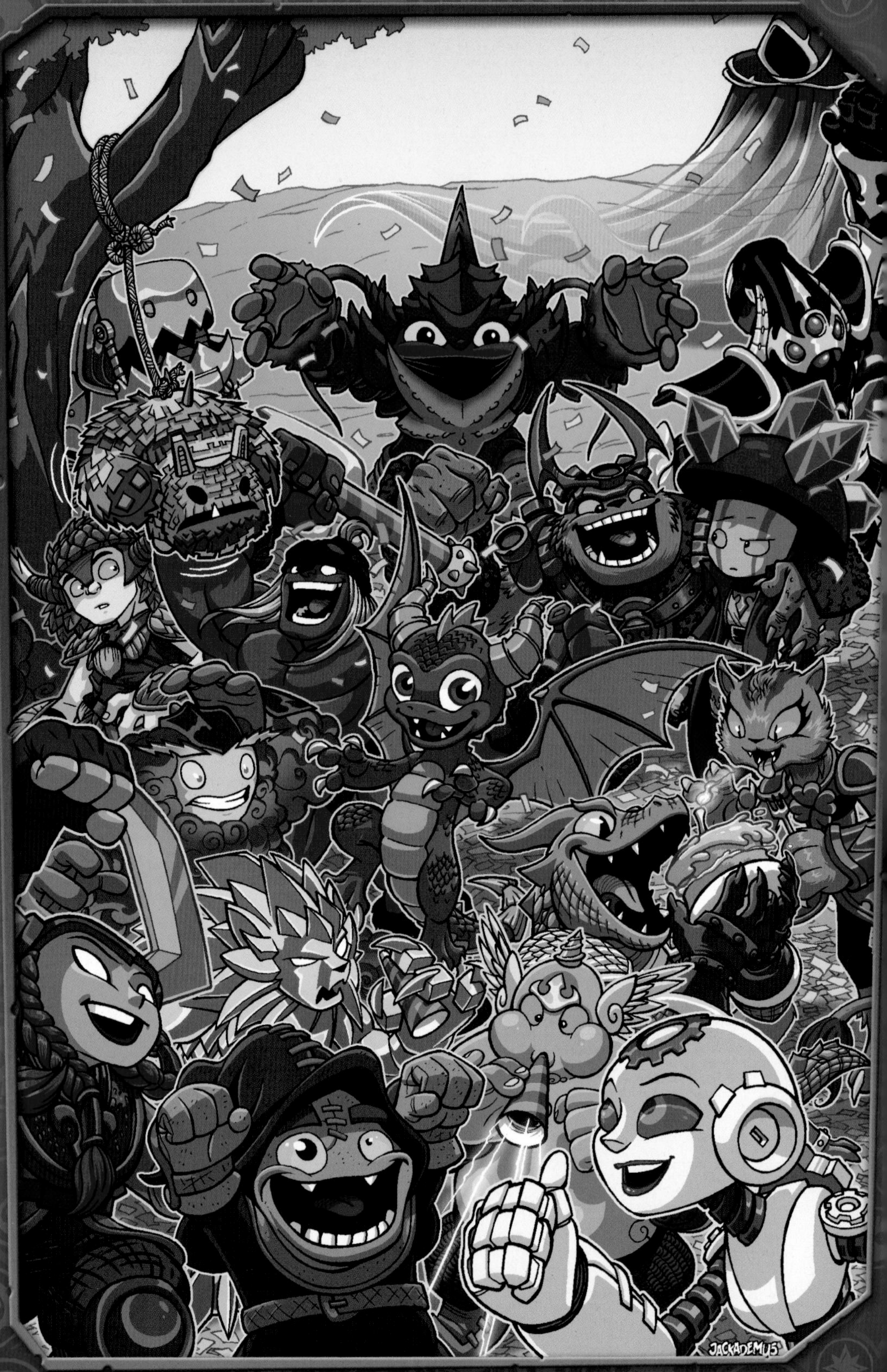
JACKADEMUS

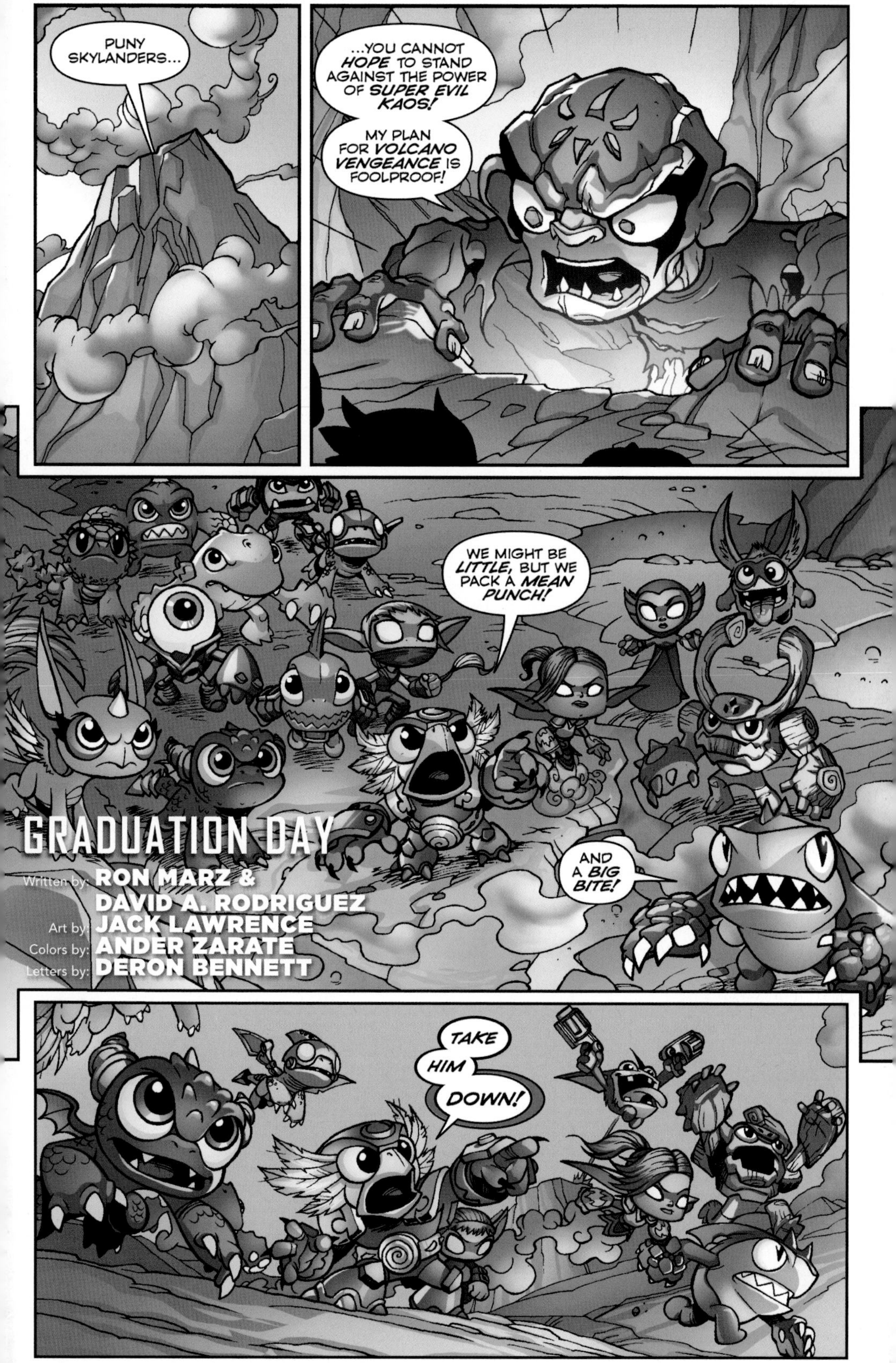
PUNY SKYLANDERS...
...YOU CANNOT HOPE TO STAND AGAINST THE POWER OF SUPER EVIL KAOS!
MY PLAN FOR VOLCANO VENGEANCE IS FOOLPROOF!
WE MIGHT BE LITTLE, BUT WE PACK A MEAN PUNCH!
GRADUATION DAY
Written by: RON MARZ &
DAVID A. RODRIGUEZ
Art by: JACK LAWRENCE
Colors by: ANDER ZARATE
Letters by: DERON BENNETT
AND A BIG BITE!
TAKE HIM DOWN!

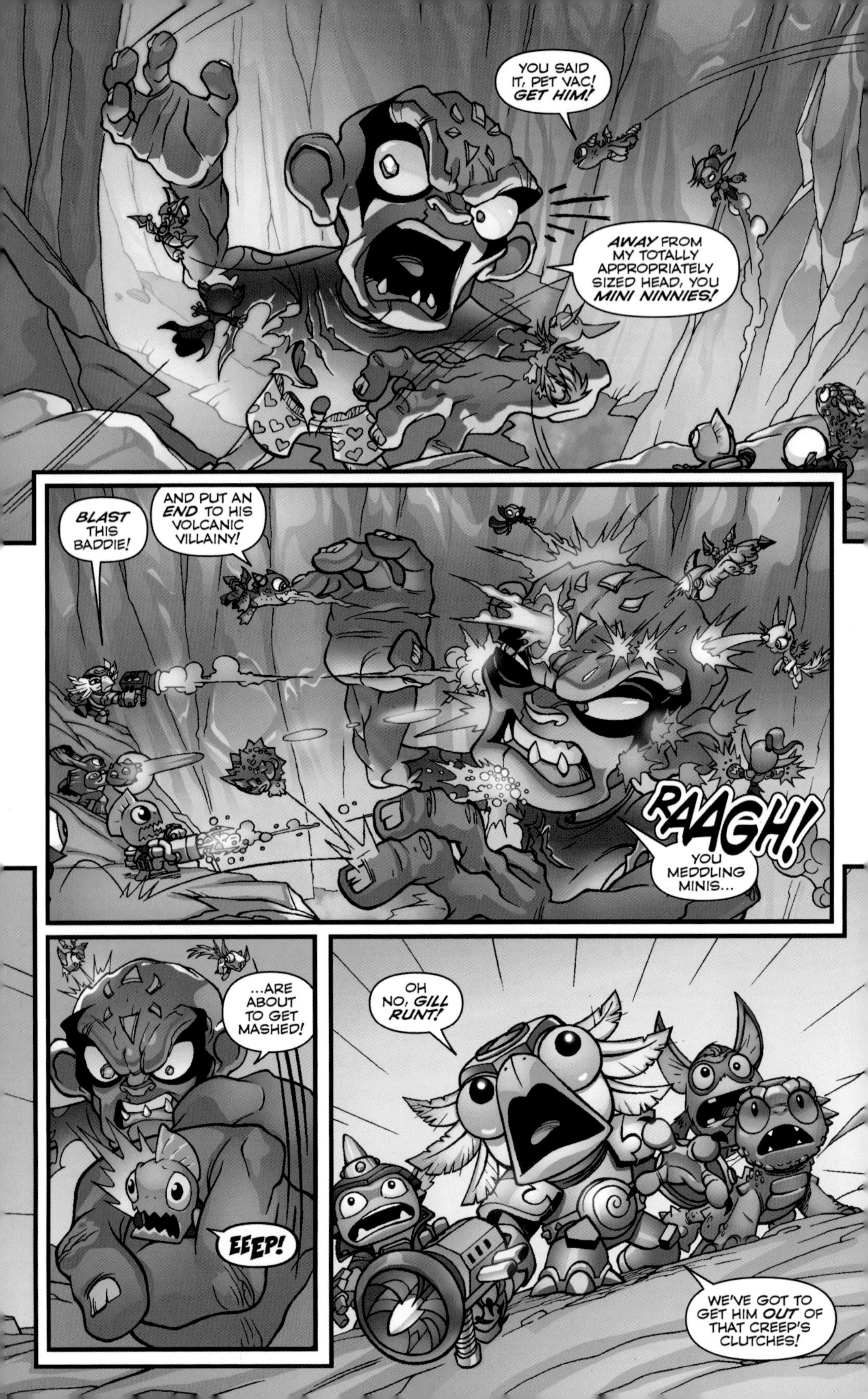

YOU SAID IT, PET VAC! *GET HIM!*
AWAY FROM MY TOTALLY APPROPRIATELY SIZED HEAD, YOU *MINI NINNIES!*
BLAST THIS BADDIE!
AND PUT AN *END* TO HIS VOLCANIC VILLAINY!
RAAGH!
YOU MEDDLING MINIS...
...ARE ABOUT TO GET MASHED!
EEEP!
OH NO, *GILL RUNT!*
WE'VE GOT TO GET HIM *OUT* OF THAT CREEP'S CLUTCHES!

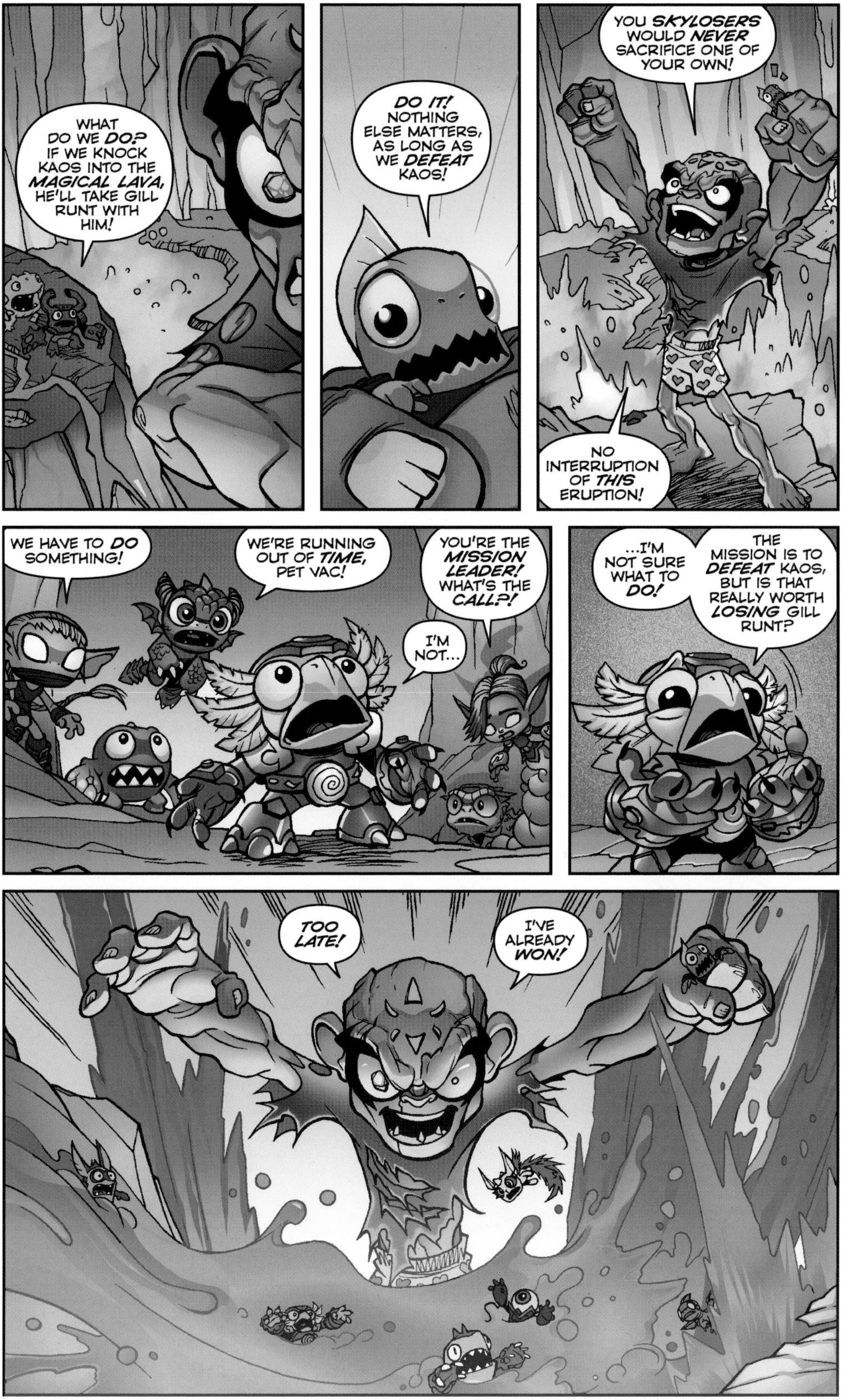
WHAT DO WE DO? IF WE KNOCK KAOS INTO THE MAGICAL LAVA, HE'LL TAKE GILL RUNT WITH HIM!
DO IT! NOTHING ELSE MATTERS, AS LONG AS WE DEFEAT KAOS!
YOU SKYLOSERS WOULD NEVER SACRIFICE ONE OF YOUR OWN!
NO INTERRUPTION OF THIS ERUPTION!
WE HAVE TO DO SOMETHING!
WE'RE RUNNING OUT OF TIME, PET VAC!
YOU'RE THE MISSION LEADER! WHAT'S THE CALL?!
I'M NOT...
...I'M NOT SURE WHAT TO DO!
THE MISSION IS TO DEFEAT KAOS, BUT IS THAT REALLY WORTH LOSING GILL RUNT?
TOO LATE!
I'VE ALREADY WON!

PAUSE SIMULATION.

YOU HAVE *FAILED* THE TEST, PET VAC. DO YOU KNOW *WHY?*

BECAUSE KAOS *WON.*

THE MISSION WAS TO *DEFEAT* KAOS, BUT I COULDN'T *STOP* HIM. I WAS THE TEAM LEADER, SO IT'S *MY* FAULT.

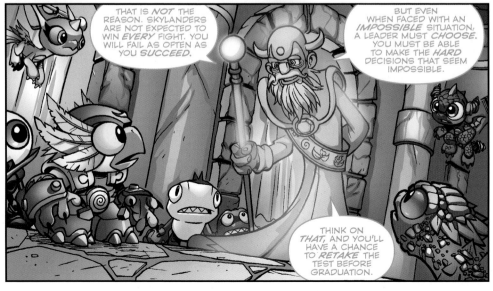

THAT IS *NOT* THE REASON. SKYLANDERS ARE NOT EXPECTED TO WIN *EVERY* FIGHT. YOU WILL FAIL AS OFTEN AS YOU *SUCCEED.*

BUT EVEN WHEN FACED WITH AN *IMPOSSIBLE* SITUATION, A LEADER MUST *CHOOSE.* YOU MUST BE ABLE TO MAKE THE *HARD* DECISIONS THAT SEEM IMPOSSIBLE.

THINK ON *THAT,* AND YOU'LL HAVE A CHANCE TO *RETAKE* THE TEST BEFORE GRADUATION.

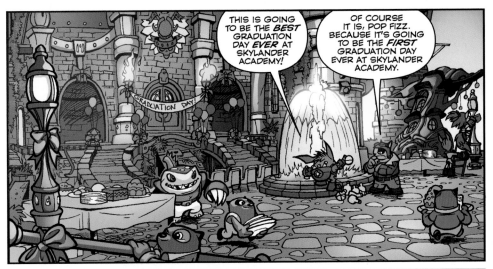

THIS IS GOING TO BE THE *BEST* GRADUATION DAY *EVER* AT SKYLANDER ACADEMY!

OF COURSE IT IS, POP FIZZ. BECAUSE IT'S GOING TO BE THE *FIRST* GRADUATION DAY EVER AT SKYLANDER ACADEMY.

UM...YOU SURE THAT SPECIAL *PUNCH MIX* OF YOURS ISN'T GOING TO TURN EVERYONE INTO RAGING *BLUE MONSTERS?*

NOTHING TO WORRY ABOUT, FLYNN!

PROBABLY.

I THINK.

I WISH WE HAD A FEW MORE SKYLANDERS AROUND TO HELP GET THE ACADEMY *READY*, CALI.

EVERYBODY'S BEEN DEPLOYED TO HANDLE ANY LAST-MINUTE *SITUATIONS* THAT MIGHT ARISE, TESSA, SO WE'RE ON OUR OWN.

BUT EVERYONE SHOULD BE BACK FOR THE *CEREMONY*.

INCOMING AIRSHIP! YOU GUYS EXPECTING *COMPANY?*

THAT'S NOT COMPANY, THAT'S THE *BAND!*

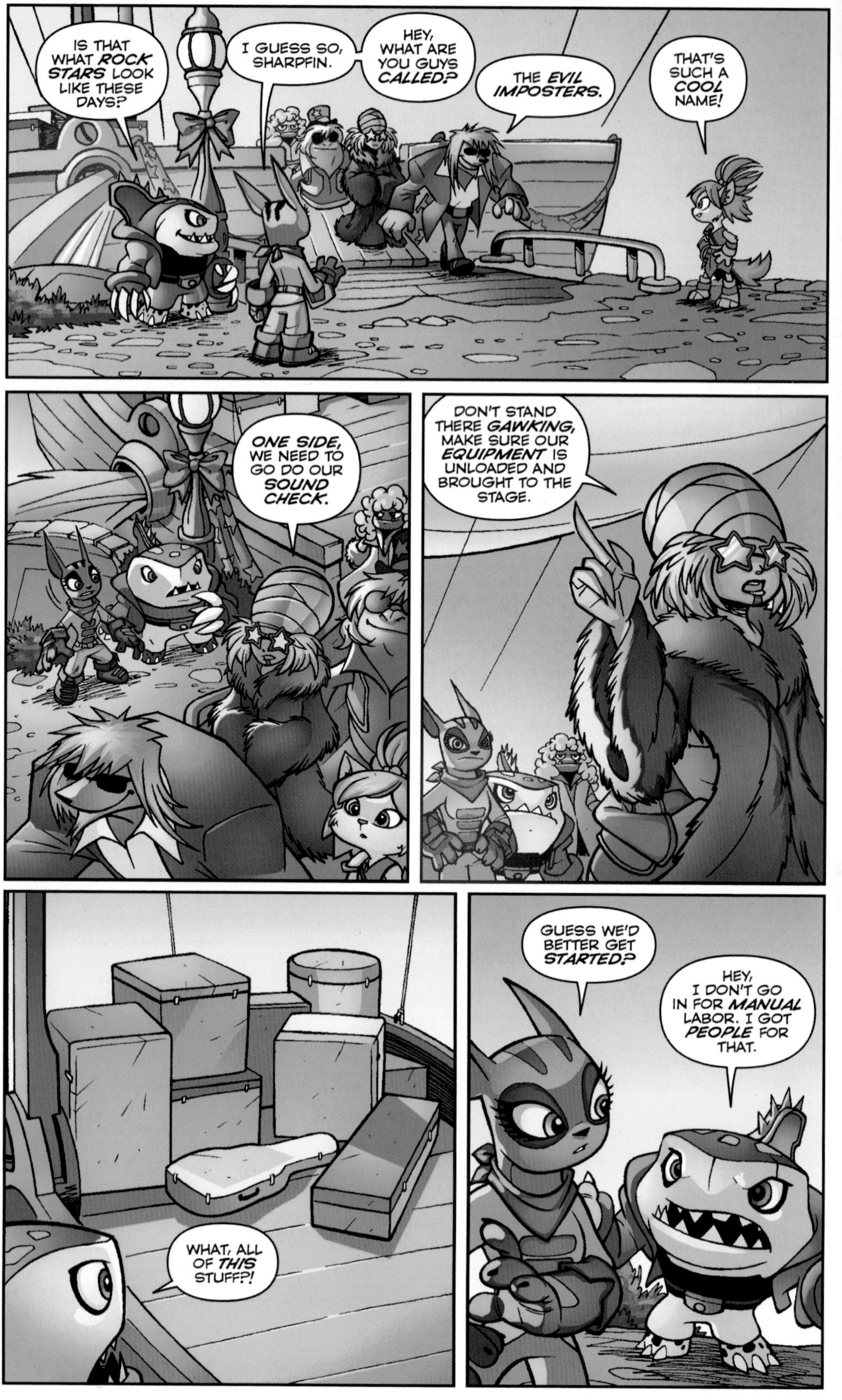
IS THAT WHAT ROCK STARS LOOK LIKE THESE DAYS?
I GUESS SO, SHARPFIN.
HEY, WHAT ARE YOU GUYS CALLED?
THE EVIL IMPOSTERS.
THAT'S SUCH A COOL NAME!
ONE SIDE, WE NEED TO GO DO OUR SOUND CHECK.
DON'T STAND THERE GAWKING, MAKE SURE OUR EQUIPMENT IS UNLOADED AND BROUGHT TO THE STAGE.
WHAT, ALL OF THIS STUFF?!
GUESS WE'D BETTER GET STARTED?
HEY, I DON'T GO IN FOR MANUAL LABOR. I GOT PEOPLE FOR THAT.

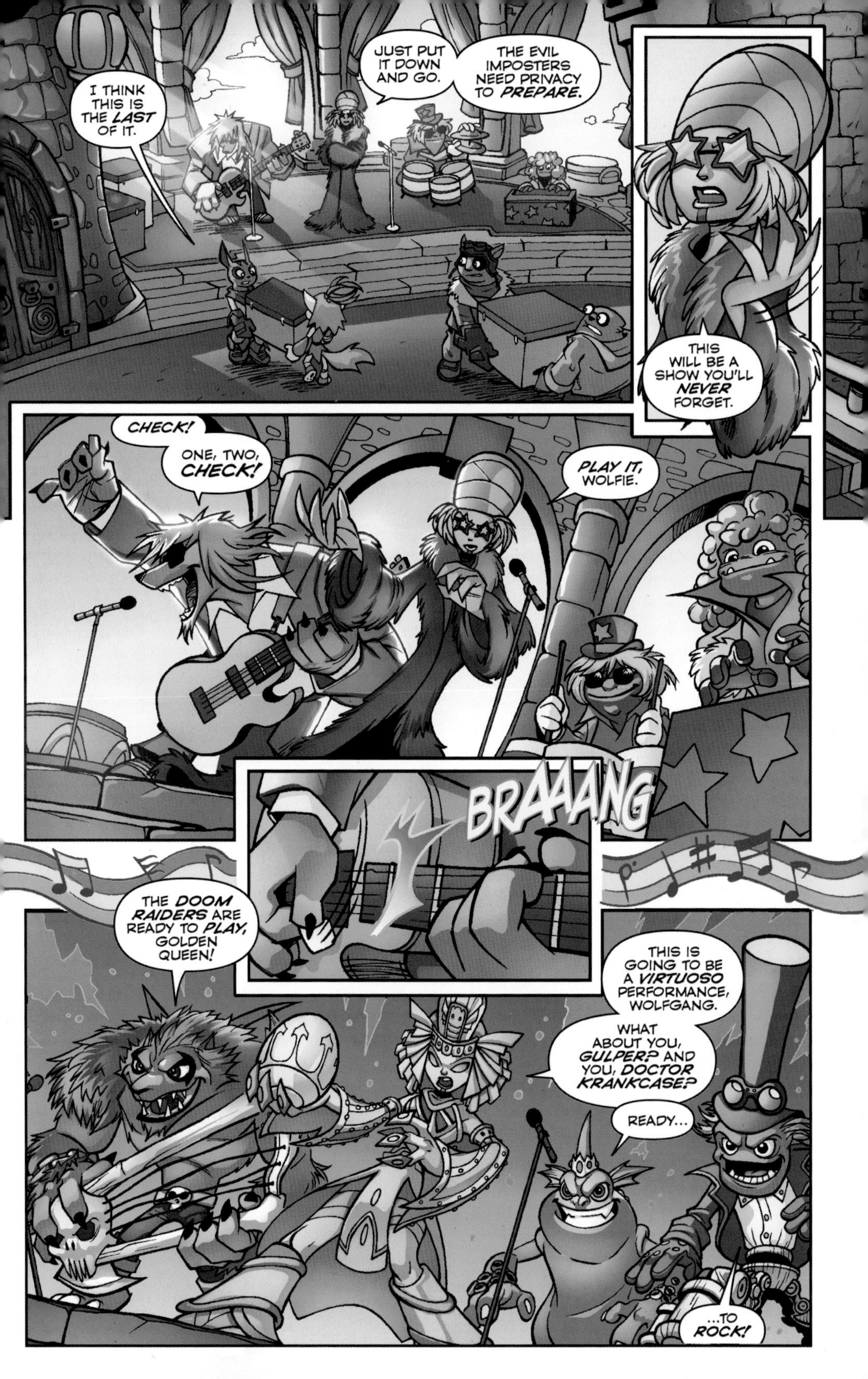

I THINK THIS IS THE *LAST* OF IT.
JUST PUT IT DOWN AND GO.
THE EVIL IMPOSTERS NEED PRIVACY TO *PREPARE.*
THIS WILL BE A SHOW YOU'LL *NEVER* FORGET.
CHECK!
ONE, TWO, *CHECK!*
PLAY IT, WOLFIE.
BRAAAANG
THE *DOOM RAIDERS* ARE READY TO *PLAY,* GOLDEN QUEEN!
THIS IS GOING TO BE A *VIRTUOSO* PERFORMANCE, WOLFGANG.
WHAT ABOUT YOU, *GULPER?* AND YOU, *DOCTOR KRANKCASE?*
READY...
...TO *ROCK!*

THIS LIBRARY IS SO HUGE...

...BUT I THINK WE'VE FOUND EVERY BOOK THAT CAN HELP YOU, PET VAC.

THANKS, HIJINX. THANKS TO ALL YOU GUYS...

...BUT I'M NOT SURE ANYTHING'S GOING TO HELP ME.

I'LL NEVER BE A LEADER, WHICH MEANS I'LL NEVER BE A TRUE SKYLANDER.

YOU HAVE TO BELIEVE IN YOURSELF, PET VAC.

EASY FOR YOU TO SAY, WEERUPTOR. YOU'RE NOT A FAILURE.

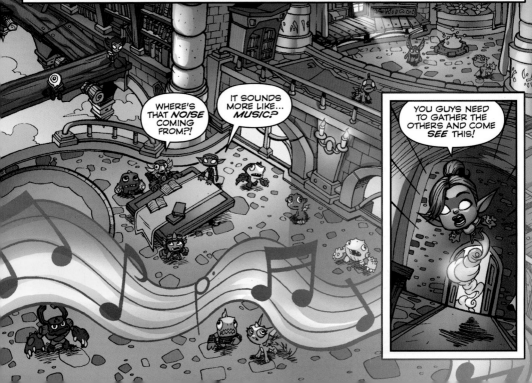

WHERE'S THAT NOISE COMING FROM?!

IT SOUNDS MORE LIKE... MUSIC?

YOU GUYS NEED TO GATHER THE OTHERS AND COME SEE THIS!

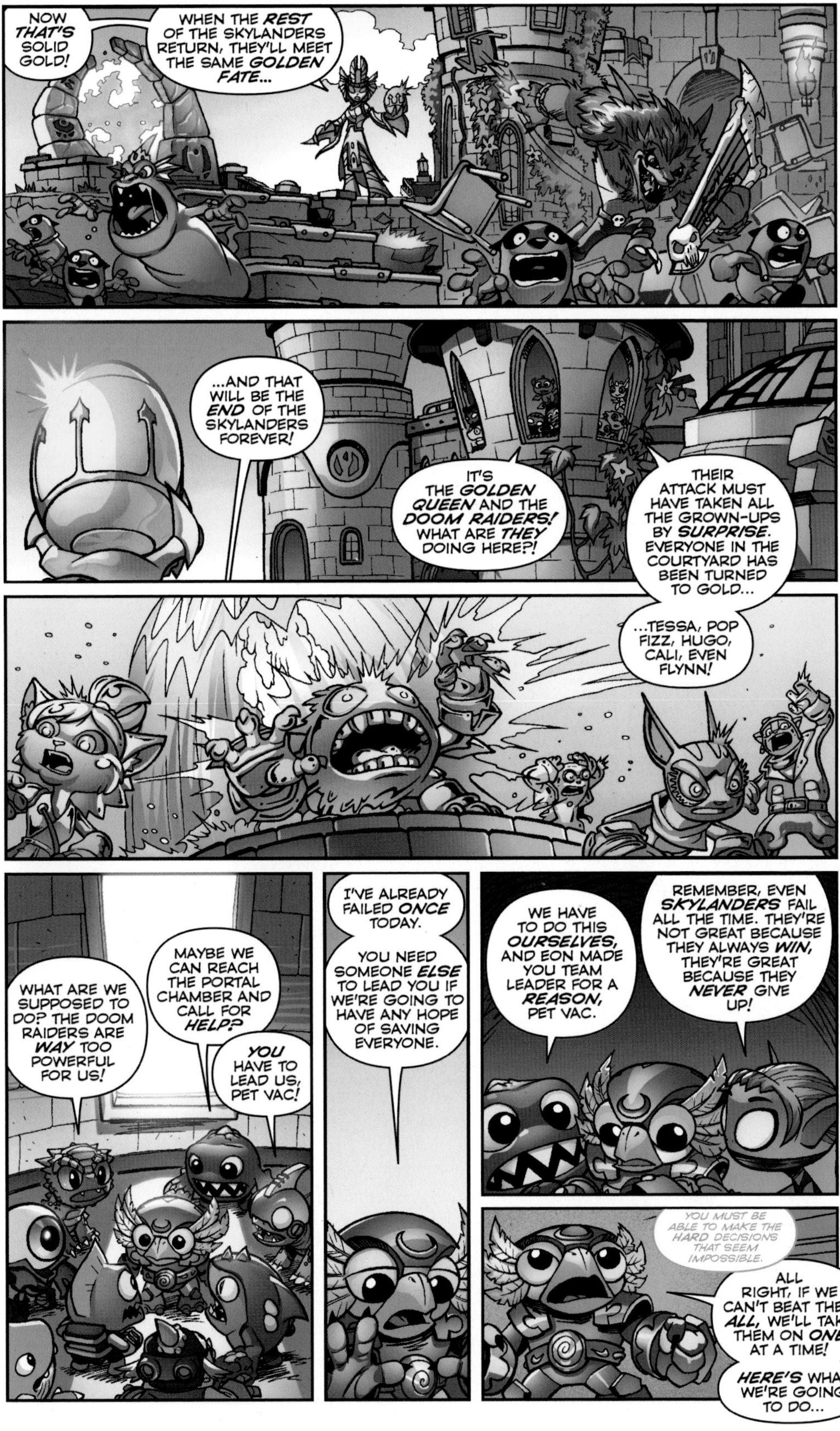
NOW THAT'S SOLID GOLD!
WHEN THE REST OF THE SKYLANDERS RETURN, THEY'LL MEET THE SAME GOLDEN FATE...
...AND THAT WILL BE THE END OF THE SKYLANDERS FOREVER!
IT'S THE GOLDEN QUEEN AND THE DOOM RAIDERS! WHAT ARE THEY DOING HERE?!
THEIR ATTACK MUST HAVE TAKEN ALL THE GROWN-UPS BY SURPRISE. EVERYONE IN THE COURTYARD HAS BEEN TURNED TO GOLD...
...TESSA, POP FIZZ, HUGO, CALI, EVEN FLYNN!
WHAT ARE WE SUPPOSED TO DO? THE DOOM RAIDERS ARE WAY TOO POWERFUL FOR US!
MAYBE WE CAN REACH THE PORTAL CHAMBER AND CALL FOR HELP?
YOU HAVE TO LEAD US, PET VAC!
I'VE ALREADY FAILED ONCE TODAY.
YOU NEED SOMEONE ELSE TO LEAD YOU IF WE'RE GOING TO HAVE ANY HOPE OF SAVING EVERYONE.
WE HAVE TO DO THIS OURSELVES, AND EON MADE YOU TEAM LEADER FOR A REASON, PET VAC.
REMEMBER, EVEN SKYLANDERS FAIL ALL THE TIME. THEY'RE NOT GREAT BECAUSE THEY ALWAYS WIN, THEY'RE GREAT BECAUSE THEY NEVER GIVE UP!
YOU MUST BE ABLE TO MAKE THE HARD DECISIONS THAT SEEM IMPOSSIBLE.
ALL RIGHT, IF WE CAN'T BEAT THEM ALL, WE'LL TAKE THEM ON ONE AT A TIME!
HERE'S WHAT WE'RE GOING TO DO...

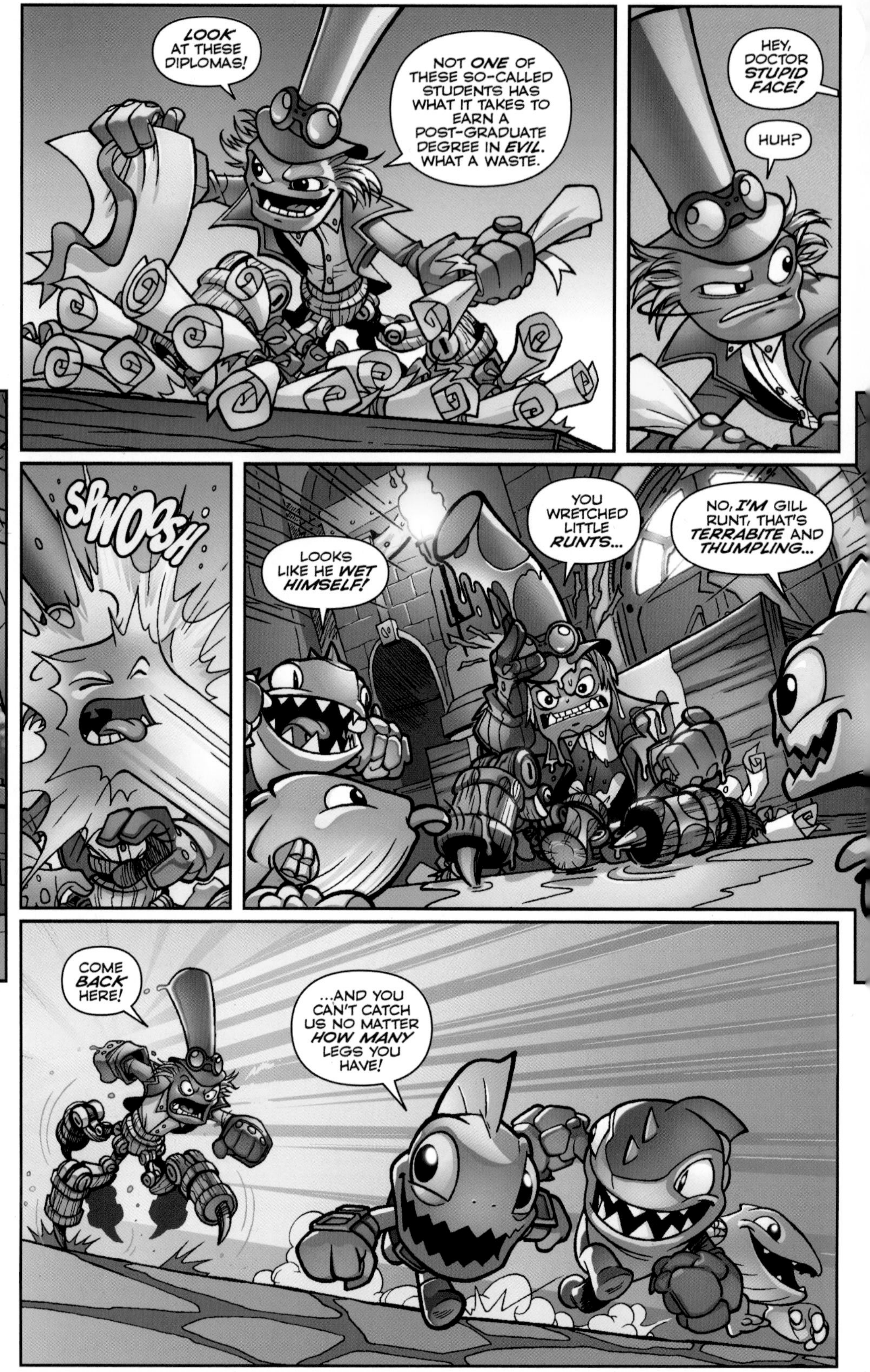
LOOK AT THESE DIPLOMAS!
NOT ONE OF THESE SO-CALLED STUDENTS HAS WHAT IT TAKES TO EARN A POST-GRADUATE DEGREE IN EVIL. WHAT A WASTE.
HEY, DOCTOR STUPID FACE!
HUH?
SPWOOSH
LOOKS LIKE HE WET HIMSELF!
YOU WRETCHED LITTLE RUNTS...
NO, I'M GILL RUNT, THAT'S TERRABITE AND THUMPLING...
COME BACK HERE!
...AND YOU CAN'T CATCH US NO MATTER HOW MANY LEGS YOU HAVE!

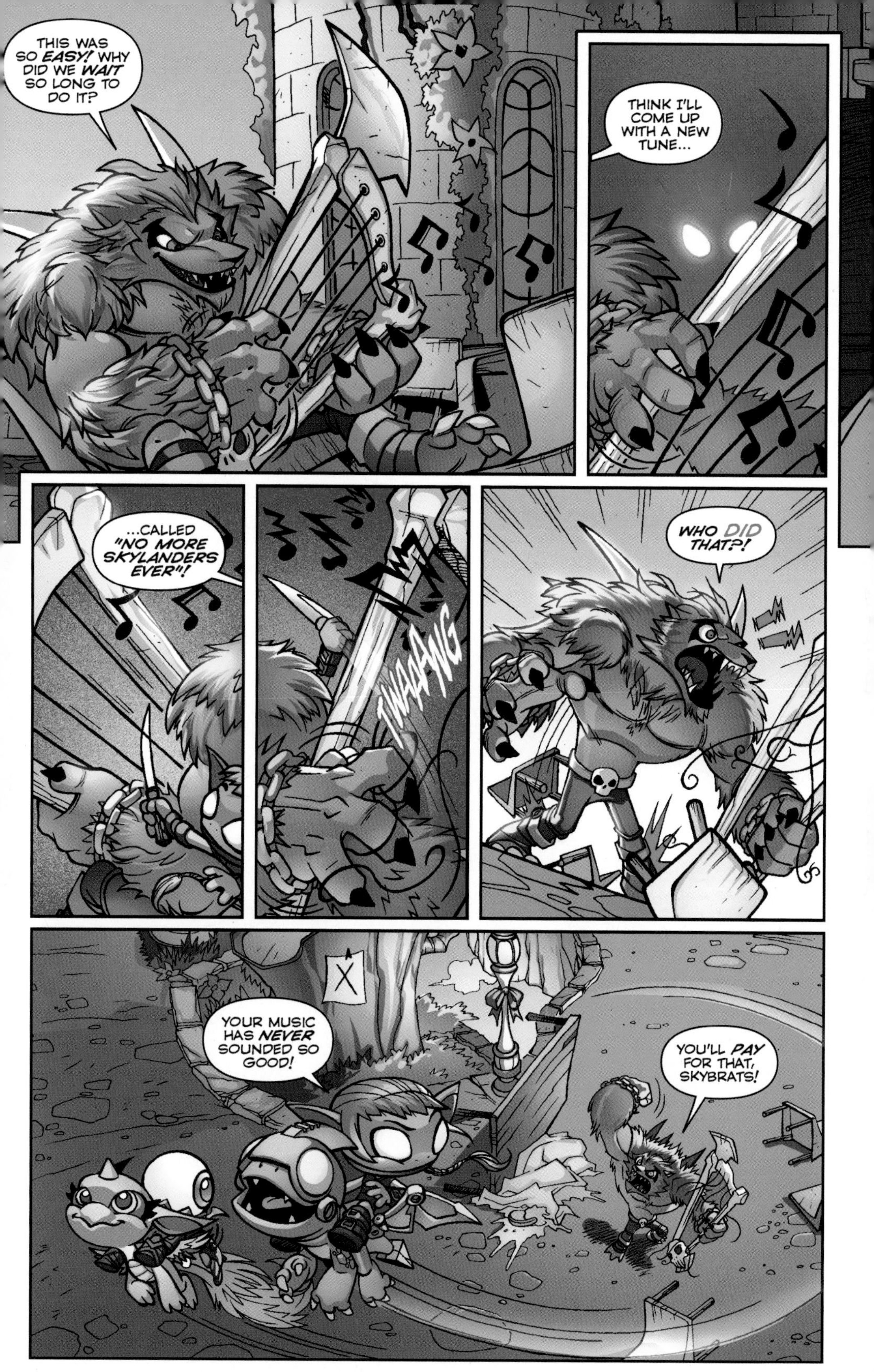
THIS WAS SO EASY! WHY DID WE WAIT SO LONG TO DO IT?
THINK I'LL COME UP WITH A NEW TUNE...
...CALLED "NO MORE SKYLANDERS EVER"!
TWAAANG
WHO DID THAT?!
YOUR MUSIC HAS NEVER SOUNDED SO GOOD!
YOU'LL PAY FOR THAT, SKYBRATS!

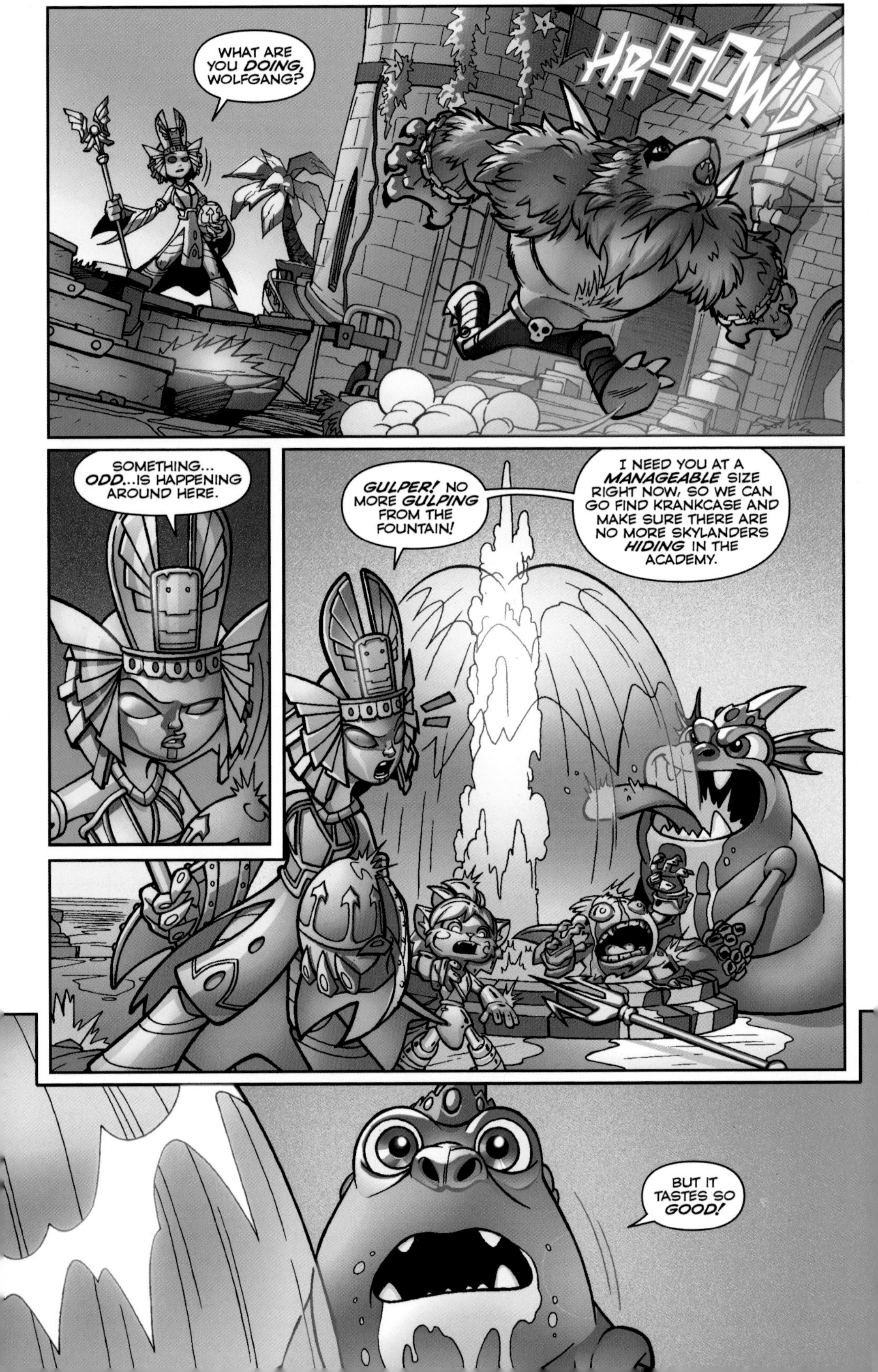
WHAT ARE YOU DOING, WOLFGANG?
HROOOOWL
SOMETHING... ODD...IS HAPPENING AROUND HERE.
GULPER! NO MORE GULPING FROM THE FOUNTAIN!
I NEED YOU AT A MANAGEABLE SIZE RIGHT NOW, SO WE CAN GO FIND KRANKCASE AND MAKE SURE THERE ARE NO MORE SKYLANDERS HIDING IN THE ACADEMY.
BUT IT TASTES SO GOOD!

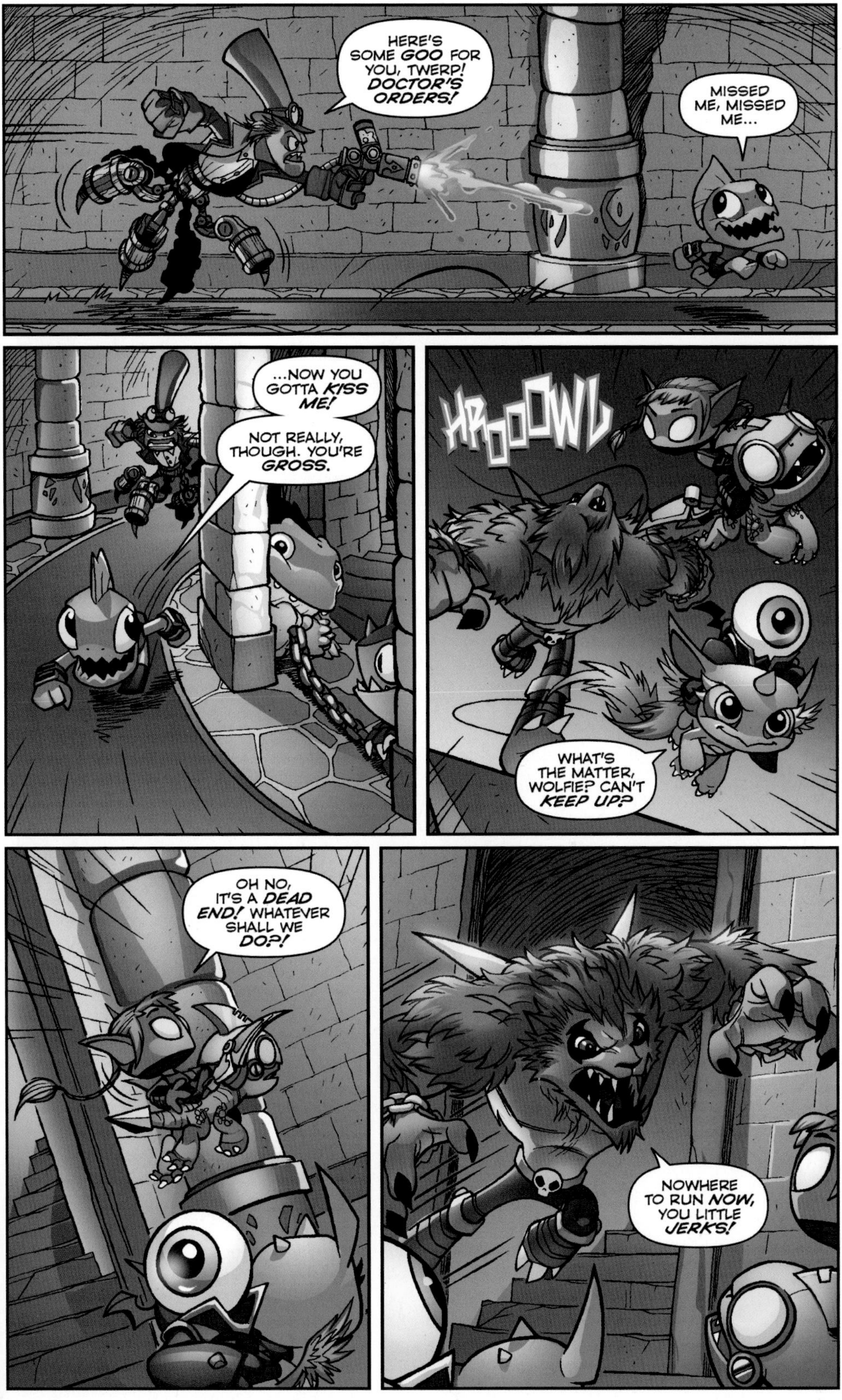
HERE'S SOME GOO FOR YOU, TWERP! DOCTOR'S ORDERS!
MISSED ME, MISSED ME...
...NOW YOU GOTTA KISS ME!
NOT REALLY, THOUGH. YOU'RE GROSS.
HROOOOWL
WHAT'S THE MATTER, WOLFIE? CAN'T KEEP UP?
OH NO, IT'S A DEAD END! WHATEVER SHALL WE DO?!
NOWHERE TO RUN NOW, YOU LITTLE JERKS!

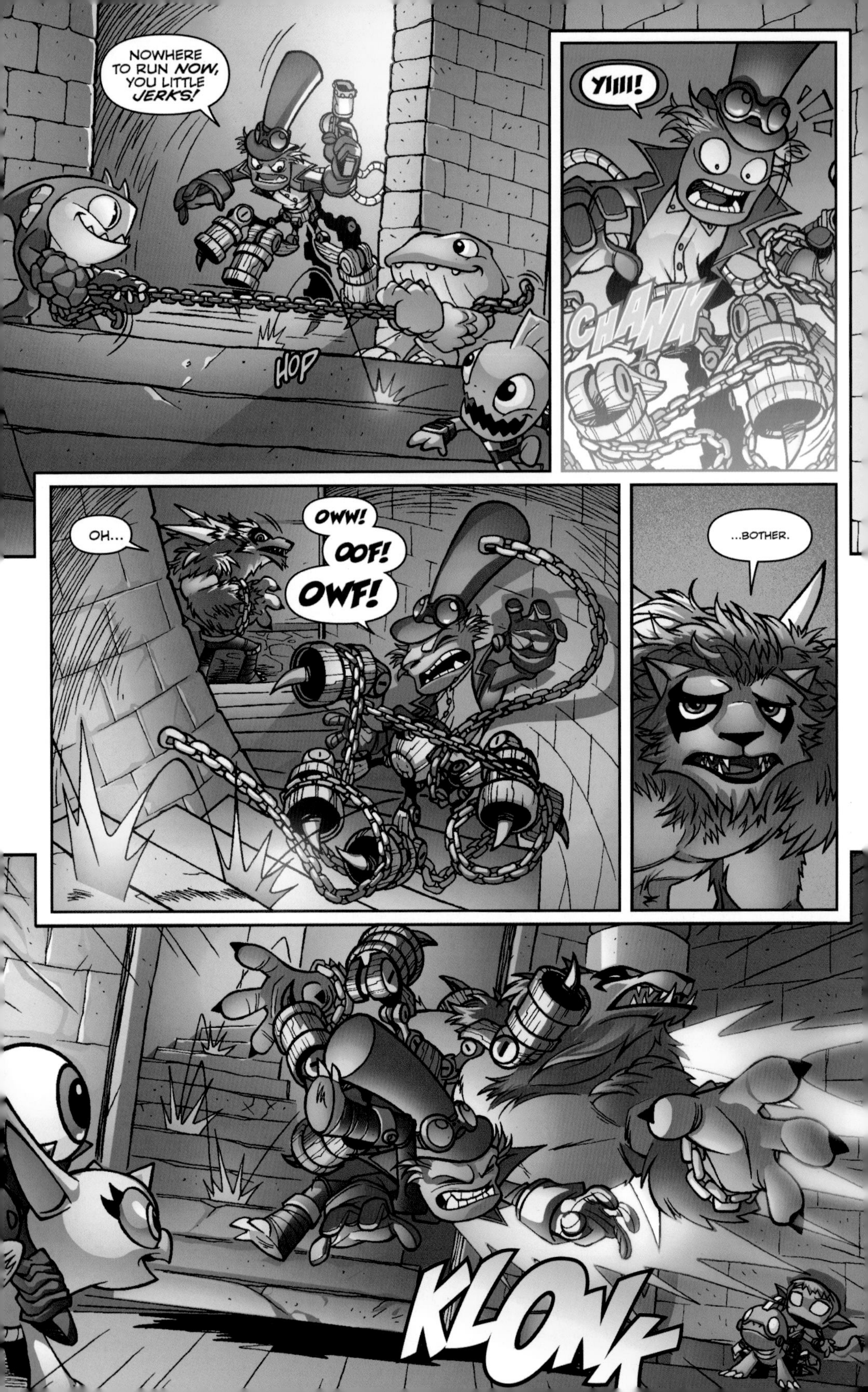
NOWHERE TO RUN NOW, YOU LITTLE JERKS!
HOP
YIIII!
CHANK
OH...
OWW!
OOF!
OWF!
...BOTHER.
KLONK

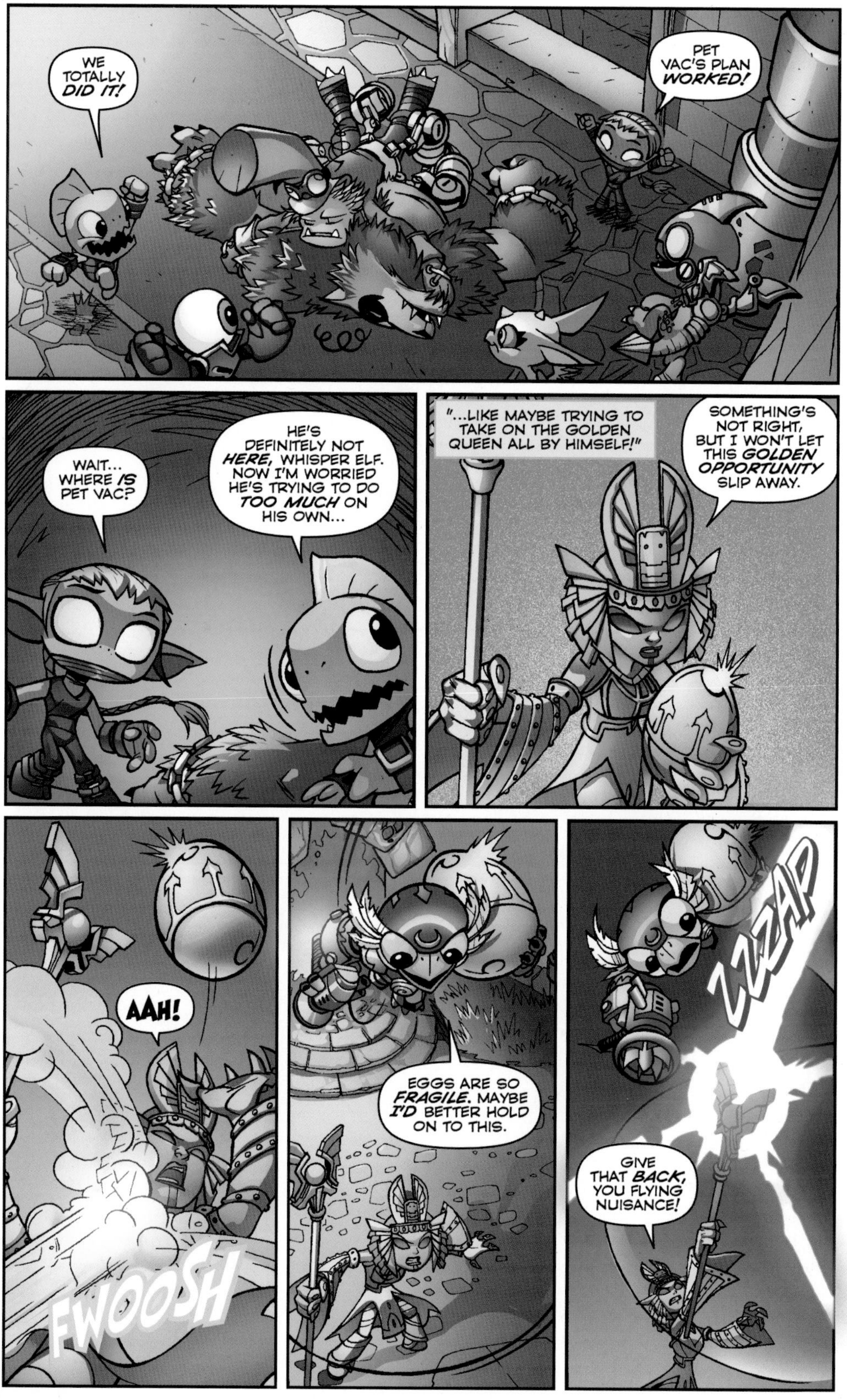
WE TOTALLY DID IT!
PET VAC'S PLAN WORKED!
WAIT... WHERE IS PET VAC?
HE'S DEFINITELY NOT HERE, WHISPER ELF. NOW I'M WORRIED HE'S TRYING TO DO TOO MUCH ON HIS OWN...
"...LIKE MAYBE TRYING TO TAKE ON THE GOLDEN QUEEN ALL BY HIMSELF!"
SOMETHING'S NOT RIGHT, BUT I WON'T LET THIS GOLDEN OPPORTUNITY SLIP AWAY.
AAH!
FWOOSH
EGGS ARE SO FRAGILE. MAYBE I'D BETTER HOLD ON TO THIS.
ZZZZAP
GIVE THAT BACK, YOU FLYING NUISANCE!

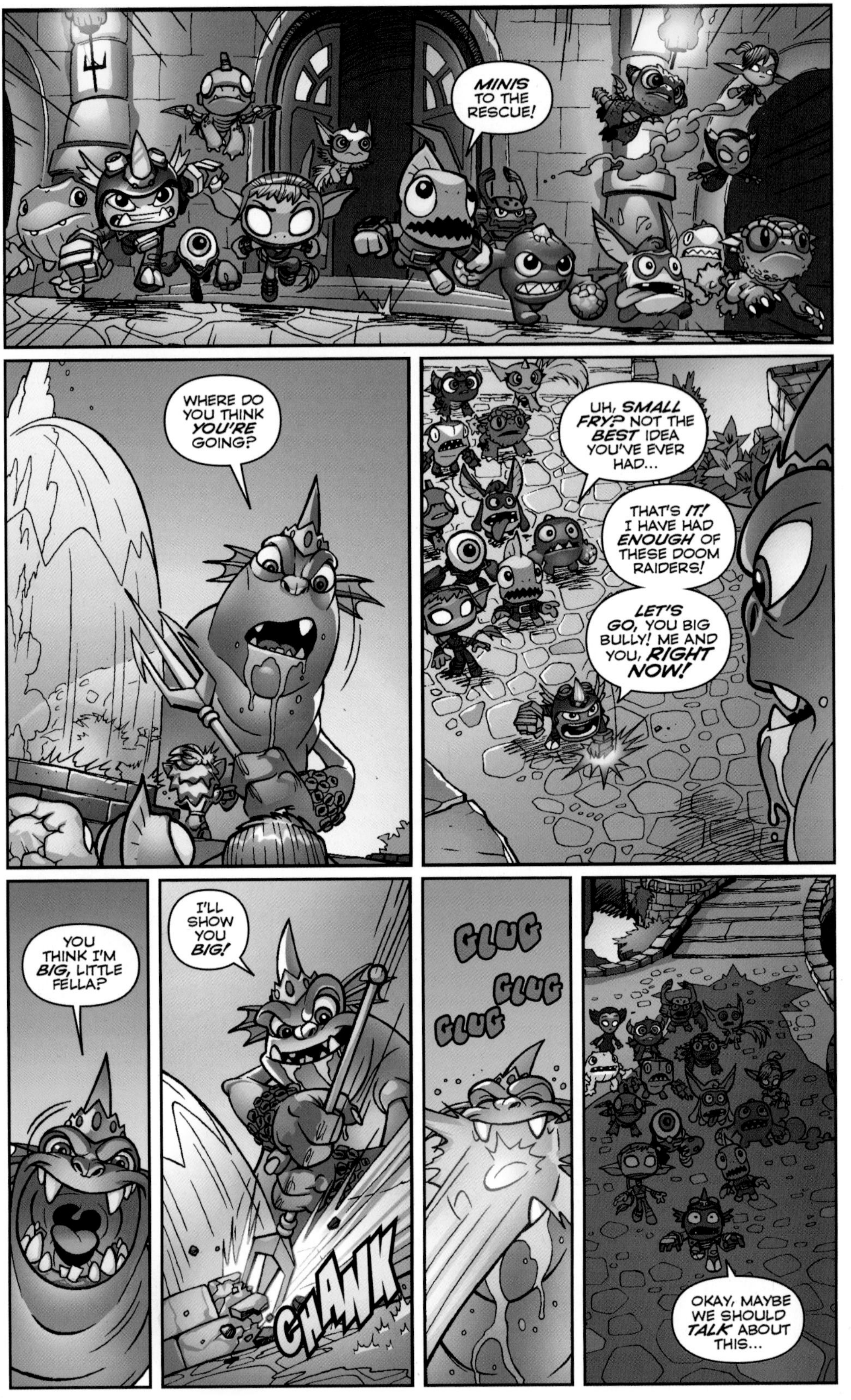
MINIS TO THE RESCUE!
WHERE DO YOU THINK YOU'RE GOING?
UH, SMALL FRY? NOT THE BEST IDEA YOU'VE EVER HAD...
THAT'S IT! I HAVE HAD ENOUGH OF THESE DOOM RAIDERS!
LET'S GO, YOU BIG BULLY! ME AND YOU, RIGHT NOW!
YOU THINK I'M BIG, LITTLE FELLA?
I'LL SHOW YOU BIG!
CHANK
GLUG
GLUG
GLUG
OKAY, MAYBE WE SHOULD TALK ABOUT THIS...

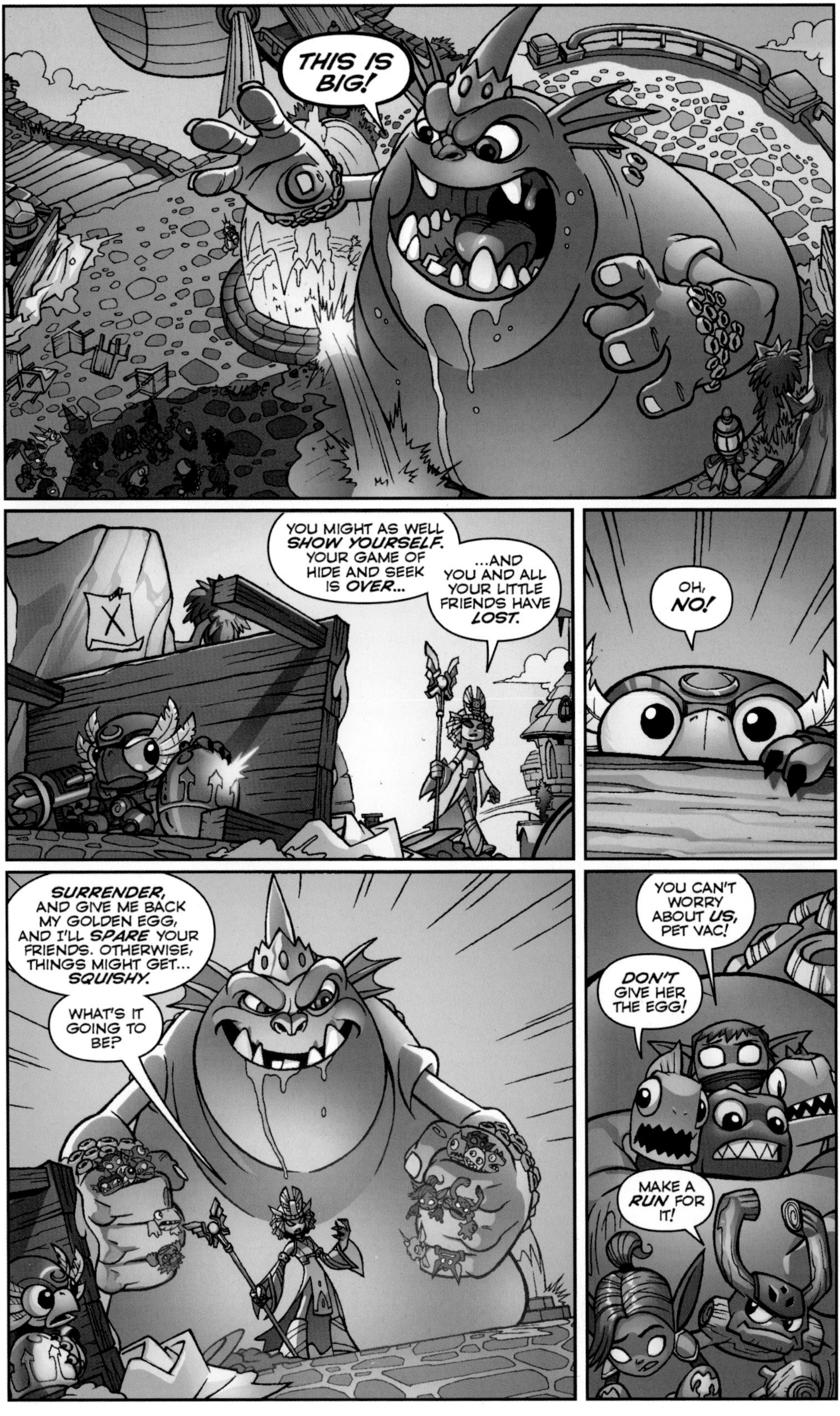
THIS IS BIG!
YOU MIGHT AS WELL SHOW YOURSELF. YOUR GAME OF HIDE AND SEEK IS OVER...
...AND YOU AND ALL YOUR LITTLE FRIENDS HAVE LOST.
OH, NO!
SURRENDER, AND GIVE ME BACK MY GOLDEN EGG, AND I'LL SPARE YOUR FRIENDS. OTHERWISE, THINGS MIGHT GET... SQUISHY.
WHAT'S IT GOING TO BE?
YOU CAN'T WORRY ABOUT US, PET VAC!
DON'T GIVE HER THE EGG!
MAKE A RUN FOR IT!

FINE. IF YOU'RE GOING TO MAKE ME CHOOSE...

...I CHOOSE MY *FRIENDS*. I SURRENDER. NOW LET EVERYONE *GO*.

FIRST, YOU THROW THE EGG HERE. AND DON'T TRY ANYTHING *FUNNY*.

A BREEZE FROM THAT *LEAF BLOWER* WON'T SAVE YOU NOW.

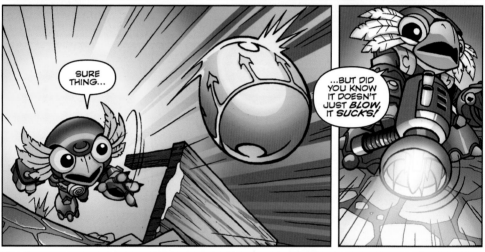

SURE THING...

...BUT DID YOU KNOW IT DOESN'T JUST *BLOW*, IT *SUCKS!*

MY *STAFF!*

IS NO MATCH FOR MY *SUCTION GUN!*

VROOSH!

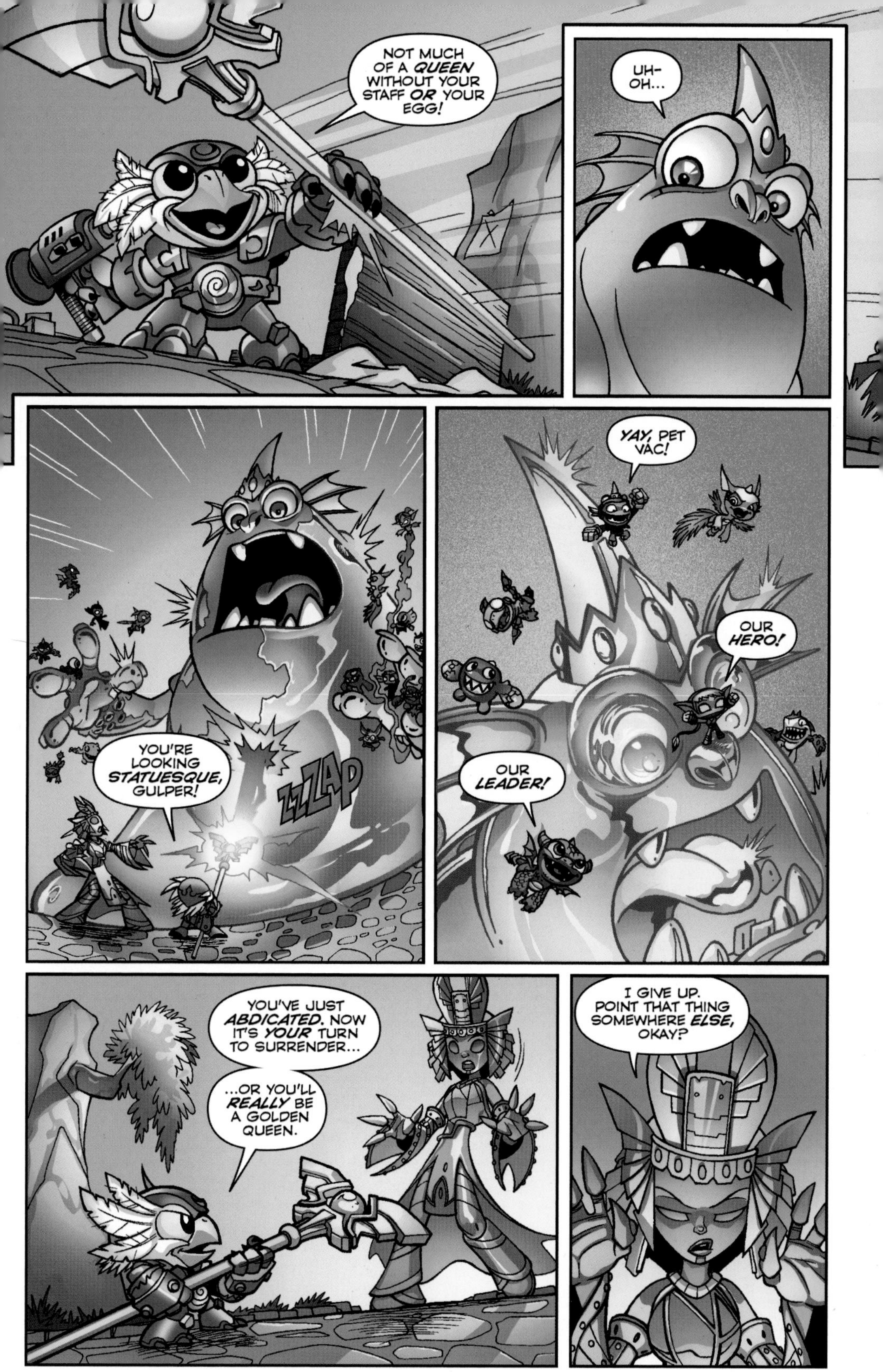
NOT MUCH OF A QUEEN WITHOUT YOUR STAFF OR YOUR EGG!
UH-OH...
YOU'RE LOOKING STATUESQUE, GULPER!
ZZZAP
YAY, PET VAC!
OUR HERO!
OUR LEADER!
YOU'VE JUST ABDICATED. NOW IT'S YOUR TURN TO SURRENDER...
...OR YOU'LL REALLY BE A GOLDEN QUEEN.
I GIVE UP. POINT THAT THING SOMEWHERE ELSE, OKAY?

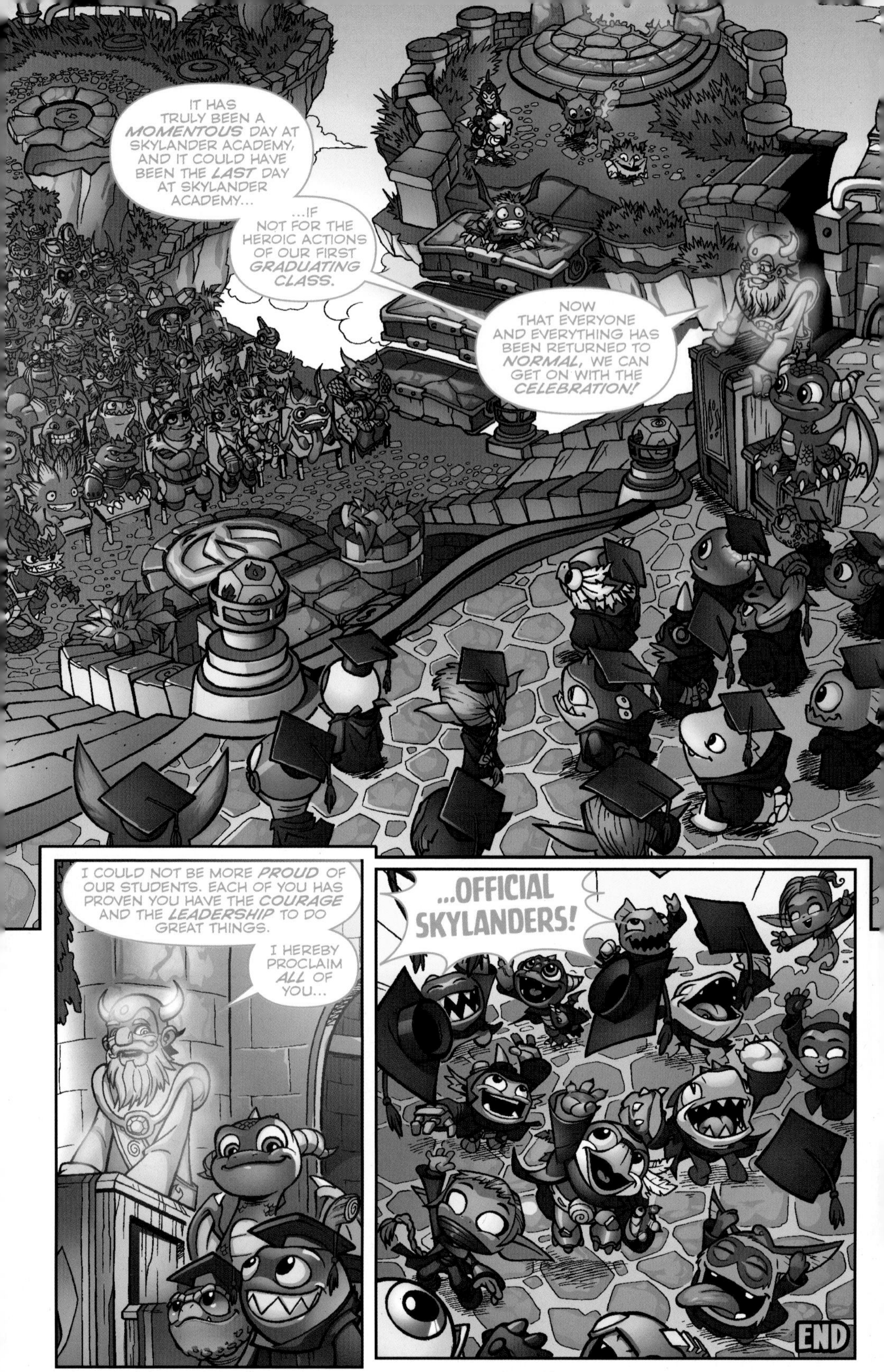
IT HAS TRULY BEEN A MOMENTOUS DAY AT SKYLANDER ACADEMY, AND IT COULD HAVE BEEN THE LAST DAY AT SKYLANDER ACADEMY...
...IF NOT FOR THE HEROIC ACTIONS OF OUR FIRST GRADUATING CLASS.
NOW THAT EVERYONE AND EVERYTHING HAS BEEN RETURNED TO NORMAL, WE CAN GET ON WITH THE CELEBRATION!
I COULD NOT BE MORE PROUD OF OUR STUDENTS. EACH OF YOU HAS PROVEN YOU HAVE THE COURAGE AND THE LEADERSHIP TO DO GREAT THINGS.
I HEREBY PROCLAIM ALL OF YOU...
...OFFICIAL SKYLANDERS!
END

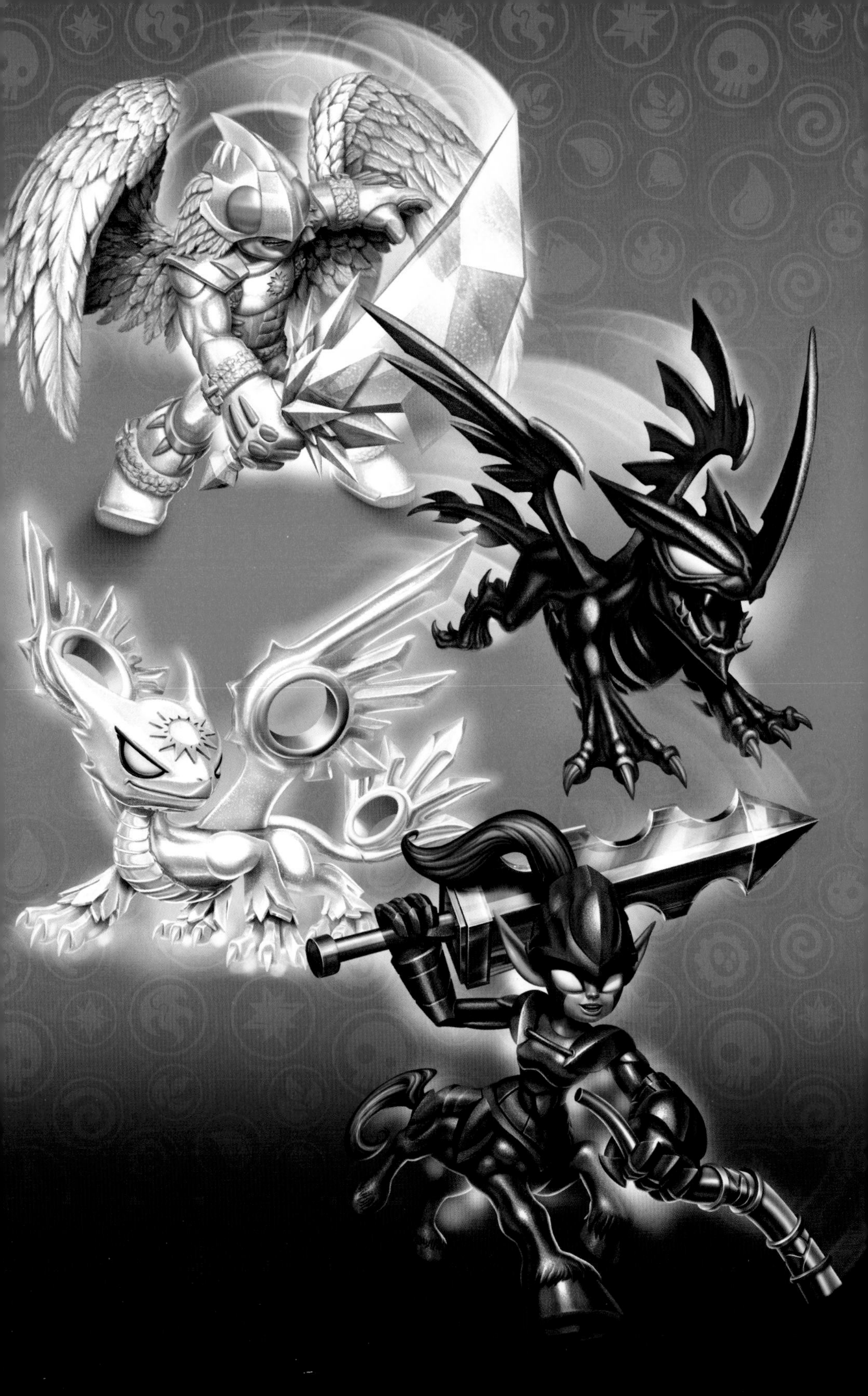

SPOTLIGHT

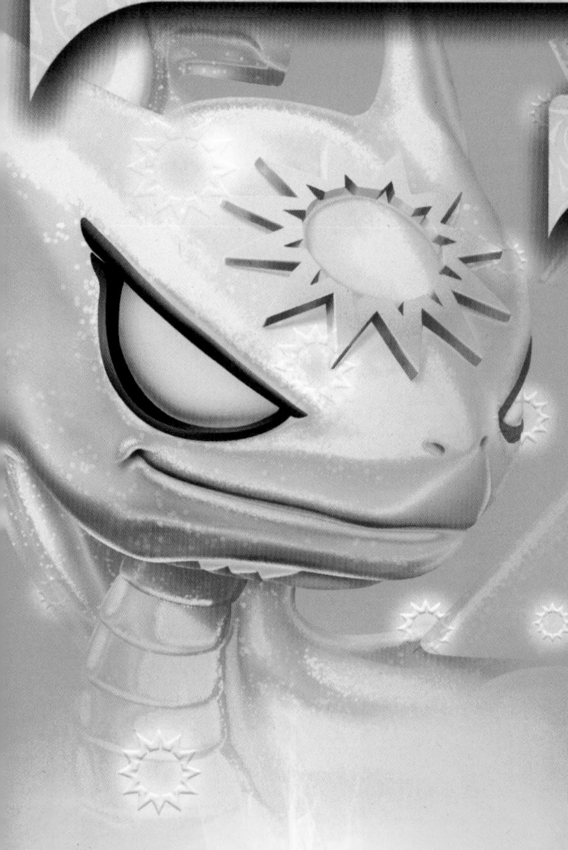

BIO

Spotlight was discovered by Master Eon in the Prismatic Palace, where the Portal Master had ventured seeking the Crystal Orb of Light. Upon finding the Orb, Eon reached out and gently touched it—causing a brilliant light to emanate in all directions. Having been infused with Eon's magic, the Orb glowed magnificently. And when Eon slowly lowered his hand from his shielded eyes, Spotlight stood before him in a respectful bow. Her power of Light was unknown to him, for it was not of the eight common Elements in Skylands. But sensing that the Ancients sent Spotlight to him for a reason, he took her to the Core of Light and trained her to defend it as a member of the Skylanders. And when none other than evil Portal Master KAOS destroyed it—***Spotlight*** vanished!

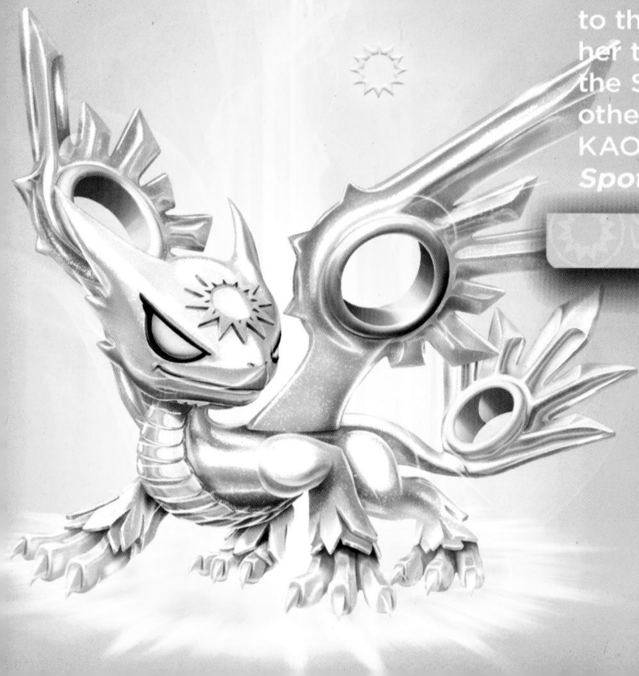

BLACKOUT

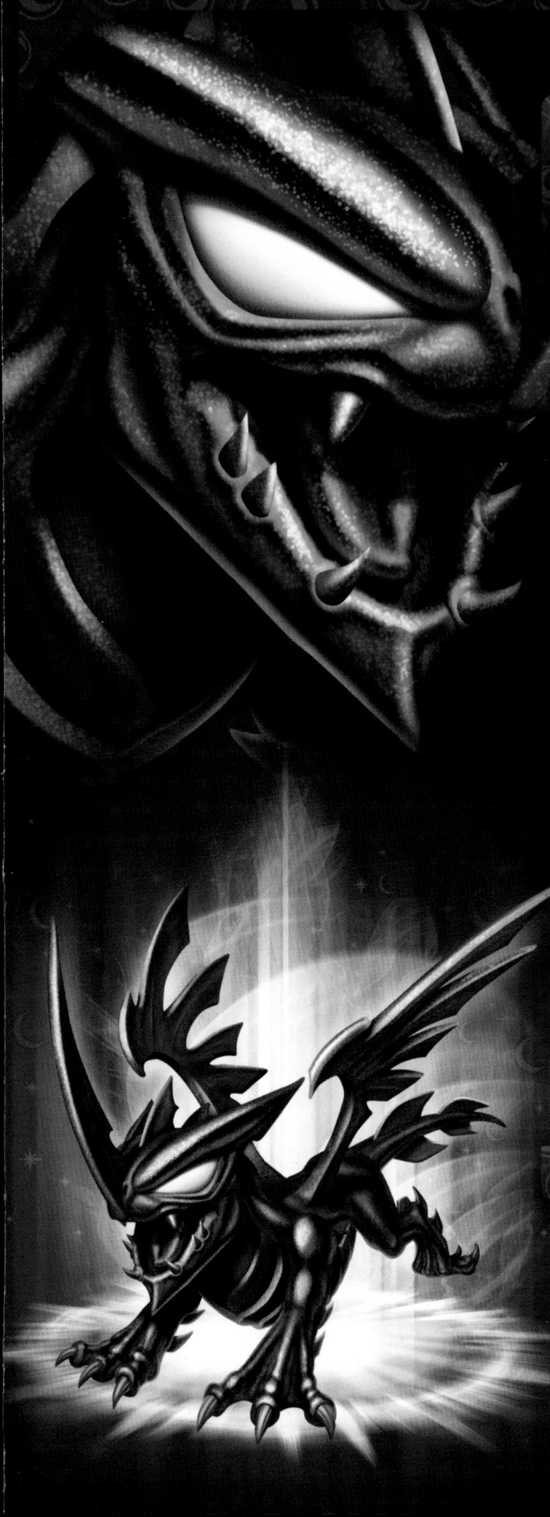

BIO

Blackout hails from the Realm of Dreams, where the collective imagination of all the creatures in the universe comes together to create beautiful wonders... and terrible nightmares. At a young age, he was recruited into the Dark Stygian—a Dragon Clan whose chief responsibility was to create nightmares for evil creatures as a way to discourage them from doing more villainy. But the clan began to abuse its power and soon spread nightmares far and wide for its own amusement. But Blackout would not stand for it. So he learned to teleport directly into the nightmares the clan created and fought the creatures within. Eventually, the nightmares reached as far as Master Eon, who witnessed Blackout's courage within his own dreams. After helping him put a stop to the Dark Stygian, Eon then made Blackout a Skylander, serving as the protector of the Realm of Dreams and beyond!

KNIGHT MARE

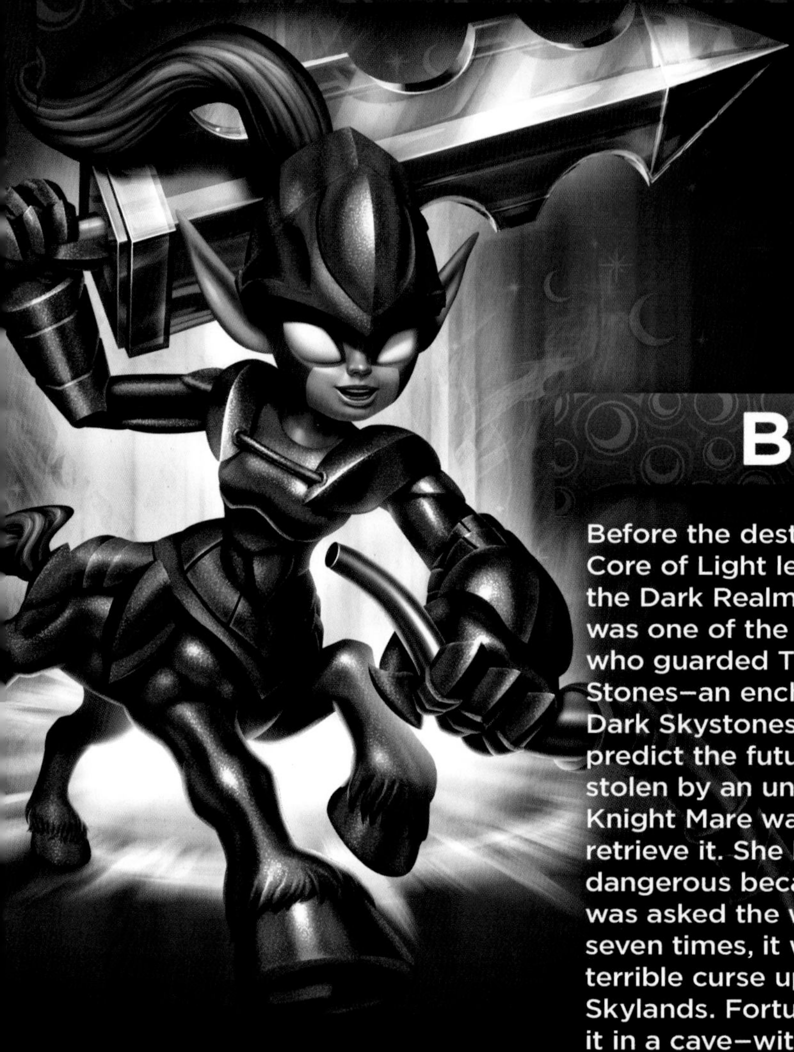

BIO

Before the destruction of the Core of Light left her stranded in the Dark Realm, *Knight Mare* was one of the Dark Centaurs who guarded The Oracle of Stones—an enchanted game of Dark Skystones that could predict the future. When it was stolen by an unknown force, Knight Mare was called upon to retrieve it. She knew it would be dangerous because if the Oracle was asked the wrong questions seven times, it would unleash a terrible curse upon all of Skylands. Fortunately, she found it in a cave—with a gang of Bicyclopes about to ask their seventh wrong question. With no time to lose, she charged forward, beating the fierce Bicyclopes and saving Skylands from the terrible curse. Now having joined the Trap Team, Knight Mare uses her hunting skills and Traptanium Lance to bring down evil everywhere!

KNIGHT LIGHT

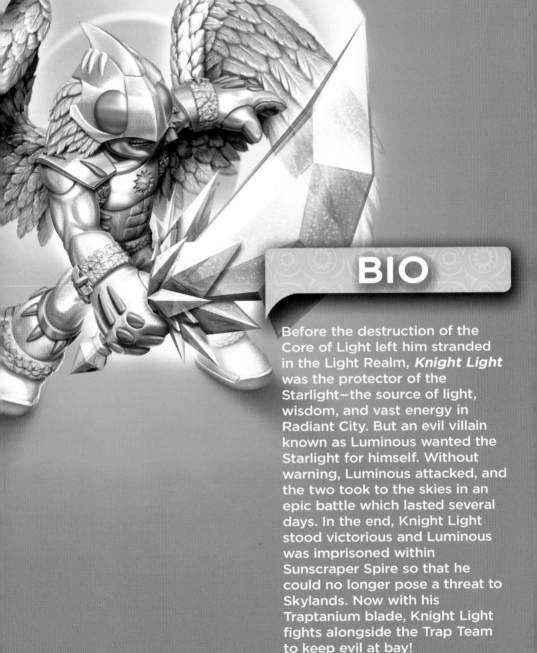

BIO

Before the destruction of the Core of Light left him stranded in the Light Realm, *Knight Light* was the protector of the Starlight—the source of light, wisdom, and vast energy in Radiant City. But an evil villain known as Luminous wanted the Starlight for himself. Without warning, Luminous attacked, and the two took to the skies in an epic battle which lasted several days. In the end, Knight Light stood victorious and Luminous was imprisoned within Sunscraper Spire so that he could no longer pose a threat to Skylands. Now with his Traptanium blade, Knight Light fights alongside the Trap Team to keep evil at bay!

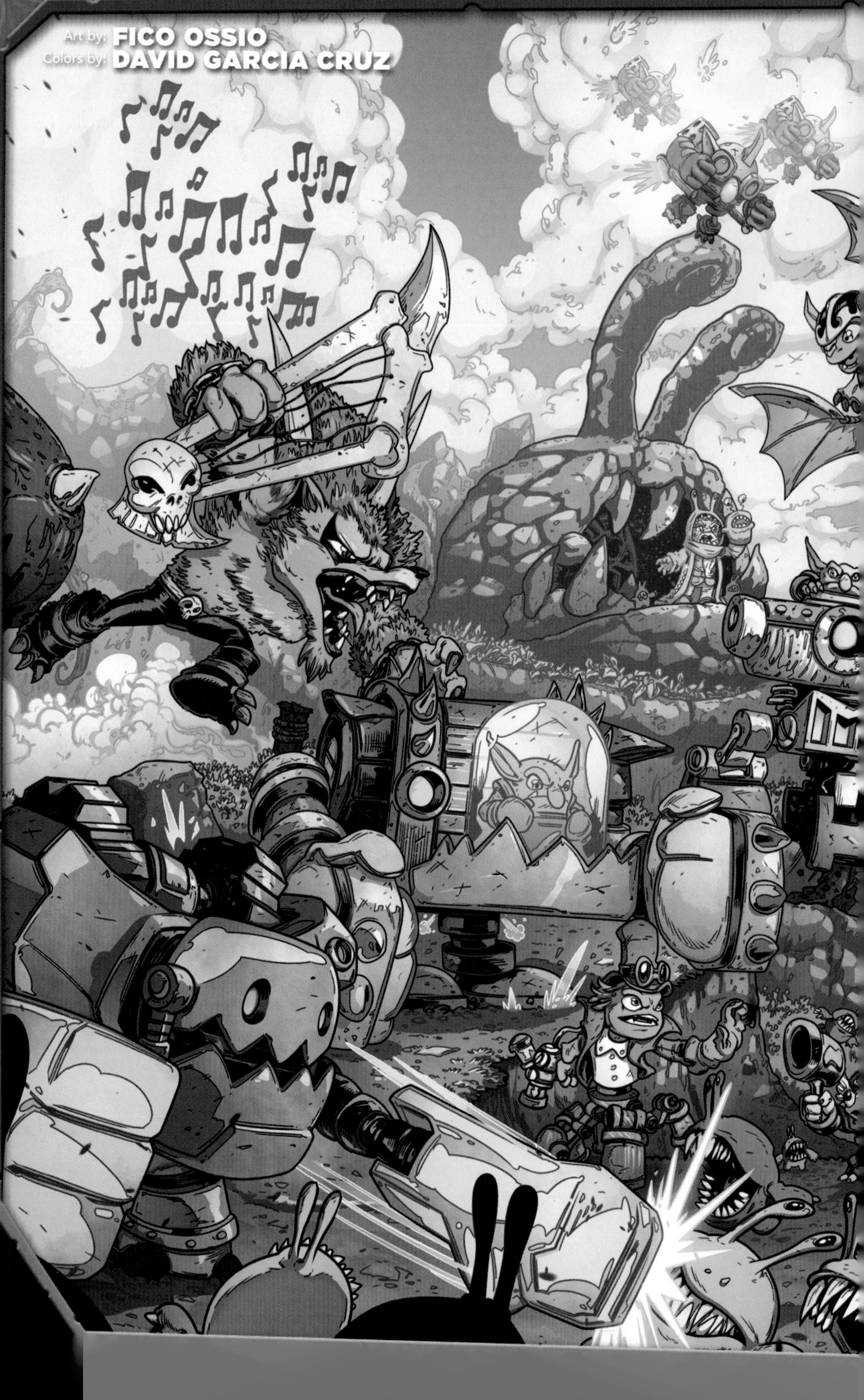
Art by: FICO OSSIO
Colors by: DAVID GARCIA CRUZ

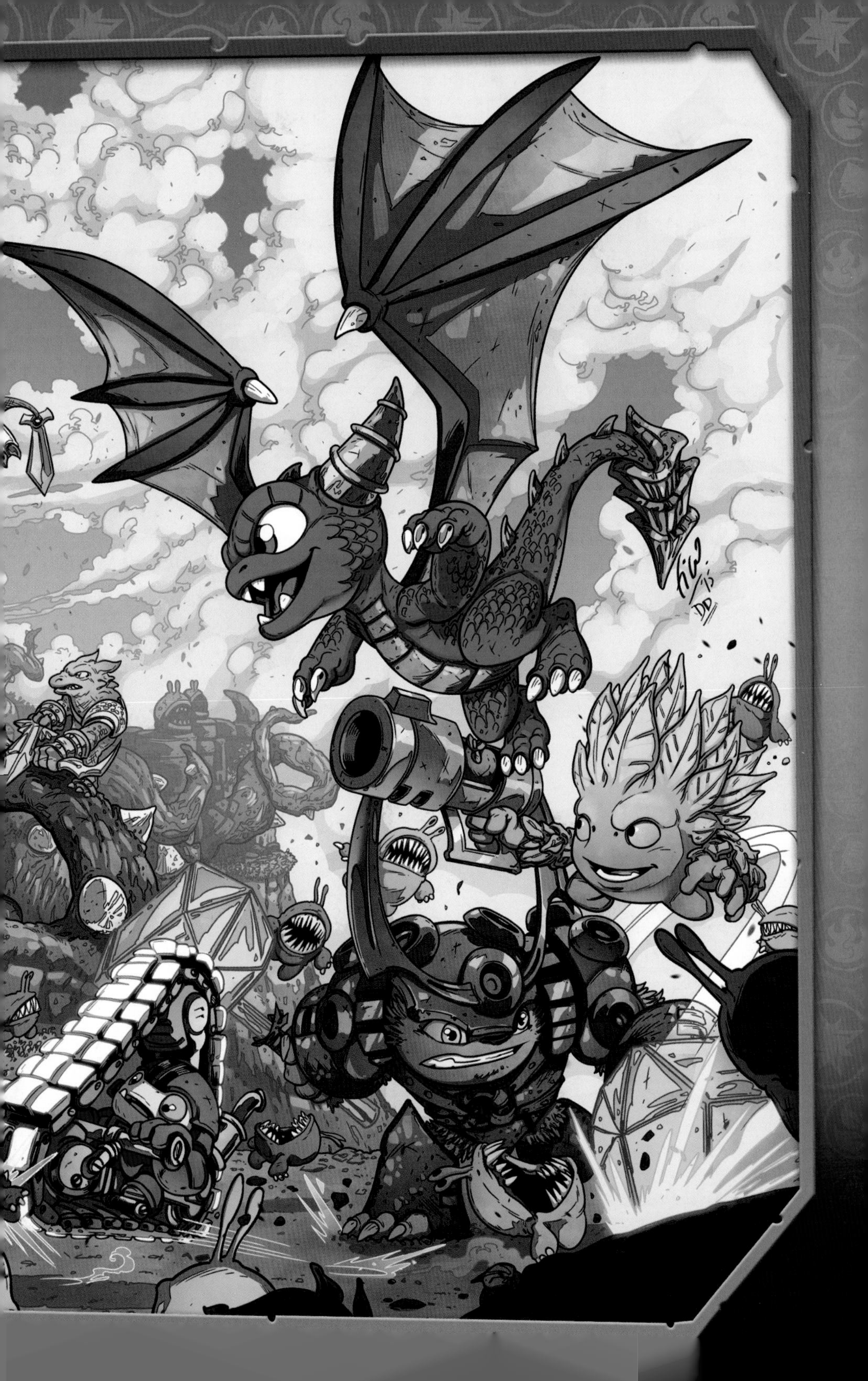